# "Why have you never married, Miss McNeil?"

The question had exactly the effect Gabe had hoped. The wind went completely out of Lucie, and he almost regretted asking. Still, he could not seem to stop himself from continuing, "I mean, you'll forgive me, but you appear to be of age." He allowed his eyes to roam over her from head to foot.

"You are saying *past* the age, are you not, sir?" she said stiffly. "My maidenly status is of my own choosing and, with respect, sir, it is not your business. If there's nothing more I can do for you, I'll check on your mother."

It was clear to Gabe that her opinion of him was less than complimentary. But why should this woman's opinion of him matter? What did he care what she thought of him? Whether she liked it or not, Miss Lucie McNeil would just have to get used to him.

**Books by Anna Schmidt**

Love Inspired Historical

*Seaside Cinderella*

Love Inspired

*Caroline and the Preacher* #72
*A Mother for Amanda* #109
*The Doctor's Miracle* #146
*Love Next Door* #294
*Matchmaker, Matchmaker* #333
*Lasso Her Heart* #375

## ANNA SCHMIDT

is a two-time finalist for the coveted RITA® Award from the Romance Writers of America as well as twice a finalist for the *Romantic Times BOOKreviews* Reviewer's Choice Award. The most recent *Romantic Times BOOKreviews* Reviewer's Choice Nomination was for her 2006 novel, *Matchmaker, Matchmaker...* The sequel, *Lasso Her Heart,* inspired readers to write to Anna via her Web site (www.booksbyanna.com) and declare that its theme of recovery from tragedy brought them comfort in their own lives. Her novel *The Doctor's Miracle,* was the 2002 *Romantic Times BOOKreviews* Reviewers Choice Inspirational Category Winner. In 2008, Anna's novels (in addition to this one) include *This Side of Heaven* (Harlequin Everlasting Love), *Slingshot Moves* (Harlequin NASCAR series) and *Mistletoe Reunion* (Love Inspired). A transplant from Virginia, she now calls Wisconsin home and escapes the tough winters in Florida.

# ANNA SCHMIDT
## Seaside Cinderella

Steeple
Hill®

Published by Steeple Hill Books™

STEEPLE HILL BOOKS

Steeple
Hill®

ISBN-13: 978-0-373-82792-3
ISBN-10:    0-373-82792-X

SEASIDE CINDERELLA

www.SteepleHill.com

**Printed in U.S.A.**

For Jehovah is good; His loving-kindness
is to time indefinite and His faithfulness to
generation after generation.
—*Psalms* 100:5

For my parents and the love story they lived.

## Chapter One

Lucie McNeil noticed the yacht's approach as she swept the front steps of the large Queen Anne-style house positioned high on a bluff overlooking Nantucket Bay. The Hunters' home had originally been built as a spacious summer cottage for the then-prosperous Hunter family. It was near enough to town to allow shopping for supplies to be convenient, yet far enough away that it offered privacy and solitude.

She glanced across the yard to where sixty-year-old Emma Hunter sat under the lone tree that broke up the spare landscape. Her employer suffered from heart palpitations and shortness of breath, which often left her so weak she could barely stand without assistance. A quilt frame dwarfed her as she sewed row after row of tiny, perfectly matched stitches across the face of the gaily colored quilt.

At the far side of the pasture, Emma's husband, Colonel Jonathan Hunter, worked on the repair of a fence, his snow-white hair blowing in the gentle breeze of the unseasonably warm May morning. In just three months

Lucie had come to think of him as the father she'd never had—not that she hadn't known her father or lived in his house back in Ireland. But he had been cruel and self-centered. Jonathan Hunter was not only a gentleman—he was a gentle man, at peace with his world and God and wishing the same for anyone he met.

Lucie put the broom aside and crossed the yard to Emma. She adjusted the lap robe that covered the older woman's increasingly useless legs.

"Now, y'all just stop fussing over me, Lucie," Emma chided in the sweet Southern drawl that had not disappeared in spite of over forty years living in the North.

"Yes, ma'am," Lucie replied, but adjusted the cover anyway.

Emma frowned. "Now, Lucie, we have discussed this enough. I am Emma—not 'ma'am' or 'Mrs. Hunter' or any such nonsense. I stood on ceremony growing up in Charleston and even after the colonel and I were married, and where did it get me, or anyone else for that matter?" She let the threaded needle drop to the stretched fabric as she collapsed against the pressed back of her wooden wheelchair.

Still unused to these energetic outbursts of conversation, often followed by sheer exhaustion, Lucie knelt next to Emma's chair. "Would you like to go inside?"

"I met my Jonathan on a morning like this," Emma said dreamily, as if Lucie hadn't spoken. "It was at the end of the war and he was a naval officer for the Yankees. Daddy had a plantation overlooking the Charleston harbor and when I saw the deep blue of the man's uniform and the sun glinting off his gold officer's buttons, I just knew he was about to change my life."

Accepting the fact that she might as well sit and make

herself useful by helping with the quilting, Lucie pulled an extra needle from the unbound edge of the quilt top and threaded it. As she knotted the thread, she glanced toward the harbor and saw that the yacht was not passing as she had assumed, but had moved closer and seemed prepared to drop anchor. Emma was oblivious to the possible approach of visitors as she continued her story. "Mama insisted that I mind my manners and offer the gentleman a cool drink and a seat on the veranda while she sent Sudie, our house slave—our servant—to fetch Daddy. 'Be sweet,' she told me." Emma sighed. "Mama was weak—maybe it was the war. It had made her so afraid…" Her voice drifted off and Lucie glanced over to see if the older woman had dozed off, as she often did.

"Not me," she mumbled. "The war had made me stronger—and angrier," she added and returned to her quilting as if she'd never begun the story. "Did you say we are to have seafood chowder for the noon meal, my dear? Colonel Hunter will be famished."

"I'll just go stir the chowder." When she looked back, Emma was fast asleep. Lucie smiled, guessing that having begun the story, Emma would dream of her first meeting with her beloved colonel. Emma's dreams always seemed to bring her such pleasure. Not at all like the nightmares that haunted Lucie's own sleep. She glanced out to sea as she walked back to the cottage. The yacht bobbed in the light, choppy waters of the bay. Perhaps it was an outing for some rich city dwellers after all.

After checking on the chowder and the bread she had placed in the oven of the old wood-burning kitchen stove, she returned to the porch and her sweeping. She kept her eye on the yacht, now part of a seascape against a background of the deep blue waters of the bay and the translucent blue of the sky. She shaded her eyes against the morning sun and watched as a dinghy with a single occupant was lowered into the water by the yacht's crew. The man began to row toward the shore.

Lucie fingered the small silver cross that hung from a thin chain at her collar as she watched the man drag the dinghy to a spot high above the tide line and start hiking across the beach. A thick field of sea oats at the crest of the dunes parted as he kept coming. When he reached the top of the bluff, he lifted his head and fixed his gaze on her and the cottage. Lucie had the sense that nothing— short of God himself—would deter this man from his purpose.

*Bill collector,* Lucie thought, her eyes narrowing. Back in Ireland, she'd seen them often enough, striding across the fallow, dead fields that had once been farmed by her father. More times than she liked to recall, her mother had hustled her and her siblings inside the tiny, dark cottage, barring the door against the pounding of the bill collector. Her father was usually off at the local pub, drowning his sorrows and using the last of their meager funds to do it.

The Hunters were responsible and cautious souls— religious and pious people who firmly believed in "rendering unto Caesar." But they were also up in years. Perhaps Colonel Hunter had failed to meet some deadline for paying the mortgage or rent? Or it might be a tax collector.

But as the stranger came closer, she realized that everything in his demeanor spoke of money and power and the expectation that his word would be obeyed. This was a man like those she'd seen come down from the fashionable mansions of Boston to see how they might squeeze one more rent-producing space out of an already overcrowded tenement. No matter that the risk of disease, fire or other calamities grew with every additional tenant. She had seen men like this one evict a woman and her crying children into the night with no more thought of where those souls might go than he might give to whether he would have jam or jelly for breakfast.

Halfway across the grassy expanse that lay between the fenced yard and the dunes, the man paused and shed his coat, throwing it over one arm as he continued his trek toward the cottage. Every motion was performed with elegance and dignity. He was obviously a man of refinement and polish, and Lucie had learned that in America, those were men to be carefully watched. Yet in spite of her doubts, she felt drawn to him, curious to find out who he was and what he wanted of the Hunters.

She crossed the yard to where Emma dozed. "Emma," she said quietly as the man opened the gate and closed it carefully behind him.

Emma Hunter glanced up and looked around, a little confused as she came back to the present from the past she seemed to prefer these days. She saw the man and smiled. "Why, it's Gabriel," she said with obvious surprise and delight. "Where is the colonel?"

"Repairing the fence in the pasture," Lucie replied, glancing back at the man. "Shall I go and fetch him?"

"No, meet our son first and then you can go for the colonel."

So, this was Gabriel Hunter. His name had come up frequently in the weeks since Lucie had come to work for the Hunters. The parents often spoke of the boy—their only child, who had delighted them so and then gone to Boston at sixteen to make his fortune. They were extremely proud of him.

"How do I look?" Emma asked nervously, pinching her cheeks to bring color.

Lucie understood that Emma was asking not about her beauty but about her robustness. In her short time with the Hunters Lucie had learned that their son was a successful and powerful man in Boston. The younger Hunter wanted his parents to move to the city to live with him. The Hunters wanted to stay where they had shared their happiest times. They planned to die on this island, and since that day might come sooner than later for Emma, they had hired Lucie, believing her presence would help reassure their son that they had everything they needed right here.

"You look just fine," Lucie assured her, pressing her hands over her apron and tucking an errant strand of hair back into her tight bun as she sat in the vacant chair across from Emma and looked up to judge the man's progress.

Her breath caught. She recognized him, and yet could not say from where. He removed his hat out of respect for his mother. Lucie picked up her needle and began a fresh row of stitches.

"Mother," he called.

"Hello, Gabriel dear. Lovely of y'all to visit, and on a weekday, too."

Lucie hid a smile. Emma's Southern roots were showing in both the hint of a drawl and the very subtle reprimand. But all traces of levity were forgotten as Lucie glanced up and into the ocean-blue, deep-set eyes of Gabriel Hunter. He looked at her as if in a single glance he knew all there was to know of her, and had dismissed her entirely from his thoughts. His brow furrowed as he returned his attention to his mother.

"You're looking well."

"It's the sea air. I've always told you that. From the time I was a child back in Charleston…" Her voice trailed off as she stared across the yard and out to the sea beyond.

Lucie had grown used to these momentary lapses, but feared that Emma's son would look upon them with alarm.

"Perhaps a glass of water, young woman," Gabriel ordered without so much as a glance in Lucie's direction.

"Don't be rude," Emma instructed, snapping back to the present from whatever daydream had captured her momentarily. "Miss McNeil is our boarder, not your servant, Gabe. If you want a glass of water, surely you haven't been gone so long that you've forgotten how to locate the pump yourself."

"Yes, ma'am," he said immediately. "I thought perhaps… The water was for you."

"Well, that's thoughtful, dear, but I also know where the pump is and can serve myself in my own home. Now, why have you come?"

Lucie noticed that Gabriel Hunter seemed unsure of himself for the first time since his arrival. He shifted from one long leg to the other as he slowly turned his hat in his hands.

"Oh, now where are my manners?" Emma chastised herself before he could reply. "Lucie, dear, this is our son, Gabriel. You've heard the colonel speak of him. Lucie comes to us from Ireland, Gabe. She has the loveliest lilt to her speech, though certainly the cat seems to have taken her tongue at the moment. Lucinda, isn't it? Lucinda McNeil, my son, Gabriel Hunter."

Lucie paused in her sewing and nodded her head. "I'm pleased to…"

"I wonder if my mother and I might have a moment alone, Miss McNeil."

"Lucie," Emma corrected. "And anything you and I have to talk about can be said with Lucie right here. She is like family."

Gabriel frowned and looked directly at Lucie. Clearly he expected her to excuse herself, but she took her direction from her employers and those were Colonel Jonathan and Mrs. Emma Hunter, not Mr. Gabriel Hunter. She picked up her needle and resumed her sewing, risking a glance up at Gabriel and seeing that her action had further irritated him.

"Father wrote that he had hired a housekeeper— someone to help out," he said in a voice that was barely audible.

"Well, Lucie is more boarder than hired girl," Emma explained. "She has taken one of our upstairs rooms and has her meals with us. In return she cooks and helps with just about everything else." Emma flung her arm in a wide arc that encompassed the cottage and the grounds. "It's in her nature to be helpful, but the true bonus lies in the companionship. She's an angel from God."

"When did you start using the wheelchair?" Gabriel asked, ignoring this last comment.

"I…"

Lucie saw that the question had been unexpected and had flustered the older woman. "It was my suggestion," Lucie said. "Using the wheelchair makes it easier for her to traverse the uneven ground between here and the house. There isn't enough space inside to set up her quilt frame, and she wants to finish this project and begin her next. It's a wedding gift—for your wedding, I believe."

Lucie continued her quilting but could feel his eyes on

her. He was frowning. She suspected that her response had been neither expected nor wanted.

He focused his attention on Emma. "Then you should have ample time to finish it, mother, since, as you well know, I am not betrothed."

"That's not what the Witherspoons think," Emma muttered as she filled her mouth with straight pins that she proceeded to poke into the layers of the quilt with unnecessary fervor. "Gabe has a business partner," Emma explained to Lucie as if Gabriel had suddenly vanished. "Thurgood Witherspoon—silly, pretentious name, but it suits. Thurgood has a daughter, Jeanne, and…"

Lucie's fingers froze midstitch. Thurgood Witherspoon had been the owner of the factory where she had worked—the factory where her friends had died in the fire she had escaped. She *had* seen this man before—the Hunters' beloved son had been at the garment factory, the day the gossip had spread from one sewing machine to the next that he and the stocky older man with him had just purchased the factory. With hands that shook in anger at the very memory of the disaster those same girls had endured just a few months later, Lucie resumed her sewing, stabbing at the cloth with each stitch.

She watched as Emma's son paced a little ways from them, his hands locked behind his back as if he was a ship's captain surveying the sea. Now she understood why there had been more about him that she had recognized than just the general demeanor of wealth and power. Gabriel Hunter had been at the factory—not on the day of the fire, but earlier. In the summer, when he had stood on the catwalk with Mr. Witherspoon and the floor manager, standing in this same position and surveying the legion of women hunched over sewing machines below.

Now he looked out at his father, who was repairing a fence at the far side of the pasture where several sheep grazed. "The sun is warm. Shouldn't my father have a hat, Miss McNeil?"

"Your father abhors hats and you know that," Emma replied. "It is you who seems to have taken a fancy to hats."

Only the sound of gulls circling the beach and the occasional distant pounding of Jonathan's hammer broke the sudden silence. Having rethreaded her needle as she'd chattered away, Emma resumed her quilting.

"Were you planning to stay for lunch, Gabe?" she finally asked.

"Frankly, I had thought that I would stay for a few days if you have the room." He glanced in Lucie's direction.

"Your room is there, sir," Lucie said softly. Did the man honestly think she might have usurped his place in the house? "Your mother keeps it ready for your visits." She saw that he understood the unspoken accusation that Emma did this in spite of the fact that his visits were infrequent and usually did not include staying the night.

"Your father could probably use some help, Gabe. Why don't you let him know you have arrived while Lucie and I see to some lunch?"

Lucie realized Emma was looking for a way to distract her son so she could get back to the house and get settled without him noticing how weak she really was. Normally Jonathan or Lucie lifted the tiny woman from her chair and carried her into the house. The wheelchair was useful only to move her short distances or change her position when the sun grew too warm or the wind too cool.

*Please make him go,* she prayed silently, and then her

eyes fell on the footpath that wound through a cluster of low, twisted bayberry bushes.

"There's a path here through the pasture," Lucie added, glancing down at Gabriel's dusty, though likely previously highly polished boots.

"I know the way," he replied without looking at her.

"I just meant that it's less muddy than the field. May I take your coat to the house for you?"

Without a glance, Gabriel thrust his coat at her, donned his hat and struck out on the narrow, rutted path she had indicated.

"Hurry, dear," Emma urged Lucie in a soft voice. "We want to be all settled when the gentlemen come for lunch." Her tone indicated her excitement at this unexpected opportunity for a social occasion. Lucie was more concerned that they get Emma positioned so she could get through the lunch without further raising her son's suspicions.

"It may be too much for you, Emma," she said cautiously as she wheeled the older woman up the boardwalk the colonel had built for her and around to the side of the house, hidden from Gabriel's sight. She waited to be sure Gabriel's view of her next action was fully blocked before half lifting, half balancing Emma against her hip as she helped the woman up the steps and into the house.

"Pshaw! I'm perfectly fine, and how often does Gabriel give me this opportunity for a real visit? Let's set the dining-room table and use the good china, dear."

Gabe saw his father pause in his work and squint into the sun. When he realized that the tall young man coming across the pasture was his son, he hooked the claw of the hammer onto a rail in the fence and wiped his hands on a kerchief he carried in his back pocket. "Gabe," he called out happily.

Gabriel acknowledged his father's welcome with a wave that was more of a salute. He did not smile. He had come on business. For Gabriel there was very little in life that did not come down to business—even the task of persuading his aging parents to leave the island they loved and live with him in the city. But his purpose was clear. He wanted his parents to have the best care. Gabe was frustrated by their stubbornness, although his father often pointed out that he and Emma were grateful for the money and supplies Gabe sent them monthly—even if they rarely used anything but the most perishable items. Gabe suspected they shared everything—including the money—with others in need.

Gabe's parents took great pride in his dedication to his work, to building a successful business and a powerful fortune in the city. But they also felt that the time had come when he should be satisfied enough with that to think about finding a woman to love, and about raising a family of his own. But Gabe had little interest in such things. He enjoyed his work.

As he closed the distance between them, Gabriel stuck out a hand for shaking, knowing his father would have preferred an embrace. "It's been a while," the older man observed with no hint of reprimand as he accepted the handshake. "Can you stay for lunch?"

"Lunch and supper and the next few days," Gabriel replied with no pleasure in his tone. "We need to make some decisions, Father, and I intend to stay for as long as that takes."

The two men stood in the middle of the field, studying

each other for a long moment. Jonathan's brow was furrowed. Gabe felt his jaw set with stubborn determination. He only wanted the best for his parents. Why couldn't he make them see that?

"Sounds as if you've already made up your mind and you'll be staying until you get your way," Jonathan challenged, without taking his eyes off his son. Jonathan rarely reverted to the tone he used to take with the men under his command, but Gabe well knew that there was a time and a place for everything. He could not help but admire his father's restraint in not allowing his temper to overcome his reason.

Gabe looked down at his shoes then out toward the horizon. "I prefer not to argue about this, Father. You knew the day would come. She's taken to a wheelchair. And what about this woman? When you wrote, I assumed that she was someone local and certainly someone older. Do you know anything about her past? Her reasons for coming to a place so deserted in the dead of winter?"

"Well, now, we know her name and that she came over from Ireland and found work in Boston, but then fell on some hard times. She doesn't like to talk about the past much."

"All the more reason for you and Mother to be wary." Gabe surveyed the surrounding landscape. While he could not deny that the trip to town could be accomplished in less than half an hour, there wasn't another house in sight—only fields and the sea. "You're isolated here. The very least you might…"

"Now, what was that about not arguing?" Jonathan replied, his good spirits restored. He wrapped his arm around his son's waist and started back toward the house. "Did you see how well your mother looks? There is color in those cheeks, a sparkle in her eye. I suspect having Lucie's company is part of it, don't you think?"

"As I mentioned, Mother is in a wheelchair—something different than when I was last here for Christmas. Then she relied on a cane, which was cause enough for concern. Your hired woman claims that it's just a convenience, but…"

"Now, Gabe, if you refer to Lucie as a hired woman in front of your mother, you're asking for trouble. She's become your mother's friend and confidante and frankly, I've taken a shine to her myself. It's like having a daughter around the place."

"She's been here what—three months?"

"Let me think." Jonathan did the mental calculation. "Yes, three months now. Wait until you see what a fine cook she is and how she's made the house sparkle."

"But what do you know about her?"

"I've just told you. She takes good care of your mother. She's a help to us both with the housework and cooking and such. We enjoy having her with us. A good Christian woman—goes to church every Sunday. Even has us back to saying grace at meals—something we'd not done for some time. There's a sadness about her, though—a deep grieving."

"How did she get here?"

"Adam O'Hare brought her to us. He had taken his last catch to market just before the bay froze for the season and—"

"Adam knew her?"

"Not exactly," Jonathan muttered as they reached the house. "Ah, smell that bread. As I've said, Lucie is a wonder in the kitchen, son."

* * *

While both men wiped their feet and washed up, Emma switched from her wheelchair to one of the dining chairs. From there she watched as Lucie set the table.

"Yes, the lace cloth," she murmured. "Oh, and let's use my grandmother's good china and silver, and Mother's crystal."

As soon as the table was set, Lucie returned to the stove and ladled hot chowder into a tureen and set it on a tile in the center of the table. Surrounding it were platters of sliced cheeses, cold meats, bread Lucie had baked earlier and bowls of fruit.

"They're coming," Emma whispered as the back door opened, and they heard the thud of boots on the wood floor. "Hand me that plate of cheese, dear."

As the two men entered the room, Emma pushed herself up from the chair and set the dish in place as if she had just come in from the kitchen and was sitting down for the meal. "Well, it's about time," she said in a gay voice. "Lucie and I were ready to start without you handsome men. Sit here, Gabe, across from Lucie."

Lucie saw Gabe take note of the wheelchair, positioned now in the hall by the door as if waiting to take Emma back out into the yard. She also saw him study his mother closely.

"You seem a bit flushed and out of breath, Mother," he observed as he reached for the platter of bread next to his father.

Emma laughed. "You try putting together a meal served properly on good china in such a short time," she said. Then she looked at Lucie and raised her eyebrows in exasperation. "Men," she declared, then took Lucie's hand and Gabe's and nodded to Jonathan.

Jonathan and Emma bowed their heads. Lucie noticed that Gabe did not, just before she lowered hers.

"For all that we are about to receive and for the special pleasure of our son's visit, we thank thee, Lord. Amen."

"Amen," Emma and Lucie murmured.

Lucie offered Emma some cheese then passed the dish to Gabe across from her. Their fingers touched briefly and the dish wobbled dangerously. "Sorry," she murmured, steadying it with her other hand.

"I've got it."

"Gabe tells me he's here to stay for a few days," Jonathan announced. "A bit of a holiday."

"Oh, Jonathan, you are such a romantic," Emma chided. "The boy hasn't taken a holiday in years. We both know why he's here. Lucie, dear, our son is determined to have us come live with him. You lived in Boston. Can you honestly imagine Jonathan and me anywhere but right here?"

Lucie lifted her eyes and risked a glance at Gabe. "I expect that Mr. Hunter's Boston is quite different than the parts of Boston that I knew," she replied quietly.

Her comment brought her the immediate and unwanted attention of Gabriel Hunter. "How so?" he asked.

"I only meant that Boston is a large city," Lucie replied, meeting his gaze. "Neighborhoods differ—as do the occupants."

"Lucie was a seamstress," Emma said. "Quite talented, judging by the work she's done on my quilts."

"Really, Mother, then—"

"He's taken to calling us 'Mother' and 'Father,'" Emma continued. "When he was little, it was 'Mama' and 'Papa,' but…" She shrugged and reached over to cover

Gabe's hand with hers. "He's gotten quite high society in his adult years."

Lucie was surprised when Gabe took his mother's hand in his own and gave it an affectionate squeeze. She realized that he was not immune to Emma's charm. It was clear that he was quite fond of her.

The conversation moved to people from the fishing village that Gabe had known as a child, then on to Jonathan's plans for plowing the kitchen garden after lunch. Emma cut large servings of the thick, heavy lemon poppyseed cake and added a generous dollop of clotted cream. During all this, she entertained them with the tale of her mother acquiring the glass dessert plates on a trip to Paris.

Once the cake was served, Lucie watched as Emma allowed the conversation to falter under the guise of them all enjoying the cake. Then she sank back in her chair and pushed her plate away. "Oh, heavens, I'm afraid this heavy meal has gone straight to my head," she said. "Gabriel, if you're planning to stay here in the cottage, you should get settled in. Go bring your things up from the yacht. Unless you want to help Lucie clear and then get your things." She glanced at Lucie. "I'm afraid I've left you with all the work, dear girl."

"Not at all. It was a lovely lunch. We should do this more often…with the possible exception that we serve lighter fare," Lucie teased.

Emma laughed. Lucie took her cue from Emma.

"Now, Mr. Hunter…what's it to be? Get your things or help me with the washup?" Never in her life would she have dared such cheek if it hadn't been the perfect way to get the man out of the room so she and Jonathan could move Emma and get her settled for a much-needed nap. She softened her challenge with a smile.

Jonathan laughed. "That's putting it plain, Lucie, my girl. My advice to you, son, is that you head for that yacht of yours before she takes away the option."

Gabe was left with little choice but to leave the house and make the trek back down to the beach where he had left the dinghy. As he rowed out to his yacht, he focused on the cottage, imagining Lucie McNeil going about her chores. From everything he had observed she was efficient and skilled at managing the responsibilities of a housekeeper. He had no doubt that her duties went beyond cleaning and cooking to include nursing care for his mother. If any one of them thought he had missed observing that his mother had yet to walk a single step in his presence, they were sadly mistaken.

He saw the McNeil woman come out onto the porch and shake out the lace tablecloth. She was tall and slender with thick black hair pulled harshly away from her face into a sensible but entirely unflattering bun at the nape of her long neck. Mid- to late twenties, he guessed. Certainly past marriageable age. In checking her nails and knuckles for cleanliness, it had not escaped his notice that she was small-boned and that her skin was amazingly unblemished for one who had worked hard her entire life. Only her hands gave her away. They were reddened and freckled with exposure to the sun and harsh soap. It also had not escaped his notice that at one time she had burned the palms of both hands.

He tried to put the memory of her eyes from his mind. That first instant she had looked up from her quilting to meet his gaze, he had been captivated by their color. His initial impression had been that she was of little interest—

plain, even dowdy. But her eyes were the most unexpected and arresting shade of violet and they sparkled with intelligence and humor and a surprisingly healthy dose of cynicism. Bold, they were, in their appraisal of him—and condemning, he realized now. What gave her any right to judge him?

She finished shaking the crumbs from the cloth and folded it carefully. He thought she might be watching him, but it was difficult to tell. He frowned. What was her game? What would bring such a woman out here to this desolate setting?

He had admired her obvious intelligence. But in a person dependent on others for her very existence, was there not some possibility of the conniver in that bold look? He thought of his business partner. Thurgood Witherspoon was a man who believed one could ignore certain proprieties as long as in the end it was all to the good. Good for him—and Gabe—and their business.

He turned his thoughts from his business partner back to the hired woman. His father had said Adam had brought her to them. Adam O'Hare was a simple fisherman. No doubt the woman had told some tale to win his sympathies and then begged him to aid her in her escape from the city. He could just see Adam, eager as always to do something for Jonathan and Emma—the people who had once employed him and who now counted him as their dearest friend. He would have leapt at the opportunity to bring them this woman as the answer to their prayers for staying on the island.

Of course the McNeil woman would side with his parents in their fight to stay. After all, if he were successful in moving them, she would lose her position. For the first time since arriving, Gabe smiled. He knew just how to play this game—it was no different than the dealings he had with business associates every day.

*She needs this job,* he thought, *and she will stand with them unless I can find a way to convince her that persuading my parents to move into the city with me is no threat to her. In fact, she will be far better off.*

It wasn't the first time Gabe had sought a way to turn a potential enemy into an ally. It was at the very foundation of his success in business. Lucie McNeil had met her match.

## Chapter Two

By the time Gabe gave the crew instructions for docking
the yacht in town while he returned to the house with his
belongings, his mother was sleeping. He was certain that
the excuse of a heavy noon meal making her drowsy had
been a ruse. The truth was that over the course of the meal
his mother had grown increasingly wan and pale in spite
of her obvious efforts to present a lively front.

He looked around the downstairs rooms for his father,
then caught sight of him through the parlor window. He
was wheeling a small hand plow across the yard, obviously intent on plowing the kitchen garden. Gabe decided
to take his things upstairs to his room and then have a
word with his father.

When he reached the top of the stairs, he heard the snap
of a sheet from the end of the hall. When he reached the
doorway to his room, Lucie was tucking in the fresh, crisp
linen neatly under the corners of the feather mattress.

Lucie had heard his footsteps on the worn carpet that
ran the length of the hallway. She'd tensed but gone on

with her work. "I'll be finished in a minute," she said when he stopped at the door.

"No need to rush," he said, moving around her in the close quarters to set down his bag next to the room's single side chair. "I wanted to talk with you."

She let the top sheet float to the mattress. "You want to know why I'm here, I suppose."

She saw a flicker of surprise at her directness. "Among other things," he replied as he sat on the edge of the side chair, filling the room even more than he had when standing. He waited, his eyes following her every movement.

She continued her work, stalling for time. *Give me the proper words—words that will calm rather than further alarm him.*

She took a deep breath. "I left Ireland two years ago. I came to Boston because there were people my family had known back in the old country. They took me in for a while and helped me get work in the garment factories. Unfortunately, the man of the house thought that entitled him to certain favors." She looked directly at Gabe for the first time. "I moved out and found a room in the basement of a tenement with some cousins on my mother's side. I continued working at the factory and took in piecework so that I could contribute as much as possible to the household and also send something home to my mother. I saved as best I could, but the cousins had several small children."

"So, you are a seamstress by trade?"

"I know how to run a sewing machine and do passable handwork."

"What happened?"

Lucie turned away. *You know what happened,* she

wanted to scream at him. *You and your business partner well know.* She plumped a pillow and stuffed it into a lace-edged pillowcase. "The factory closed—after a fire."

"That must have been difficult." There was not a hint of sympathy in his tone. Behind the words lay the un-spoken message of men like him. *Such things happen.* Lucie wondered if for one single instant it occurred to him that this might have been his factory.

She shrugged then pinned him with those violet eyes. "At least I only lost my position—not my life." *Too much,* an inner voice warned. She took a calming breath and added, "There have been situations where others were not so fortunate." She turned her back to him as she folded a blanket so its threadbare state was less noticeable.

He looked away. "So, you came here."

"Yes."

"Why?"

She sighed wearily and placed the folded blanket across the foot of the bed. "It was— That is, I was unem-ployed and homeless. I had nowhere else to go. My mother's cousin was also out of work. She and her hus-band had all they could handle to keep a roof over the heads of their own children without having to worry about me."

"Still, Boston has many opportunities. You might have been able to get a position in one of the fashionable up-town shops. After all, you speak well, and…"

Lucie wheeled around and glared at him. "Is that what men like you think? That women like me could make a change as simple as that?" She snapped her fingers and actually took a step toward him. "Therefore, we must *choose* to stay where we work and live with no air, no sunshine, no relief? To be sure, if it were so very terrible, we would just pick up and move on to other things, would we not? After all, you would."

*Calm me. I am making matters worse by insulting him.*

"It seems that this is exactly what you did," he said, standing as he met her gaze. "Did you know someone here on the island?"

She straightened the lid on the chamber pot before placing it under the narrow bed. "No. One of the girls I worked with came from here. The way she talked of Nantucket, it made me think of home—of Ireland."

Gabe said nothing as she placed fresh towels on the washstand.

"And is it like home?"

His voice had lost its harshness and for a moment she felt the tears that were never far from the surface threaten. "Our cottage in Ireland was nothing as grand as this, but it did look out to the sea."

"And tell me again, how did you come to work for my father?"

She saw that he hoped to catch her in some lie. "Mr. O'Hare brought me here. He said your father was seeking a housekeeper." She had almost said "nurse" for that was how Adam had described the position.

Gabe turned to the window. "I'm sure that when my father employed you, you had no idea it would be quite so isolated. It must have been lonely for you these last several weeks with no one but two old people for company."

"On the contrary, Mr. Hunter, I count myself as blessed. Your parents have taken me in as a member of the family. They are as dear to me as my own parents, and I count my good fortune each and every day. Now, if there's nothing further—"

Gabe heard her run her hands over the bed to smooth nonexistent creases from the coverlet. She released a soft sigh of satisfaction. Gabe thought it was as good a time as any to test the waters.

"I love my parents, Miss McNeil," he said without turning to look at her. "Very much."

There was a brief moment in which neither of them moved or spoke.

"Then perhaps you'd be coming to visit more often now that the weather has turned nicer," she said. "Your mother would like that very much, and I expect your father misses you every bit as much, although he defends your need to attend to business matters."

Gabe turned. "It appears to me that you have influence, Miss McNeil, and surely you can understand that my wanting my parents with me where they can have everything they need and access to the finest doctors and…"

Her eyes narrowed and she placed her hands at her waist as she met his look. "Your parents, Mr. Hunter, have a home here. This is their place—their land. Your mother has already lost her home twice—once when she was a girl and the war came to her very door. Then again when Mr. Hunter's finances collapsed and they were left with only this house and land. What kind of thing would it be to take this home from her a third time? Perhaps it's the property that's important to you, for word has it that the appeal of the islands for city dwellers has turned the tide for many people living here now. According to your father, tourism is a profitable enterprise. This property, with its isolation and views, could be quite valuable."

Gabe bristled. So she had considered the value of the property and cottage, and apparently had pumped his father for information. How dare she accuse *him* of less-than-pure motives. "That is out of line, young woman."

"I meant no disrespect. It's just that some of the people I met in Boston, the landlords and factory owners, knew the value of the land. I expect from what your mother has told me of her heritage—where land was everything—she has probably instilled that same respect in you."

He studied her for a long moment. This was the closest he had been to her other than at lunch. At the table he had barely glanced at her, but now she seemed to fill the small room with her flashing eyes and her accusatory speeches barely tempered with the respect due him, given his station—and hers.

"Why have you never married, Miss McNeil?"

The question had exactly the effect he had hoped. The wind went completely out of her. He almost regretted asking, because she looked so completely taken aback. Yet he could not seem to stop himself. "I mean, you'll forgive me, but you appear to be of age." He allowed his eyes to roam over her from head to foot.

"You are saying *past* the age, are you not, sir?" she said stiffly. "My maidenly status is of my own choosing and, with respect, sir, it is not your business. However, I am twenty and four. And now, if there's nothing more I can do to make you comfortable, I'd like to check on your mother."

"I'll go with you," Gabe said, and took pleasure in her surprise.

"Very well," she said as she led the way down the stairs to his parents' bedroom on the first floor.

Emma was smiling as they entered the room, but still sound asleep.

"As you can see, she's resting," Lucie whispered, and bent to pull the cover over Emma's thin shoulders.

Gabe stood on the other side of the bed, looking down at his mother. "She looks…" He turned to the window so Lucie would not see the emotion he felt looking at his mother, so tiny and frail…and peaceful. He watched his father as he awkwardly pushed the manual plow through the tough and rocky soil.

"She's dreaming. She has such sweet dreams," Lucie said almost wistfully, then she, too, turned to the second window overlooking the garden. "I should help the colonel," she said, more to herself than to him, and in the next instant she was gone.

It was clear to Gabe that her opinion of him was less than complimentary. He believed that unspoken in that statement had been the fact that he should be the one going to help his father. He frowned as he watched her exit the house and walk across the yard to where Jonathan struggled with the plow. Something she said made his father stop and laugh and then hand the plow over to her.

Why should this woman's opinion of him matter? What did he care what she thought of him or his plans for his parents? Whether she liked it or not, he knew that his was the best possible solution. Miss Lucie McNeil would just have to get used to that. She would have to find another way of making her way in this world. She was not his problem. Satisfied that he had put the woman from his mind, Gabe bent and kissed the forehead of his sleeping mother, then left the room. He rolled back his sleeves and went out to help his father.

"I can manage that, Miss McNeil," he said heartily, as he reached to relieve her of the plow.

"It's almost done," she replied, refusing to let go. "There's just one more row." She started forward, pushing the plow with surprising ease. "You could start to pull out those stones if you're of a mind to help out," she added, and Gabe could have sworn she grinned at his father as she passed him.

"Well, now, with you two young people in full charge here, I'll just be going down to check the traps," he said, and headed off toward the dunes. "Fresh lobster for supper," he called.

"Aye, if you're lucky," Lucie called back.

As Gabe wrestled with the large stone that turned out to be two-thirds buried in the freshly plowed earth, he tried to stave off the unfamiliar rush of envy he felt at her easy banter with his father. He glanced up and saw her looking back at him. Needing to impress her with the fact that he, too, knew how to work, he gave a mighty heave on the rock. It popped free and sent him sprawling onto his backside in the fresh dirt. The sun was behind her so he couldn't be sure, but he could have sworn the woman was laughing at him.

Later, as Lucie set three places at the kitchen table, she heard Gabe come down the hall. "I thought my father was taking a tray with mother," Gabe commented. He smelled of soap and wore a freshly laundered white shirt with no collar, his suit vest left unbuttoned and the same trousers, although he'd obviously brushed away the dirt from the garden mishap.

"He is," Lucie replied, forcing herself to concentrate on the food preparations rather than the smell and look of Gabe Hunter.

"Are we expecting a guest?"

She saw that he was perplexed by the three place settings. "Adam takes his suppers with us most nights."

"I see."

"Your mother tells me that you and Adam spent a great deal of time together when you were a boy. Adam talks fondly about those days sometimes. It's a bit as if he looks upon you as the son he never had. I expect the two of you will have some catching up to do."

He watched her carefully. "Adam is still fishing for a living, is he?"

She nodded.

It should have been an unexpected pleasure to get reacquainted with Adam O'Hare. Somehow that pleasure was spoiled by the presence of Lucie McNeil. Not that she did anything untoward. She was a model hostess, making sure each man's plate was kept filled until Adam protested that it was enough. When she was at the table, she remained silent, allowing the two of them to share memories and catch up on what had happened in the years since they'd last seen each other. But it disturbed Gabe that she was there, that he could see her, smell her, hear the rustle of her skirt as she moved between the kitchen and dining room. He felt self-conscious having her hear how much he enjoyed reminiscing with the old man who had first taught him to fish, swim and set a proper lobster trap.

"I want to thank you for everything you've done for my parents," he told Adam. "I know my father relies on you."

Adam shrugged and leaned his chair back on two legs as he lit his pipe and studied Gabe. "You come to take them away?" he asked.

Gabe had positioned himself at the dining table so he could observe Lucie's actions in the kitchen. He saw her hands grow still as she rinsed the dishes. Her back was to him, but he knew she was waiting for his answer. "Nothing has been decided. I just came to spend a few days with them," he said.

"I know your Ma's enjoying your visit," Adam replied with a broad smile. "The way that woman does talk about you, you'd think you were bigger than the president himself."

"You were the one who urged me to follow my dream," Gabe replied, remembering the day Adam had confided that he'd once dreamed of having his own fishing business. "Funny how we both got what we wanted."

"Took me a sight longer," Adam said as he stretched out his long legs and folded his gangly arms behind his head. Then he let out a sigh of pure contentment. "Yep, I never could have imagined that Nantucket would end up as the place for rich city dwellers to spend their time, or that they'd want to go fishing in the bargain. It's been a good life, son. Unexpected in many ways, but good, mostly thanks to your folks."

Lucie set the kettle back on top of the stove, then bent to bank the fire underneath.

"You need more wood, Lucie?" Adam stood and waited to do her bidding.

"I'll get it," she replied with a gentle smile. "You'd best see to repairing those traps for Jonathan."

Adam gave her a cockeyed grin. "Yes, ma'am. Come on, Gabe. I'll bet you've forgotten everything you ever knew about lobstering." He wrapped his arm around Gabe's shoulder and led him toward the door.

* * *

Lucie watched the two men head for the beach. Gabe's neatly clipped dark hair was in sharp contrast to the unkempt and thinning white that peeked out from beneath Adam's worn knit cap. It was impossible to believe that Gabe had once idolized Adam—at least according to Emma. Adam was such a simple man, content with his life. He'd never lived anywhere but right here on this island. Oh, she was sure he'd had bigger dreams, as did she, but they were the impossible kinds of dreams that practical souls like them often had. Just knowing that they were out of reach somehow made whatever they faced in life more bearable. After all, if you could not achieve a dream, then it would always be just that—a dream to comfort you in your exhaustion.

Gabe Hunter apparently had realized all of his dreams, and look where it had gotten him. If one measured contentment by satisfaction with the way things were and happiness with what had been achieved, then he had to be the most discontented man she'd ever seen. He was also the most confusing. After arriving with the express purpose of taking his parents back to Boston with him, he'd been here for several hours and as far as she could tell he'd made no progress with that intention. Gabe did not strike her as a man who was patient when he wanted something. She would guess he was accustomed to reaching out and taking what he wanted.

She felt a shiver race through her and blamed it on the cool spring night and the breeze off the ocean, not on the fact that the memory of accidentally touching hands with Gabe Hunter earlier at lunch had just skittered across her mind. She shook it off and went across the yard to get wood for the stove. She had spent far too much of her day thinking about Gabe Hunter and worrying about what he might think of her. *Get thee behind me,* she murmured as she stacked several pieces of kindling in the basket she made of her apron.

Lucie was sitting in the small parlor darning a pair of his father's woolen socks when Gabe came back to the house.

"Adam went back to the village," he told her.

She glanced up. "I expected that he would. He goes out early most mornings for his catch." She returned to her darning, but cut her eyes once or twice to where he remained standing in the doorway. "Your parents have retired for the night," she added. "They asked that I let you know they would see you at breakfast."

He took a couple of steps into the room, which was filled with mementos from his mother's home in South Carolina and the mansion his parents had once owned in Boston. These treasures were mixed in with the accumulations of summers spent here on the island before his father's financial troubles began. After that this place had become their permanent home—their only home. He picked up a photograph of himself as a small boy and studied it. "Hard to believe I was ever that young," he said, more to himself than to her as he replaced the frame on the mantel.

Lucie cut the thread and folded the socks. "I'm sorry. Of course, you want to sit for a while. I can finish this tomorrow."

"No, stay. That is, if you don't mind." He took the chair opposite hers, dwarfing it and looking quite uncomfortable. "Tell me about my mother's health."

Lucie straightened in her chair and folded her hands

in her lap. He did not miss the way she gripped her fingers tightly. "What is it you wish to know?" She made an obvious attempt to keep her tone light but respectful.

He leaned forward, resting his elbows on his knees. Next to him the dry logs popped in protest as they surrendered themselves to the flame. "You see, Miss McNeil, I'm nobody's fool. I am very aware that in the many hours that have passed since my arrival in this house, my mother has not taken a single step in my presence. As a matter of fact, she has spent most of that time in her bedroom—a room, I might add, that used to be located at the top of the stairs but now seems to have replaced my father's study."

"Your father was not really using his study, and when I came here to live, Emma—your mother—had the idea that it would give us all more privacy if they moved down here and I took their room upstairs."

"Nevertheless, none of that answers my original question. I would like to know what the true status of my mother's health is."

He watched as she considered her options. He planned to stay for at least a couple of days. There was no way she and his mother could keep him from learning the extent of her mother's frailties. She chose her words with care. "As you well know, your mother wishes to live out her days in this house on this island," she said quietly.

"And how close is that end?"

"That isn't for me to say. It's in God's hands."

Gabe threw up his hands in exasperation as he stood and paced the room. "She has been in your hands—not God's—for the last three months, Miss McNeil. I'm asking you to tell me how far she has slipped."

Lucie stood and pulled herself to her full height.

He stopped pacing and turned. "Well?"

"We are all in God's hands, Mr. Hunter. As for your mother, she has difficulty walking and she has difficulty getting her breath sometimes. As with most women of her age she tires a bit more easily than someone younger. Fortunately for her, she has people who love her around to help her through the bad days. Fortunately for me, your mother is one of the sweetest, most charming and kind souls I have ever met, and I count it God's blessing on me that I can spend this time with her and your father." She delivered all of this in a quiet and even tone. "If there is nothing more, I will bid you a good night, sir."

He was about to protest, but then stepped aside to let her pass.

## Chapter Three

Lucie had not expected the dream that night. For one thing she had fallen into bed more exhausted than she could ever remember. She knew why. This wasn't the usual physical exhaustion she felt at the end of a long and busy day. No, physical exhaustion was almost always accompanied by mental and emotional exhaustion, and it allowed her a deep and dreamless sleep.

But from the moment Gabriel Hunter had walked up from the beach, Lucie had suspected trouble. When she had recognized him as one of the owners of the garment factory, she had felt the pent-up fury she had not permitted herself to acknowledge—a desire for revenge like nothing she had ever known. She had never spoken of what she had seen that horrible day, but it had been all she could do not to lash out at him for the devastation that pure, preventable negligence had caused when the factory had burned. She had steeled herself against an outburst out of respect for Jonathan and Emma.

She had also fought to control her temper throughout the long day and evening as she waited for the challenge she knew would come. It would have nothing to do with his recognizing her from the factory. To her knowledge he had only visited the place the one time, and men like Gabriel Hunter took little notice of people like her unless he was given cause. He had certainly noticed her now that his parents had taken her in. Further, Emma had made it clear that Lucie was not only their boarder and helper. She had become their friend—and ally.

He had bided his time, watching her, questioning everything he saw in the house with a lift of his dark eyebrows, a furrow of his brow or a knowing glance from those piercing blue eyes. By the time the challenge she'd been anticipating all day came, it was late, and she was weak from fatigue and from being on her guard since he'd arrived. He had what he'd planned to have all along—the upper hand. She had stood her ground and he had allowed her to leave the room, but she was not fooled. When she woke and went to tend to her morning chores, Gabriel Hunter would still be waiting for answers.

Lucie closed her eyes and forced herself to concentrate on more pleasant things, like Emma's quilt and the rhythm of the old woman's steady hand as she pushed the needle through the fabric, forming stitch by exacting stitch the pattern that would bring the fabric to life. Lucie smiled and pulled the covers to her chin as the clock in the parlor chimed the hour. The dream came just before dawn.

*She was walking—no, running—through the alley. It was winter, yet the weather held the promise of an early spring. A church bell was calling parishioners to evening vespers. The twilight air was sweet and the slight wind pleasant. Lucie tugged at her woolen scarf as she rounded the corner and saw the factory looming ahead of her. She was late, but if she hurried...*

*No, wait. The smell. Not sweet at all. It was acrid and pungent. The air stung her eyes. Then it was snowing, and she thrust out her tongue to catch some of the cooling flakes. But instead of providing solace, the flakes were warm and powdery—ashes and soot. She blinked and tried to swallow. Smoke. There was so much smoke rolling through the streets and engulfing everything in its path.*

Lucie sat up, pushing the covers away. She was drenched in sweat, her breath coming in heaves as if she actually had been running. Her cheeks were wet—not with perspiration but with tears. It had been months. How long would the memory of all she had seen and heard and felt that day haunt her?

Knowing there would be no further sleep that night, Lucie threw back the covers and stood by her narrow bed. In the dark she poured water from the pitcher into the bowl and splashed it over her face and neck. She brought her braided hair over her left shoulder and used her fingers to work through the plait. With a practiced hand she brushed through the few tangles and then twisted and looped the length into a tight knot that she secured with pins.

She reached for the dress she had worn the day before, then changed her mind and took out another dress along with fresh undergarments from the shallow, curtained space that served as her wardrobe. In all of this she never once looked in a mirror or lit a lamp. For Lucie it was vanity enough that she had decided on the clean clothing. It was because of him. It was because she needed to be at her best in order to face him.

By the time the sky had lightened in the predawn mist,

Lucie had the fires going, bread baking, eggs gathered, chickens and other livestock fed and the table set with Emma's best breakfast cloth and crochet-edged napkins. She had cut thick slices of bacon from the slab in the smokehouse. They lay on a plate, ready to fry. She had an hour before she would need to wake Emma and help her dress. Emma would insist on coming to the table for breakfast in spite of the fact that she rarely ate breakfast, and if she did, it was always on a tray in her room.

Lucie pulled out the small, worn book she carried in her apron pocket. She would sit on the side porch in Emma's rocking chair and read a passage and then watch the sun rise. Both would calm her and give her strength to face the day—to face Gabriel Hunter. But when she stepped out onto the porch, Gabriel was already there— sitting in Emma's chair.

Gabe had slept fitfully, the ghosts of his youth haunting the small room in the dark. How many nights had he spent lying awake, plotting his future—his escape from the island and the poverty it represented? As a grown man—successful beyond his wildest childhood imaginings—he had stretched out on the bed, his arms folded beneath his head as he stared out the window.

Throughout the night he had watched the branches of the large ash tree whip back and forth in the wind. A storm brewing, he had thought, and had remembered how, when he was a boy, such impending storms had only added to his sense of imprisonment. Forcing himself into the present, he had thought of his yacht and had mentally gone over each step he'd observed the crew of three take to secure the vessel. Only after he'd given his men explicit instructions, and retrieved his personal effects before the steward rowed him to shore, had he been comfortable sending them on to dock in town. Gabriel Hunter was a cautious man—especially when it came to the people and possessions he prized.

As he shifted to find a more comfortable position in the rocker on the porch, he had to ask himself why he hadn't stayed the night on the boat. He would have been far more at ease. Yet he hadn't even considered the idea. From the moment his mother had sent the Irish woman to prepare his room, he had never once thought of suggesting he stay in town or on the yacht. Perhaps it had been the delight at his unexpected visit that he'd seen in his mother's dark-circled eyes. Perhaps he had feared insulting his parents' hospitality. Far more likely, it had been the hired woman. She did everything expected of her and more, but there was not a subservient bone in her tall, reedlike body.

Her violet eyes flashed and glittered with emotions she obviously knew better than to risk stating aloud. She could be goaded, though. He had seen that the evening before. In the parlor, after his parents had retired, he had deliberately baited her and she had come close to responding in a way that no true servant would ever consider.

"Good morning, Lucie," he said when she stepped out onto the porch. He remained seated and turned away from the wind to light his cigar.

"Good morning."

No "sir" accompanied her greeting. Gabe frowned up at her, wondering if she had deliberately positioned herself so that he saw only her silhouette, and had to squint in the rising sun to see that.

"Shall I prepare you some breakfast?"

"I'll wait for my parents," he replied, and turned his attention to the horizon, dismissing her by his indifference.

To his surprise she sat down on the top step and opened a small leather book. The text was printed on an onionskin paper that crackled as she lifted the blue ribbon marking her place and placed a finger under a page, prepared to turn it.

"Don't let me keep you from your chores," he said. "There's no need for you to attend to my needs until my parents are up and about."

She did not look up from the page, but marked her place with her forefinger as she replied, "The chores are done for the moment and, unless I can prepare a plate for you, I'm not sure what I can do to attend to your needs."

Gabe considered several retorts. The woman calmly turned the page and continued reading.

"What are you doing?" he asked.

"Reading," she replied, and turned another page. Either she was a practiced student or she was pretending to race through the text. He suspected the latter.

"Reading what?" he asked, and in the same moment reached over and took the book from her hands, an action he regretted as soon as he saw the title on the spine of the small book.

*The Book of Psalms.*

He handed it back to her, and without comment she found the page she'd been reading, marked the place with the ribbon and closed the book. "Your mother should be awake soon," she said as she stood and smoothed her apron. She did not wait for his reply, but turned and went inside.

She had planned the whole encounter. He was sure of it. She'd seen him there and had decided to play her little scene of piety. He wasn't fooled. Women he knew often used game-playing to get their way. Jeanne Witherspoon was a master at the craft. Once she and her mother had concocted an elaborate plan to get Gabe to accompany them to a chamber music concert. Their scheme had been impressive enough that he had gone—and hated every moment of it. Such antics might amuse him in a drawing-room setting, but there was no diversion in such tactics from a servant girl.

Gabe puffed on his cigar and stared out to sea. In some ways she was indeed more girl than woman—first impressions notwithstanding. Up close her face had the unlined skin of youth. Her hair was thick and shiny, as black as a night sky. Her form... He stopped himself from thinking of her further. It was not her physical attributes that promised to be the problem for him. Lucie McNeil might be younger than he had first thought, but she was clearly an intelligent and literate young woman. Still, there was another side to her—barely concealed characteristics of pride and willfulness that exceeded her station in life.

From the far side of the porch, he heard the low murmur of voices, then the stronger voice of Lucie McNeil as she apparently came to the window. It would be open, he knew, because in all weather his mother had always insisted the window be open at least a crack.

"'Tis another lovely day," Lucie said. A pause and then, "Yes, a good day for plowing and planting—as long as you let me do both." Laughter. Hers. His father's.

Her voice faded as she apparently stepped away from the window, and he could not make out the words. When he heard a door open and close, and then his father's slow, heavy tread in the hall, he went inside.

"Ah, Gabriel. Did you sleep well?"

Gabe wondered if it was only his imagination or if his father had taken on some of the woman's Irish brogue. "The first night in a strange bed is always difficult," he replied, and did not miss the brief look of hurt that crossed his father's expression.

"Aye, it's been awhile since you spent the night in that bed," he agreed with a forced smile. "A bit cramped, no doubt. You weren't nearly as tall or filled out when…" His voice trailed off on a smile.

Gabe understood that his father had been about to say "when you left home." He cleared his throat and glanced around the spotless kitchen, spying the bacon slices and the freshly baked bread on the side table. "Where's Mother?"

"She'll be here directly. You know your mother and her beauty rest. It's the Southern belle in her," Jonathan added with a wink. "Bacon?" he asked as he lifted the eye of the cook stove to check the fire. Then he set a cast-iron skillet on the hot surface and speared a slice of bacon from the platter.

"You have a cook," Gabe reminded him.

For a moment Jonathan stared at him with eyes that showed no comprehension, then he laughed and dropped the bacon into the now-hot pan. The bacon fat caught and sizzled, releasing a tantalizing aroma that carried Gabe back to the days of his youth. He barely heard his father's reply.

"Lucie? Lucie's attending to your mother." Jonathan continued to prepare the breakfast. He was dressed in worn, rough clothing—the garb of a farmer or fisherman, when once he had been a prosperous businessman attired in the finest wares that Boston haberdashers had to offer.

Jonathan jerked his head toward the open shelves above the dry sink. "Dishes are still kept there," he said. "Set places for four. Adam won't come for breakfast. Out on his boat at this hour."

Gabe opened his mouth to protest. If they insisted on having this woman, they could at least expect her to do the work of a hired woman. "How much are you paying her?" he asked.

His father's eyebrows were thick and expressive. The slightest lift of them had spoken volumes even before they had turned the same snow-white as his full head of hair. The obvious spoken response that this was really not Gabe's business was unnecessary, as Gabe—chastised into the need to turn away—reached for plates, cups and saucers from the shelf.

"Ah, here comes the prettiest girl on all of Nantucket," Jonathan called out as if announcing the arrival of a special guest at a grand ball.

Gabe stepped into the doorway in time to see his mother leaning heavily on her cane and on Lucie McNeil's forearm. Both women were short of breath, and as she slowly made her way to the table, Gabe noticed that his mother's cheeks were flushed. He moved closer to see if this was natural coloring or the result of a bit of rouge applied to fool him.

"Good morning, Mother," he said, and bent to kiss her cheek as he pulled her chair away to allow her room to sit. The color was natural. Her cheek was warm. "Did you sleep well?"

The four of them endured a breakfast laced with stilted conversation. Afterward, Gabriel insisted he drive Lucie to the village for supplies. Normally Lucie would have walked and enjoyed it, but Gabriel had dismissed her protest with the statement that it had been some time since he'd been to town.

Lucie made no attempt at conversation on the ride into the village. She sat stiffly erect and concentrated on maintaining as much space between Gabe and herself as the narrow wagon seat allowed, while the wagon bounced its way over the ruts and gullies left by the spring rains. He seemed equally determined not to speak, although she suspected his reasons had more to do with his sense of her place than anything else. Men like Gabriel Hunter did not make small talk with hired help. Bereft of any orders to give he was probably at a loss for words. She soon realized he was almost as uncomfortable as she was, and the thought permitted her to relax slightly.

She risked a glance his way as he guided the wagon over a particularly uneven patch of the dirt road. Was he deliberately pushing the team of horses so that the wagon bounced and teetered with every slight turn in the way? His jaw was clenched, and the scowl that seemed to be his usual expression furrowed his brow beneath the brim of his hat.

"There's a sharp curve ahead, just before the downhill road to the village," Lucie said. "It's best to take it slow, especially after last week's rain."

"I am well aware of the twists and turns of the way," Gabe said, but he slowed the horses with a tug of the reins. "After all, I grew up here."

"Not entirely," Lucie replied without thinking, then bit her lip, determined to keep her words to herself.

His jaw clenched. "Meaning?"

"I just recall your mother telling me that the family

made Nantucket your permanent home when you were nine, and you left just before you reached sixteen, so…"

*Be quiet, Lucie.*

"And how long have you been here? And how many times have you driven this road?" He kept his eyes straight ahead as he added, "Or perhaps you've traveled this way with some village man who's come calling once my parents were asleep."

Lucie sucked in her cheeks in an effort to remind herself to remain civil, subservient. It did no good. "As you no doubt know, I have been here for three months. I have never driven the road myself but have traveled it often with Adam, who is kind enough to help when I need to do a heavier shopping. Otherwise I walk."

To her consternation the man had the audacity to split the air with a snorting laugh. "Please don't take me for the fool that my parents and Adam obviously are, Lucie McNeil. You may have wound your way into their hearts, but I am not so easily persuaded."

"Meaning?" she shot back, reverting to his informal, not to mention insulting, manner of addressing her.

He feigned a look of shock. "Why, Miss McNeil, you're still relatively attractive in spite of your years. I suspect even you might get lonely for companionship. You may wish to consider that the selection of eligible men is far greater in Boston than you'll find on this island."

Lucie glared at him until she saw that in spite of his attempts to ignore her, she had caused him discomfort. "You have no right to judge me, Gabriel Hunter," she said.

"Nor you me," he replied as he snapped the reins, sending the horses into a trot for the remainder of the journey.

## Chapter Four

Although Gabe was well aware of the island's recovery from decades of economic devastation, he could barely conceal his astonishment at the magnitude of that recovery. On his visits to his parents, he went directly to their beach, spent an hour or so at the house with them and returned to Boston. The last time he'd traveled this road it had been by foot.

On his way to the docks on the eve of his sixteenth birthday, he'd passed shuttered and abandoned houses and shops, and fishing shanties. In such places lone residents like Adam eked out a living catching the fish they would later sell at market on the mainland. Then every landmark he passed had been further proof of his assertion that there was nothing for him here. If his father was satisfied to simply give up and refuse to rebuild what had once been his, Gabe was not. He would go to Boston, find work and, dollar by dollar, amass more wealth than his father had ever imagined.

Now, on this cloudless May morning, he slowed the horses through streets bustling with traffic—carriages, wagons, the occasional family taking an early holiday out for a bicycle excursion or strolling in and out of the many shops along Main Street. Ahead on the square he saw the impressive brick exterior of the Pacific Bank—the bank his father had helped establish. Across the street stood the clothing store once owned by Rowland Macy's father. Rowland had been every island boy's hero, having first abandoned the stodgy business of haberdashery to follow his dream of whaling, and then headed for California for the gold rush.

Gabe smiled slightly as he recalled that eventually Rowland had come full circle, returning from California to settle in New York City and open his own clothing business in the heart of Manhattan. It occurred to him that he, too, had come full circle—leaving the island intent on making his way and his fortune and, having achieved that, now finding himself fighting to protect that fortune from the same total ruin his father's had suffered.

He shook off his business worries and continued his visual and mental tour of his boyhood hometown. Next to the bank he spotted the familiar Doric columns of the United Methodist church his family had attended in his youth.

"Are my parents still members of the church there?" he asked.

Lucie started at his sudden question after several moments of silence between them. As usual she appeared to weigh her words carefully before replying. "We have taken to attending services at the small church we passed closer to their home. I began attending there shortly after I arrived, and one Sunday your parents asked if I minded if they joined me."

"I see." He steered the horses to the public watering

hole in the square. By the time he had secured the horses and come round to her side, Lucie had just climbed down and was smoothing her skirts. Gabe involuntarily reached out a hand to steady her but withdrew it immediately. When she turned, he was standing close enough to touch her. "It would appear that in the short time you've been with my parents, Lucie, you've had quite an influence on their lives," he said, and wondered why he had taken note of the way the top of her head barely reached his shoulder.

"On the contrary," she replied, moving past him with as little contact as possible when he made no move to step aside. "It is your dear parents who have influenced me."

She busied herself retrieving her shopping list from the pocket of her dress. "I won't be long," she assured him. "Shall I meet you here or—"

He stepped to her side. "I'll come with you," he said, and when she hesitated, added with a wave of his hand, "Lead on, Miss McNeil."

Lucie had no misconceptions about why Gabriel Hunter had decided to accompany her on her rounds. The man did not trust her. He was watching her every move, his eyebrows raised in surprise when shopkeepers welcomed her warmly or a fellow church member called out a greeting in passing.

After a stop at the dry-goods store to purchase thread and other sewing supplies for Emma, Lucie had had enough. "I can complete the rest of the shopping on my own," she said with barely concealed ire. "Perhaps you would care for a refreshment before the drive home," she said as they passed a tavern.

"I do not partake of spirits." He took the list from her and studied it. "Let's see." Silently, he ticked off each item, then crushed the paper in one hand. "It would appear that we have everything."

"Your father asked me to shop for a small gift for your mother—and your mother requested the same. I would like to give them a gift, as well. After all, tomorrow is their anniversary, but no doubt you are aware of that." She took some satisfaction in the downcast eyes and sudden interest in his boots that told her he'd had no idea.

"And have you funds for such extravagances?"

Lucie sighed. "Not everything comes at great cost, Mr. Hunter. In cases like these a token is as treasured as something far more grand but equally as frivolous."

He blinked as he worked through the logic of that.

"I have some money left from the household funds," Lucie said.

"And your gift to them will also come from those funds?"

Lucie forced herself to take a deep breath, more to restrain herself from slapping the man than because she needed air. "Why, Mr. Hunter, a businessman like you must know of the age-old practice of bartering." She did not wait for his reply but stalked off down the street and turned the corner.

Sean Connors had been Gabe's best friend in the five years Gabe had lived on the island. Together the boys had explored every inlet and beach along the island's shore. They had fished together in the summer, harvested cranberries in the bogs for spending money in the fall, tracked small game through the snow in the winter and dreamed of escape in the spring. It was Sean who had helped Gabe stow away for the boat trip to New Bedford and from there Gabe had made his way to Boston. It was Sean who had held firm to his dream of captaining a ship that traveled to exotic ports. It was Sean who had never left the island.

Now Gabe stood in the doorway of a corner shop and waited while Lucie spoke with Sean. Gabe was shocked at the change in his boyhood friend. Old beyond his years—grizzled and stooped—Gabe would not have known the man except for the smile and the sound of his laugh. That laugh had echoed across the dunes on more than one occasion as the two boys pursued their youthful adventures. Gabe watched as Sean handed Lucie a package wrapped in brown paper and tied with the rope fishermen used for repairing nets.

In return Lucie removed a locket that Gabe hadn't noticed until now and dropped it into Sean's hand. Gabe started forward then held back. Lucie was coming his way. She had just turned to wave and laugh at some comment Sean had made. In that instant Sean saw him and his face sobered. Shaking his head as if tossing off an apparition, he turned and went inside the tiny shanty.

Gabe stepped quickly into a doorway as Lucie rounded the corner.

"One gift in hand," she said as she passed him without a glance and placed the package in the cloth bag she'd used to store the thread and sewing notions she'd purchased earlier. She paused and without turning added, "Well, come along. You might be able to help me decide."

Feeling like a schoolboy caught by his teacher, Gabe fell into step behind her as she entered a shop where the window featured the kinds of lacy items that would have sent Jeanne Witherspoon into spasms of delight.

Inside the tiny shop, Lucie fingered several items—a lace-trimmed blouse of the sheerest cotton lawn, an intricately woven blue shawl that looked as light as air and finally a silk bed jacket with roses and vines embroidered over its entire surface. She spent some time on the bed jacket, holding it up to the light, discussing the handwork with the shopkeeper and finally, after hearing the price, replacing it with great care in the display.

She turned to the counter displaying an array of ladies' handkerchiefs. The shopkeeper assured her that initials could be embroidered while Lucie took care of any shopping she had yet to do. Lucie nodded and prepared to give the clerk the order.

Gabe picked up the bed jacket. "If that is my father's gift for my mother, I believe he would be more pleased with this item, Miss McNeil."

Her cheeks colored and she turned to the clerk. "Excuse us a moment, please," she said, and walked as far away from the ears of the clerk as the small space would permit before speaking. "The price is too dear," she whispered.

"How much has my father allotted?"

She murmured a figure, then added with more conviction, "And he would not like it if you paid the difference. This is his gift—not yours."

"And what is the total sum you have for both gifts?"

Lucie pulled some bills and coins from the small purse she had pinned to her pocket and turned her back to the clerk, using Gabe as cover as she counted it.

"Very well," Gabe said, holding out his hand for the money.

Lucie hesitated and then gave it to him.

Gabe turned to the shopkeeper, "Ma'am, are you the proprietress?"

"Yes, sir," the shopkeeper replied, her eyes excited at

the prospect of a greater sale. "I own the shop and make most of the items you see here."

"I see several items that suit my needs." He selected the shawl, the blouse and the bed jacket and placed the items on the counter. "The bed jacket is a separate sale," he said, handing her all of the money Lucie had given him.

Lucie stepped forward as if to protest, but before she could the clerk smiled sadly. "I am sorry, sir, but you are short by—"

"Here is my offer," Gabe said, leaning in close to the proprietress so that Lucie had to step closer to hear. "You can either have sales today of…" He mentally calculated the total as he fingered the price tag on each of the remaining items. Then he laid out the money for the sum, making sure to keep his money distinctly separate from the amount he'd placed on the counter for the bed jacket. "Or you can have no sale at all."

Lucie started to protest but Gabe held up his hand, his gaze remaining fixed on the shopkeeper. He smiled at the woman, who batted her eyelashes flirtatiously. "You drive a hard bargain, Mr.—?"

"Hunter. Gabriel Hunter." He gathered all the money and handed it to her. "Please wrap the bed jacket as a gift and we'll be back to pick up our purchases in twenty minutes." And with a tip of his hat, he headed for the door, started out then paused and held the door for Lucie. "Where next?"

"Home," she said angrily. "I'll just have to come up with something else for Emma to give Jonathan now that you've spent all the money."

Gabe smiled. "Why, Miss McNeil, have you never heard of bartering?"

He led the way down the street and turned at a narrow lane. He glanced at signs and window displays as he made his way down the lane, turned a corner and entered the next street. Lucie hurried to keep up with his long, purposeful strides. "Where are you—"

He stopped abruptly and peered through a small window that was covered from the inside with sawdust and grime. Hanging in the window like slabs of meat were three hand-carved violins. "That quilt that my mother is finishing, Lucie—is it promised?"

"I believe she plans to give it to some needy family."

"And is it near to complete?" he asked, ignoring the explanation.

"Well, yes. Emma—Mrs. Hunter—is quite intent on beginning a new project, the quilt for your wedding, so—"

Gabe nodded and opened the door to the shop. Inside, the place smelled of freshly carved wood and finishing oils. Shavings and chips covered the floor and surrounded a workbench that practically filled the space. Aside from the violins in the window there was little stock.

"Hello?" Gabriel called.

A curtain separating the shop from living quarters in the back stirred, and a young man hurried forward. Obviously unused to regular customers, he smiled uncertainly as he wiped his hands on his oil-stained and dust-covered carpenter's apron. "Yes, sir?"

Gabe had already turned to the window and taken down one of the three violins. "Did you make this, sir?"

"I did."

The curtain stirred again and Lucie could hear the giggles of several young children, as well as the shushing of a woman's voice as she obviously pulled the curious children away. She saw that Gabe had also taken note of the activity behind the curtain.

"It's good work," Gabe said as he turned the violin over, then held it to what little light could make its way through the grimy window.

The young man straightened. "It is fine work," he corrected, and Lucie saw Gabe smile. It was not a smile of triumph, but rather a smile of respect. He liked that the man had shown pride in his work and not been afraid to say so.

"You have a family?"

"Four children," the man replied, obviously mystified into confession by the sudden change in conversation.

"I should like you to consider a trade, sir," Gabe said as he placed the violin on the small display case in the corner that held a selection of bows.

"The price is—" the young man began, but Gabe cut him off.

"Are you familiar with the grove of hardwood trees on the road to Great Point?"

"Hunter's Woods?"

Lucie saw the curtain move slightly and knew the man's wife was listening.

"My father planted those trees and owns that land. There is a fine selection of wood there—wood that would make beautiful instruments as well as wood to provide warmth for a man's young family when the winter comes."

Lucie saw that this information was delivered in a conversational style, as if Gabe were discussing the weather or the day's news with the young woodworker.

"My mother is quite frail," he continued, "and tomorrow is my parents' wedding anniversary—it may be the last anniversary they share."

Lucie, the woodworker and the unseen wife were all riveted on Gabriel's words as he remained at the display case, fingering one and then another of the violin bows. Finally he selected one and handed it and the violin to the young man. "I could pay you your price for this instrument," he said, "but then it would be my gift, not my mother's."

"Aye," the young man whispered sadly.

"Or we could consider a fair trade—say, firewood for your family—gathered only from what has already fallen or been cut—and a tree of your choosing for your craft." He handed the man the violin and continued to hold the bow.

There was an audible gasp from behind the curtain. Gabe gently lifted it aside and smiled at the embarrassed young woman, four children all under the age of seven clinging to her skirts.

"And for the bow," he continued, "I thought perhaps a quilt made by my mother for your family."

Tears streamed down the young woman's face as she moved into the shop and took her husband's arm.

"How do I know—" the woodworker began.

Gabe peeled off several bills and held them up. "I am Gabriel Hunter, son of Jonathan and Emma Hunter. One of my men will deliver the quilt, as well as a statement of permission to gather wood within the next few weeks. I understand the quilt is almost complete." He glanced at Lucie for confirmation. She nodded.

"In the meantime I shall leave you this sum as good faith collateral, to be returned to my representative when he delivers the quilt and document of permission." Gabe offered the money to the man. "Do we have a bargain, sir?"

The man's wife was squeezing his arm so hard that Lucie was certain there would be the mark of her fingerprints later that evening. To the horror of the wife and Lucie the proud young man did not take the proffered payment.

"Put your money away, sir," he said as he handed the bow and violin to his wife. "When my father's business and our home were destroyed by fire, I was just a boy, but I will never forget the sight of your parents coming down our lane with a wagon filled with food and blankets and clothing they had collected for us and others who had lost everything in the fire. I'll take the offer but I don't need your money. Ginny, wrap the instrument and bow for the gentleman."

As Ginny and the children hurried away, Gabe continued his perusal of the shop. "You could do well here," he mused, more to himself than the woodworker. "Your prices are too low, of course, and you could do with more inventory on hand. People on holiday tend to buy on impulse. They won't wait for you to make something up."

"Aye," the young man murmured, soaking up the advice.

"A better sign and eventually a better location," Gabe continued. He turned suddenly and stared at the man. "Have you considered taking your instruments to Boston? You might gain some commissions—triple the price for those, of course…." He glanced at the man and then at Lucie. Both were staring at him openmouthed.

He shrugged. "Just a thought," he said, and turned his attention back to the curtain as Ginny emerged with two packages. The larger one she handed to Gabe and the smaller one she handed to Lucie.

"For your mother and father-in-law," she explained. "To celebrate their anniversary. It's a cake I baked this morning." She pressed the still-warm cake wrapped in a tea towel into Lucie's hands.

"They are not my—" Lucie began, but Gabe took her arm and ushered her to the door, pausing to shake hands with the woodworker before leading her to the street. "Well, we just have to retrieve the gift for my mother and then be on our way," he said, dropping his hold on her arm and setting out once again at a pace that Lucie was practically running to match.

As had been the case on the trip into town, the ride home was conducted mostly in silence. That earlier silence had been filled with the repressed tensions of mutual suspicion and wariness. On the return, the mood had changed to a palpable sense of heightened awareness of and curiosity about each other.

Gabe noticed that, while her hands were as tightly clasped as they had been in the morning, Lucie's posture was less rigid, allowing her to sway with the rhythm of the ride and maintain her balance without holding on to something. He was also aware that from time to time she glanced his way. If he met her gaze, she looked quickly away, down at her hands or out to the passing scenery. She seemed about to speak on any number of occasions, but all that came out was a soft sigh.

For her part, Lucie was far too aware of his hands on the reins, the closeness of his shoulder to her own on the narrow seat and the occasional sound of his gentle but deep bass voice commanding the team of horses to navigate a curve or hill. Any number of questions raged in her brain as she recalled the events of the last few hours. She felt confused and even irritated. He was not what she had thought—or was he?

"What is it?" he said, startling her after the long silence. His tone was sharp, matching her own sense of frustration.

"Nothing," she replied.

"There is clearly something you wish to discuss, Miss McNeil, and I would suggest we get to it."

To her utter astonishment, the first thing out of Lucie's mouth was an apology. "I am sorry that the woodworker and his wife took me for your…that is, they thought we were—"

"Man and wife," he said bluntly, and snapped the reins to urge the horses up the last rise. "There is no need for you to apologize for others."

"They are simple folk," she continued as if he'd said nothing.

"Miss McNeil," he interrupted, "that topic does not interest me, and if that is what has been on your mind then we have nothing further to discuss."

Lucie stiffened. There was certainly no need for him to be so abrupt. She lapsed back into a stony silence.

"What shall we tell my parents?" he asked as they crested the last rise and the cottage was within view.

"I don't understand your question," Lucie said, her suspicion of him and his motives restored.

He chuckled without mirth. "We have brought them gifts to give to each other that—as you noted—are far more dear in price than they planned. My parents are not fools, Miss McNeil. They—"

"I am well aware that Mrs. Hunter and the colonel are

quite alert, Mr. Hunter. The truth is usually the best course. At least, that has been my experience."

He turned and looked directly at her. "Has it now?"

"You doubt me?" she asked, bristling and meeting his gaze.

He turned his attention back to navigating the road to the cottage. "Should I?" he muttered, then added in a heartier tone, "The truth it shall be, then. Why don't you explain the source of the violin to my mother and I will explain the bed jacket to my father."

"And the shawl and blouse?" Lucie bit her tongue at having spoken her thoughts aloud. "That is, shall I wrap them for you?"

He kept his eyes on the road, but a smile tugged at the corners of his mouth. "That won't be necessary. I'll take care of my own purchases."

Lucie was relieved that they had reached the small barn and her day with Gabriel Hunter was finally at an end. As soon as he pulled the team to a halt, she clambered down from the wagon and stepped to the back to gather the parcels that held the bed jacket and the violin just as Jonathan crossed the yard to help unload the groceries and supplies.

"Good trip?" he asked, directing the question at both Lucie and Gabe.

"Quite successful I would say, wouldn't you, Miss McNeil?" Gabe had stopped the work of stabling the horses and turned to look directly at her.

Lucie turned her attention to Jonathan and pointed to the parcels in her arms. "I... we were able to get a splendid gift for you to give Emma. And," she added with a wink, "one for her to give you, as well."

Jonathan laughed with delight. "Lucie, you're a wonder." He turned to Gabe. "I tell you, son, you'd do well to have this young woman working for you. The way she manages finances—even limited ones—is nothing short of masterful."

Lucie risked a glance at Gabe and saw his mouth thin as he looked at his father. She realized that the expression that crossed his handsome features was not the suspicion or frustration she might have expected. Jonathan's words of praise for her had wounded Gabe's pride.

"Your financial situation does not need to be limited, Father," he said, then turned and led the team into the stables.

Having rested much of the day, Emma was in high spirits at supper, anxious for news and gossip of the townspeople from Lucie and curious about Gabe's impressions of the booming island town. "After all, it's been years since you were in town," she said with a coquettish smile.

Gabe laughed. "Now, Mother, when I come to the island, I come to see you and Father, not go into town."

"Our Gabriel was quite the romantic figure in his youth," Emma confided to Lucie without taking her eyes off Gabe. "All the single young ladies had set their cap for him, and then one night he simply disappeared, leaving a string of broken hearts in his wake."

"I was sixteen," Gabe protested, but he was laughing. "Hardly the stuff of romantic dreams."

Emma turned her attention to Jonathan. "You'd be surprised what can touch a young woman's fancy," she said. "Sometimes it's a violin played outside your window, isn't that right, Jonathan?"

Jonathan blushed and smiled. "I had to do something to get your attention."

"Oh, you had my attention," Emma assured him.

"I don't think I know this story," Lucie said, aware that this was Emma's prelude to presenting Jonathan with the handcrafted violin—the gift she had declared perfect when Lucie showed it to her and told the story of Gabe's barter earlier.

"It was the summer after Lee's surrender," Emma said.

Jonathan took up the story. "I had finally been relieved of my command and my first thought—my only thought—was to return to Charleston and persuade this lovely lady to be my bride." He took Emma's hand in his.

Emma laughed. "Well, I was having none of it. Me marry a Yankee? Horrors!"

"Not to mention the fact that I was in competition with any number of returning Confederate officers who came calling."

"I had just prepared to retire for the evening," Emma said dreamily. "My parents—everyone in the house—had already been asleep for some time. And then I heard such sweet music coming from the veranda just below my window."

From the empty chair next to him, Gabe pulled out the violin and bow and began to play. He stood between his parents as they continued to hold hands. The music and scene were so sweet and filled with love that Lucie felt like an intruder.

"I'll just—" she said as she stood, and turned away to hide her tears.

"And then," Jonathan continued softly, stopping Lucie's retreat as he took up the story, "she appeared. She was wearing the most beautiful silk-and-lace dressing gown." He nodded to Lucie, who handed him the package she'd concealed under her chair earlier.

With a squeal of delight, Emma tore away the wrappings and held up the bed jacket. "Oh, darling Johnny," she whispered, barely containing her joy. She pressed the garment to her chest. "Play for me, Johnny," she said.

Gabe passed his father the violin and bow. Jonathan ran his hands over the smooth wood, pausing to study the intricate inlay. "Oh, my sweet Emma, it's so fine." He placed the instrument under his chin and played Debussy's "Clair de lune." Emma closed her eyes, caressing the silk garment and swaying to the music.

Lucie watched this couple she had come to hold so dear in the few short months that she'd known them—this couple whose love story had become the solace for her own loneliness. She allowed her tears to run down her cheeks unchecked. When the last note stretched out for a long moment, as if reluctant to go silent, Lucie glanced up and found Gabriel Hunter watching her. Their eyes met and neither broke the connection until the note had died away. Gabriel's eyes softened as he looked at her, and the beginning of a smile played at the corners of his mouth.

Confused, Lucie looked at her hands and then back at him. Her heart seemed to slow as if she needed to stop everything while she held on to this moment—the moment when the two of them seemed to be seeing each other for the very first time.

## Chapter Five

Lucie refrained from looking at Gabe the following morning. She needn't have worried because he was equally reluctant to meet her eyes. He had spent another restless night, but this one had little to do with adjusting to strange yet familiar surroundings or working through how he was to persuade his parents to leave the island. No, his head had been filled with thoughts of Lucie McNeil. He had purchased the blouse and shawl on a whim. He might have chosen any item in the shop to make his deal, but out of the blue he had imagined her wearing the soft lawn blouse with its full sleeves and delicately trimmed bodice. During the night he had dreamed that he was placing the finely woven shawl around her shoulders as they stood together on the bluff overlooking the bay.

*Ridiculous,* he chastised himself before turning his attention to his parents—both of whom had finished their breakfast by the time he came downstairs.

"Good morning," he said as he bent to kiss Emma's

cheek. "Lovely day," he added as he pulled out his chair and sat. "I thought perhaps we might all go for a sail."

His announcement had exactly the reaction he had expected from everyone in the room. His mother squealed with pleasure. His father smiled but glanced uncertainly at Emma. And he definitely had Lucie McNeil's full attention.

"What a delightful idea," Emma said. "We'll go right after church. Lucie, do you have time to prepare a picnic? Oh, Johnny, what a wonderful way to celebrate our anniversary." She clapped her hands together in girlish delight.

Jonathan had never been able to deny Emma anything. "It's a splendid idea, son. I've been wanting to see this new yacht of yours."

"That yacht is Gabriel's one extravagance," Emma confided to Lucie, as if they were the only two people in the room. "He's quite proud of it."

"And well he should be," Jonathan said. "What is it, son—two hundred feet?"

"One-fifty." He did not wish to discuss his yacht, especially with Lucie McNeil present.

"And a crew of what—five?" Jonathan persisted.

"Three," Gabe said. "Mother, are you quite sure you're up to church, as well as sailing? That's a very full day."

"Now, stop treating me like an invalid, Gabe. I can do a great deal more than you give me credit for—especially when it involves something that will be such fun. Your father and I haven't been for a sail in years, have we, dear?"

"If you're sure," Gabe said, "then while the two of you attend church services, I'll—"

"But surely you're going to church with us, aren't

you?" Emma asked, all trace of her earlier happiness shadowed by this unexpected turn of affairs.

"Of course he's going, my dear," Jonathan said softly, his eyes meeting Gabe's and leaving no room for argument.

"Yes, we can all go to services and then perhaps have a light lunch, Miss McNeil, and allow my mother time for some rest before we set forth."

"Honestly, Gabriel, you do tend to assume too much," Emma said irritably. "If you have your way, we'll be taking this sail at midnight. Now, go get yourself ready while Lucie and I prepare the picnic and your father brings the carriage around."

There were times when his mother could still make him feel like the boy he'd been when living in this house. He often thought of those days—days when he'd had none of the pressures of adulthood and none of the fears of failing in spite of his astounding success in business. He missed those days.

Lucie had just fastened the lid on the picnic hamper when she heard Gabe on the stairs. "You should take Emma to the carriage before—" she said to Jonathan.

"Nonsense," Emma replied before Jonathan could. "It's high time we stopped this charade." She turned her attention to the doorway. "Gabriel, you may as well know the truth. I need assistance. I could use my cane and take your arm but that takes time and I do not like to be late. So please be so kind as to carry me out to the carriage before we miss the service altogether."

Without comment Gabriel scooped Emma high in his arms and strode to the back door where he paused and turned to Lucie. "I'll send word to my crew from the church to ready the yacht." It was obvious that he assumed Lucie would be staying behind.

Emma cleared up any such notion without delay. "Lucie, put away that apron and get your hat. Oh, and a wrap in case a spring wind kicks up," she added.

Lucie saw a protest rise to Gabe's lips, but he said nothing as he continued out the door and deposited his mother in the carriage that his parents used only for church and other special occasions. "I'll drive," Lucie heard him say to his father.

"It's been some time since you attended services on the island," Emma called up to Gabe as he expertly guided the team of horses over the rough road. "I imagine our little country church will be quite different from what you're used to in Boston."

"You're probing, Mother," Gabe said.

"I am at that. What's the name of that church you attend again? I'm afraid I've forgotten."

"On the contrary, your mind is quite alert and you forget very little. You never knew because I never mentioned it."

"Then shall you mention it now?" Emma said, her eyes alight with mischief.

"On those occasions when I attend formal services I am usually there as a guest of a business associate. Therefore, the place of worship varies."

Emma made a face. "Business does not belong in the church. Have you forgotten the lesson of Jesus clearing the temple? You cannot attend to God's word or the comfort it brings a troubled soul if your mind is on business," she added sternly.

With that pronouncement the four occupants of the

open carriage fell silent until they heard the church bell in the distance.

"And what of Miss Witherspoon?" Emma asked suddenly. "Does she attend church?"

"I believe she does," Gabriel replied.

"Miss Jeanne Witherspoon has set her cap for my son, Lucie," Emma said. "Or rather her father has. Thurgood Witherspoon—ridiculous name, don't you think? At any rate, he is pushing for a match."

Lucie saw Gabe's shoulders stiffen and his hand tighten on the reins, causing the horses to move into a trot.

"Now, Emma dear," Jonathan said, taking her hand. "Let's not spoil this beautiful day. Gabe is attending church here at home on Nantucket with you, me and Lucie. I should think that would make this a very special day indeed."

Her good humor instantly restored, Emma squeezed Jonathan's hand. "As if it weren't already a special day being married to you for three and a half decades now."

Jonathan laughed, but Gabe remained silent as he pulled the carriage up to the front of the church where Adam was waiting with a wheelchair for Emma. "Morning, folks, and a happy anniversary to the two of you," Adam said as he held the chair steady while Jonathan lifted Emma down from the carriage. Lucie got out on the opposite side and glanced up at Gabe.

"Are you coming?" she asked, and saw immediately by his expression that he did not think this an appropriate inquiry coming from her. "I only meant—" she hurried to add, but he interrupted her.

"Please assure my parents that I will join them as soon as I've seen to the carriage and horses, Miss McNeil."

Lucie nodded and started toward the path that led to

the entrance of the church. Expecting to hear the wheels of the carriage crunch on the rocky path as he pulled them to the side yard near the cemetery, she was surprised when there was no movement behind her. She turned and saw him watching her. All traces of his earlier irritation seemed to have melted away and he looked a bit lost, as if he had suddenly realized that he no longer belonged here.

"We're on the left—third pew from the front," she said.

He nodded and clicked his tongue to the horses. The carriage rolled forward. Instead of going into the church, Lucie stood and watched Gabe park the carriage. The young couple who owned the cranberry farm on the land next to the Hunters appeared to recognize him. Gabe smiled at them as he climbed down and dusted off his coat and trousers.

Lucie heard a sigh from just behind her.

"Isn't he just the most handsome man you've ever seen, Nellie?"

Lucie turned to see Nellie Bushnell and her sister, Gertie, staring at Gabe with moonstruck eyes. "They say he's made a great fortune since he left Nantucket," Nellie whispered, her eyes never leaving Gabe. "Oh, sister, he's coming this way. How do I look?"

Gertie snorted. "Too young for the likes of him. How do I look is more to the point." She stretched herself to her full height, lifting her chin in what Lucie was sure she thought was the kind of haughty pose that might attract a man like Gabe.

"You look ridiculous," Lucie heard Nellie reply as she brushed past her sister and followed Lucie into the sanctuary.

The church was tiny, with a pump organ at the back, the altar and a chair for the minister at the front and twelve rows of narrow wooden pews on each side of the center aisle. Behind the minister was a large stained-glass window—a gift from one of the island's wealthy whaling families before the fires and the war had destroyed the single industry that had been Nantucket's main source of income during the early part of the century.

Emma's chair was positioned in the center aisle next to the pew. Jonathan had taken the aisle seat next to Emma, so Lucie sidled down the narrow space on the side of the row of pews and slid in next to Jonathan. Less than two minutes later Gabe followed that same path and took the seat next to her. Lucie could not help but think that although the pew normally held four adults comfortably, with Gabe there it seemed crowded with just three. She inched a little closer to Jonathan.

"Do you have enough room?" Jonathan asked both Lucie and Gabe as the organist struck up the first hymn.

Lucie nodded and busied herself finding the page for the hymn. She stood and Gabe did the same. That's when she realized she would need to share her hymnal with him. There were only two copies per row and Jonathan remained seated, sharing the only other copy with Emma.

Suddenly a hymnal was thrust between Lucie and Gabe from the row behind them. Gabe turned to accept it and gave his benefactor a smile unlike any Lucie had witnessed before. She glanced over her shoulder and saw Gertie Bushnell bat her eyes at Gabe, then elbow her sister, Nellie, as soon as Gabe turned his attention to finding the correct page.

The feeling that raced through Lucie was so unexpected and so powerful she nearly dropped her hymnal.

She hardly had time to consider the source of such emotion before she felt Gabe's hand on hers as he caught the book and steadied it for her, his shoulder brushing hers in the process. Emma watched the entire scene play out, her eyes lively with interest.

Lucie straightened and held her hymnal out in front of her as she tried to find her place. Gabe's rich bass voice booming out the words was no help at all. She mumbled words in time to the familiar tune until finally the organist pounded out the chorus and Lucie had regained her composure.

Following the hymn, the minister led the still-standing congregation in the Lord's Prayer. Lucie noticed that Gabe neither spoke the words nor bowed his head in reverence. Instead he focused his attention on the hymnal, smoothing its worn leather cover restlessly with his fingers until the chorus of *Amens* had rumbled to silence and everyone had settled back into the narrow pews.

Normally Lucie loved listening to Reverend Ashford, but on this Sunday his sermon seemed nothing more than monotone played just behind the thoughts and questions racing through her head. On her left, Gabe sat stone-still and gave the minister his full attention. On her right, Jonathan fought the urge to nod off and lost the battle more than once, jumping to alertness after one of Emma's gentle prods.

Meanwhile Lucie mentally went through the preparations she'd made for the picnic. Had she remembered the mustard? Would Gabe think the meal too plebian? Was there enough food to feed the four of them plus a crew of—how many? Was it three or four? Three. She clenched her gloved hands together and forced her thoughts elsewhere.

Without a pause for a nap, the sailing would be too much for Emma, and then Gabe would have further evidence to force the issue of taking his parents back to the mainland. She had to convince Emma to rest. Perhaps if she—Lucie—feigned illness? No, they would simply go without her.

She saw that Gabe was watching her feet and then realized she was tapping her foot nervously, causing her knee to rise and fall in rhythm to the tapping. She shifted positions, forcing her feet to remain still. She was quite sure her action had caught Gabe's attention, and when she turned, he was watching her with a look that teetered between humor and curiosity.

She did not want his attention or interest. She was sure that things would be better if he were to go back to Boston and leave them all in peace. At the same time she needed to reconcile her interest in a man whose negligence had created the conditions that had led to the fire. And whenever she thought of that, she wanted to rage at him and pummel his chest with her fists. Instead she folded her hands in her lap and bowed her head.

When the service finally ended, Gabe returned the borrowed hymnal to the two young women—sisters, from the similarities of features and height—in the pew behind his. "Ladies," he said with a slight bow, "please accept my appreciation for your kindness."

The older one preened and blushed. "Well, it isn't often that we have visitors, sir. Will you be staying long?"

"Sadly, no. I have business to attend on the mainland." He retrieved his hat from the pew and nodded to the two women again as he prepared to follow Lucie and his parents up the center aisle to where the minister was receiving members of his flock at the door.

"Perhaps you could spare time to come for tea before you have to leave." This was from the younger—and more striking—of the sisters. They had pressed forward, maintaining close contact with Gabe.

Gabe saw Lucie's shoulders stiffen. Aware that she'd counted on his leaving soon, he took some small delight in assuring the sisters that he would indeed consider that. "My visit with my parents has stretched beyond my usual day trip," he added. "There may yet be the opportunity for me to accept your kind invitation. By the way, I am Gabriel Hunter, and I don't believe—"

"Nellie Bushnell," the younger one said. "And this is my sister, Gertie."

"Gertrude," the older sister corrected through pursed lips. "Charmed," she added, practically dropping into a curtsy. "Perhaps you knew our dear late father? Captain Hugh Bushnell?"

"Ah, yes—"

"Gabriel!"

Gabe looked toward the entrance where his mother was waiting and looking none too pleased with him. "Please excuse me, ladies. It was my pleasure to meet you both." He gave the sisters a slight bow and headed up the aisle to where his mother waited, her fingers drumming along the side of the wheelchair.

"I want to introduce you to Reverend Ashford," Emma said when he reached her side. He could see his father and Adam standing outside, laughing at something the minister had just told them. Lucie was nowhere in sight. Irritated that she had apparently abandoned her duties to his mother, he took command of the wheelchair and pushed his mother through the tiny foyer and out into the spring sunshine.

"Reverend Ashford, may I present my son, Gabriel?" Emma announced almost before they had cleared the doorway.

The two men shook hands and the minister made some comment about meeting him at long last. "Your parents have spoken of you often," he added with a smile that struck Gabe as overly familiar and therefore suspect. "I wondered when I might have the pleasure of meeting you."

Gabe's ears burned the same way they had when he'd been a boy and a minister or teacher had noted a lapse in his behavior with a reprimand cloaked in the niceties of ordinary conversation. He recognized his reaction as guilt and understood that it had nothing to do with the minister. "My parents—like the parents of most only children— can be overly effusive in their pride," he said.

Over the minister's shoulder, he caught sight of Lucie. She was standing in the churchyard, talking to the young cranberry farmer and his wife. Another man had joined them and the couple made introductions. The man said something that made Lucie laugh. Gabe could not help noticing that her entire demeanor was different than any time he had been with her. Gone was the tension and suspicion that seemed to color every exchange she'd had with him. In its place, she was lively and animated and— pretty. He watched as she tied the ends of her rough woolen shawl and thought about the one he'd bought the day before.

"Gabriel?"

Gabe glanced down at his mother and then at his father and the minister. Both men seemed to be waiting for a response to a question he hadn't heard. "Sorry," he murmured as he turned his back on Lucie McNeil. "I'm afraid I was—"

"Distracted," Emma said with a smile. "It was a lovely sermon, Reverend. Please do plan to come for lunch on Wednesday."

"I will," the minister replied as he shook hands with Jonathan and then offered his hand to Gabe. "A pleasure to meet you."

"The pleasure was mine, sir," Gabe replied, but he could not dismiss the uneasy sense that the young preacher had seen beneath the surface to a place Gabe was loath to explore.

"Lucie, dear," Emma called as Jonathan went to get the carriage and Gabe wheeled the chair to the road. "Whenever you're ready."

A light wind ruffled the waters of Nantucket Sound and filled the sails of Gabe's yacht. As they made their way down the pier where the crew awaited their arrival, Lucie turned her attention from Emma when she heard the snap of the heavy canvas. For a long moment she was unable to move or speak. Up close the yacht was a gleaming palace of rich polished black walnut with pewter fittings that sparkled in the midafternoon sunlight.

"Oh, my," she whispered.

"Indeed," Emma agreed. "What do you call this thing, Gabe?"

"Nantucket," Jonathan replied.

"Really?" Emma peered up at her son, shading her eyes from the bright sunlight. "That seems out of character for you—quite sentimental."

The visor of the captain's cap that Gabe had donned

as soon as they came aboard hid his eyes. "I thought it would please you," he said.

"Oh, Gabe, you're far too old to be doing such things to please your mother," Emma replied, but she giggled with pleasure and Gabe laughed.

Once everyone was settled on board, Gabe introduced the captain of the crew and the ship's steward. "If there's anything you need," he said, "just let Randolph know."

"May I take that, sir?" Randolph asked, relieving Jonathan of the worn picnic basket.

"We'll dine as soon as we're launched," Gabe instructed.

"Very good, sir," Randolph replied, then headed toward a short stairway and disappeared below deck.

"Perhaps I should—" Lucie began, and hurried after Randolph.

It took her eyes a moment to adjust after the bright sunlight on deck. Then she realized that she was in a large room, comfortably but elegantly furnished with tufted couches, a bookcase filled with volumes behind beveled glass doors that caught the light filtered through the stained-glass windows. In the center of the room was a large, round table and at the far end of the room was a fireplace with a carved cherry mantel and a nickel grate and andirons. To either side of the fireplace were doorways leading to more rooms. Everything except the dining chairs was bolted into place.

She heard the rustle of utensils and dishes beyond one of the doorways and started to follow the sound.

"Randolph can manage," Gabe said, startling her. "My parents have made it clear that they do not wish you to be treated as a…member of my staff."

She nodded and prepared to go back on deck but he

was blocking the narrow stairway. "I thought we would dine down here. That way my mother is not overly exposed to the elements."

"She'll enjoy seeing all of this," Lucie said with a slight gesture of one hand. "As will your father. It will only increase the pride they have in you fourfold."

"Really?" Gabe looked at the room as if truly appreciating it for the first time. "You like the furnishings?"

"Oh, they are very grand," Lucie assured him. "Very much your mother's taste."

"Well, then perhaps I should provide a tour before we dine." He turned abruptly and climbed the short stairway. Lucie hurried to follow and as soon as she stepped onto the deck she moved as far away as possible from Gabriel.

Emma and Jonathan were comfortably seated in deck chairs, laughing as they held hands and pointed to various landmarks along the shore.

"Grand tour leaves in five minutes," Gabe announced, and Lucie took note that his parents continued to hold hands as they turned to smile at him.

"I think if you will take one arm while your father holds the other, I can manage," Emma said when Gabe prepared to lift her in his arms. She struggled to her feet and hooked one arm firmly through Jonathan's and then the other through Gabe's. "Lead on," she called gaily.

Once they were down the narrow stairway, Emma was beside herself with wonder. "Oh, Gabe, it's all so elegant and filled with light and grace and—you. Lucie, look at that carving." She indicated the beautiful fireplace mantel. "A whale in all his glory," she added.

"Gabe could never stand the idea that those beautiful animals had once been hunted and slaughtered for their oil," Jonathan said.

Lucie glanced at Gabe with new respect. Was it possible that at last they had something in common?

"And in here," Gabe continued, "are my quarters."

"You need a quilt," Emma declared. "I'll make one for you. Lucie, come look at this so we get the coloring right."

Lucie edged closer. Somehow, even though she had been making up his room at the cottage when he came in that first day, and even with Gabe's parents present, standing in this bedroom seemed far too intimate. This was truly his; his things were on the dresser and in the small bathroom visible from the mirror mounted on the bedroom door. She gave a quick glance. "Blues and greens perhaps," she said, and then pretended her attention had been caught by something farther along the hall. "Where do those doors lead?" she asked.

"Guest staterooms," Jonathan said. "You can sleep how many? Four? Eight?"

"There are three additional rooms," Gabe said as he led Emma back to the salon.

During the tour Randolph had set places for four with fine china, silver and crystal. Lucie's bread had been sliced and displayed along with cheeses and meats on serving platters on a small sideboard. Randolph had added to the fruit she'd had on hand and created a colorful and appetizing display.

"Sit here, Mama," Gabe said softly as he helped her into one of the leather straight chairs and eased her forward until she was close enough to the table. "Papa," he said, indicating the chair at the head of the table.

Lucie reached for the remaining chair and Gabe quickly stepped forward and pulled it away from the table for her.

"Thank you," she murmured, and felt her cheeks glow at the unexpected kindness.

After lunch—which proved to be more than substantial, enough for everyone aboard—Gabe suggested they all adjourn to the upper deck and enjoy a cup of tea with their dessert.

"Lucie, come and join us," Jonathan called when she hesitated, unsure if she should come on deck or help Randolph clear. "Emma is about to tell one of her tall tales and I don't believe either you or Gabe has heard this one."

Gabe had removed the coat and tie he'd worn for church, as well as the stiff, starched wing collar. The wind ruffled his thick hair as he reached over and pulled Emma's shawl more securely around her thin shoulders. "That would be something of an accomplishment," he said as he took the chair next to Emma's.

"Ha," Emma retorted, brushing him away good-naturedly. "You'll be an old man before you've heard all my stories. Now, stop fussing and sit still. As my daddy used to say, you're more jittery than a long-tailed cat in a room full of rocking chairs."

Gabe threw back his head and laughed at that—a sound of pure delight that carried across the water and caused neighboring boaters to glance their way. He looked so young and happy as he folded his hands behind his head and turned his face to the wind and sun, that Lucie felt her breath catch at the sight of him.

Almost from the moment they'd stepped aboard his ship, Lucie had noticed a change in him. He seemed more calm and at ease, as if the sea air had blown away all his cares. Indeed during lunch he had readily entered into the conversation, asking about various people he'd known as a boy and telling his parents about contacts he'd kept with others who had left the island to seek their fortunes. It was as if the farther they moved from the shore, the more at peace he became.

Emma cleared her throat, commanding their attention. "Pay these two no mind, dear Lucie. I've yet to meet a man who truly understood a good romantic story."

Jonathan started to protest, but Emma stilled him with one raised finger. "It was a day like this—a Sunday in late spring. The boat was not so grand. The colonel had 'borrowed' it from a local. For we were in Charleston, and it was the end of the war—the end of everything, or so I thought."

"So why did you agree to go sailing with Papa?" Gabe asked. "After all, he was the enemy—the dreaded Yankee."

"He was all of that," Emma said firmly, "but one cannot forget the teachings of the Scriptures—kindness, forgiveness—"

Gabe let out a howl of protest. "Forgiveness! Mother, to this day you still believe that General Sherman was a monster."

Emma gave a derisive sniff. "Well, he was no Colonel Hunter, that's for sure—burning down whole towns and allowing his thugs to loot and pillage, and for what cause?" She reached over and took Jonathan's hand in hers. "The colonel was far more genteel. He was kind and sympathetic and seemed genuinely sorry for the devastation that had accompanied the war."

"What happened?" Lucie encouraged, both because she wanted to hear the story and because she had rarely seen Emma looking so well or sounding so strong. If

Gabe's presence had brought about such a miraculous change in her health, perhaps it would be good for the Hunters to move in with him.

"It was a lovely day," Emma said, her voice growing soft and dreamy. "The warmth of the sun and the calmness of the waters— It was as if we'd left all that devastation and horror behind us."

"You were the most beautiful woman I had ever seen," Jonathan said.

"You kissed me," Emma replied in a whisper, and Jonathan nodded.

Gabe sat up and gave his full attention to his parents. "You barely knew each other," he said, "not to mention that you were at polar ends of the spectrum regarding your values and politics."

Emma broke eye contact with Jonathan and gave Gabe a look of such disdain that he looked away. "Well, you were," he said.

"And do such trivial things as politics and wars and who did what to whom really matter when you meet the love of your life—the very person that God intended just for you?" Emma asked, turning her attention back to Jonathan.

"But in that day and time—I mean, kissing any young man, let alone the enemy, must have been…" Lucie paused, searching for the right word.

Emma giggled. "Scandalous but so very delicious, my dear Lucie."

"Mother, really," Gabe protested. "Next you'll be telling us that— Well, I don't know what, but—"

"Oh, stop worrying, Gabriel," Emma said with a wink at Lucie. "I had no idea I'd raised such a prude."

"You were in love," Lucie said, stating the obvious.

Jonathan and Emma smiled at each other. "Thunderstruck," Jonathan murmured.

"You stole my heart that afternoon," Emma whispered, cupping his cheek with her palm. "But it was months before we could be together."

"I was afraid I was taking advantage," Jonathan said.

"And I was afraid that my immediate attraction was nothing more than loneliness—desperation, even."

"What did you do?" Lucie asked.

"There was nothing I could do. He left the following day—much to my father's relief. And as the local boys came home, my mother began a campaign of matchmaking that made the battle of Charleston seem like child's play."

Jonathan laughed. "It took me less than three days to realize that I had just met the woman I would love for the rest of my life," Jonathan said.

"But it took three months before he came back."

"You waited," Jonathan reminded her.

"Yes, I did. I think I knew that it would be you or no one."

Gabe cleared his throat and stared out at the passing parade of pleasure boats.

All aboard were silent for several minutes, lost in memory or thought as the yacht skimmed over the water.

"Gabe?"

Gabe and Lucie both turned to Jonathan. "I believe your mother could use some rest. May we use your cabin, Gabriel?"

Lucie saw at once that Emma was gulping air and coughing delicately into her lace handkerchief. It always stunned her how quickly Emma could go from seeming in the pink to struggling for air. Before Lucie could move, Gabe was immediately at her side. "Mother? What is it?"

Emma waved him off impatiently, her eyes searching for Jonathan and, once finding him, issuing a silent plea.

"She'll be fine, son," Jonathan said, sounding none too sure. "She's prone to overdoing it, and last night's festivities along with everything today—"

Gabe lifted his mother and carried her below.

"Shall I—" Lucie began.

"I'll go," Jonathan replied. "She just needs a nap. She seems fine, don't you think?" He didn't wait for her answer but hurried after Gabe, who could be heard giving directions to Randolph as he hurried along the passageway toward his stateroom.

Lucie started to follow, but then stopped. This was a family matter and she suspected Gabe would not appreciate her intrusion. She walked to the railing and leaned against it, closing her eyes as the spray from the wake misted her face. She felt the pins slip and shift within her chignon as the wind clutched at tendrils of her hair and tugged them free. She held tight to her hat with one hand and clutched the railing with the other, swaying with the rhythm of the boat as she silently prayed for Emma's health.

She thought of Emma—her labored breathing, the chronic cough that at first seemed like a polite clearing of the throat until one became aware of its constancy. Over the months she'd cared for the Hunters, Lucie had grown used to the sound of it, knowing instinctively when there was cause for alarm or a need to send for the doctor. Even without hearing the cough she should have recognized the warning signs of Emma's overly bright eyes and flushed cheeks when she was telling the story. Too late

Lucie had noted Emma's utter exhaustion when making any attempt to move—even if that was as simple as waving off her son's attentions.

Lucie sighed. It had been too much, and now Gabe would have the proof he'd come for. He would take his parents back to Boston to a house no doubt as fully staffed and ready to meet the Hunters' every need as this yacht with its crew of three was. And although she could not deny that this was probably the best decision for Jonathan and Emma, she could not help but remember the faces of the elderly couple whenever they talked of leaving Nantucket. It was their home, and the one thing Lucie understood was the ideal of home, although in many ways, she had yet to find hers. She must fight for them—for their right to remain on Nantucket. She closed her eyes and hummed the prayer her mother had taught her to use whenever circumstances seemed most bleak.

## Chapter Six

As always whenever Gabe emerged from below deck, it took a moment for his eyes to adjust to the brightness of the sun reflecting off the pewter fittings and the high sheen of the wooden deck. Not at all reassured that his mother's collapse had been the result of too much excitement, he had nevertheless given in to his father's insistence that she be allowed to rest. Gabe had instructed Randolph to deliver tea with honey as his father had requested, and then tell the captain to turn around and get them back to Nantucket as soon as possible. For the time being, they would have to make do with the limited medical services the island offered, for they were far nearer to Nantucket than they were to Boston. But tomorrow—

On deck he felt the wind shift as the yacht turned, and he heard the gentle splash of the water against the sides of the boat as the captain followed orders. Bits of conversation from other boats drifted across the waves, but then he realized he was also hearing music, and that it was coming from Lucie McNeil. The woman—oblivious to his presence—was clutching the railing and leaning as far back as possible, her face lifted to the sun and cloudless blue sky, and she was humming. His mother could be direly ill, and the woman was singing.

He moved soundlessly across the boards until he was standing close enough that he might have wrapped his arms around her from behind. Instead he touched her shoulder with one finger. "Miss McNeil?"

His action had the intended result in that she was completely taken by surprise and immediately released her hold on the railing and leapt backward. It had the unintended result of sending her careening straight into his arms, leaving him only the choice of tightening his hold on her or allowing her to fall to the deck.

"Steady," he said gruffly. "I've got you."

"And you may release me, sir," she huffed, pushing him away as she reached for the railing again and eased herself into one of the deck chairs. "You startled me," she said without reproach. She removed two utilitarian hat pins from the small hat she'd worn to church and throughout the day and set it aside, then began shoving errant hairpins back into her spinster's bun.

"You seemed quite lost in your revelry," he said. "What were you singing?"

"Nothing—a song my mother used to sing," she replied, replacing her hat and jabbing the hat pin in place to anchor it against the wind. "How is your mother?"

"Perhaps if you had attended her, you would know."

Lucie released a sigh when he might have expected her to bristle and bluster out an excuse. "Your mother does not like being fussed over and treated like an invalid."

"Although she is an invalid," he replied.

He watched with interest as she worked through a number of responses. Finally she peered up at him, shading her eyes with one hand. "Your mother is a woman who prizes her independence," she began.

Gabe stiffened. "Go on."

"She is also a woman quite used to caring for others. She would take great joy in caring for you should you choose to visit more often."

"I hardly think that I owe you any explanations, Miss McNeil. However, in the interest of putting this topic to rest once and for all I shall provide you with one. Before last autumn I made regular trips out to the island to visit my parents—at least every other Sunday. Then I was called away to Europe for several weeks to finalize some important business undertakings. I returned in time to spend Christmas with my parents and then, shortly after that—as you are no doubt well aware—the winter set in."

Lucie started to say something, but he interrupted.

"As for a remedy to my mother's desire to care for me," Gabe said, giving her a sardonic smile, "there is a relatively simple solution if that is the problem."

Lucie frowned and waited. He knew he would be stating the obvious—the solution that she knew as well as he did.

"She could come to Boston and become mistress of my household there. My father could work again."

"Your father works now," Lucie said quietly.

"He is a businessman, Miss McNeil, not some fisherman or sheepherder. He was once one of the most successful businessmen in the entire northeast. Surely you have taken notice of the quality of your surroundings in spite of their run-down condition."

Once again, she appeared to consider and reject several retorts. Finally she stood, steadied herself by holding on to the railing and moved a step nearer. "My father is a sheepherder, Mr. Hunter. It is noble work, as is any profession that provides the basic services people in the world of business and profit seem to forget are essential to their success and the enjoyment of a more lavish lifestyle."

He opened his mouth, but she wasn't finished.

"As for your mother's treasures—yes, they are lovely, and all the more so because of the sentiments she attaches to each item. You see, they are not just fine china and crystal and such for her. They are her grandmother's china or the crystal vase that Jonathan bought for her on their tenth anniversary or—"

"Miss McNeil, I would suggest that you leave the sermons to others and attend your duties," Gabe snapped, and turned away. "Randolph," he shouted as he stalked off.

Lucie stood tall until she was sure he would not look back, and then crumpled into the chair once again. She had gone too far—as always. How many times had she jeopardized her very livelihood by standing up to people of power—the foreman at the garment factory or her landlord, to name two examples? How many times had she taken a stand against her father's drinking and paid for it with a lashing from his belt?

She could not fathom God's plan for her future, but for now she was in no position to risk losing this job. She had vowed never to return to the factories and yet she had not the training or references necessary to get a position in a shop. As for taking another post as a housekeeper or nurse, just the thought of working for anyone but the Hunters gave her chills. She had been successful with the

Hunters because they were kind and appreciative people. They did not see themselves as doing her a favor by hiring her. On the contrary, they saw her as a blessing, and she returned that sentiment in her nightly prayers, thanking God for sending Adam O'Hare to market that terrible day.

She realized the yacht had turned and saw that Gabriel had taken control and was steering toward town. She gathered the last of the dessert and tea dishes and took them below. When Randolph relieved her of the dishes, she made her way down the narrow passage and stood just outside the closed door of Gabe's stateroom.

Through the slatted door, she heard Emma's soft drawl. "Whatever will be," she said resignedly. "But, with God's good grace, it will be in our home on the island— not in some overdone mansion in Boston," she added, her voice rising and then collapsing in a fresh fit of coughing.

Jonathan shushed her, and Lucie knew from experience that he was holding her, consoling her. For a long moment she stood outside the closed door, and the thought flitted across her mind that she would probably only know such tenderness of a man for a woman vicariously. She was suddenly taken by the memory of Gabe's arms around her earlier when she had lost her balance— the solidness of his chest against her back, the warmth of his arms enfolding her. She shook it off as nothing more than melodramatic self-pity, and focused instead on facing the realities before her.

Her life was about to change—again. She could allow its new course to be set by the decisions of Gabriel Hunter or she could look for the opportunity her mother had taught was always hidden in even the most dire of circumstances. Lucie turned away from the closed cabin door and retraced her steps along the passageway. She took a seat on the bottom step of the polished wood stairs that led to the open deck and waited for the ship to reach port.

Before setting out on what he had rightly assumed would be a short sail, Gabriel had arranged for the carriage to remain waiting at the dock. Once the yacht docked, he took the reins himself, instructing Lucie to ride with him while his parents sat in the back. Lucie stared out at the passing scenery without really seeing it at all as she waited for Gabe to deliver a list of commands that he expected her to follow as soon as they reached the cottage.

But they passed the remainder of the trip in silence—seething for him and stoic for her. Once they reached the cottage Gabe carried his mother straight to her room and then, without a word to Lucie, he went to help his father put away the horses and carriage. When they returned, Jonathan's usual even-tempered mood had darkened considerably.

"I'll take my supper with Emma, Lucie," he said tersely. "Perhaps after supper if you would stop by and help get Emma ready for bed?"

"Of course," Lucie murmured, glancing from father to son and noting that Gabe was studying his boots as Jonathan left the room without looking his way.

"Does Dr. Fulcrum still practice on the island?" Gabe asked as he slid his arms into the sleeves of the coat he had removed just minutes earlier.

"Yes."

"Has he treated my mother?"

"He has seen both of your parents on occasion. Last month, when your father caught a terrible cold and—"

Lucie heard the slamming of the outer door and turned to find herself alone in the kitchen. A moment later she heard the clop of horse hooves moving away fast from the house, and reached the window in time to see Gabe riding off toward town.

Lucie helped Emma change into her nightclothes, spoon-fed her some broth and made sure Jonathan ate at least some cold meat and bread. Then she helped Jonathan settle Emma into the large, ornately carved walnut bed they had shared for decades. She exchanged worried glances with Jonathan over the return of Emma's labored breathing as Emma dropped off to sleep almost at once. Finally she bowed her head as Jonathan said his evening prayers, then slipped out of the room.

She wandered into the parlor but ended up pacing the room, unable to settle herself with handwork or reading. She paused once to study a photograph of a very young, broadly smiling boy, which had been the only image she'd known of the Hunters' son until he'd appeared a few days earlier. She ran her thumb over the image and wondered when the boy whose smile was so filled with trust and delight had become the man who regarded the world and everyone in it with skepticism and misgiving. It was then that she heard the creak of a wagon and the snorting of a team of horses.

She stepped to the front door and peered out through the leaded-glass panels. She heard the murmur of men's voices—one giving directions and the other responding— as they mounted the front stairway. One of the men carried a small satchel, and Lucie recognized Dr. Fulcrum. So, against Jonathan's wishes, Gabe had gone for the doctor. She opened the door.

"Doctor," she said with respect, standing aside to let

him in. The other man stayed behind, indicating his intention to wait on the porch for further direction.

"I've come about Emma," the doctor said as he handed Lucie his hat, and glanced down the hall. "Hello, Jon."

The colonel stood at the entrance to his and Emma's bedroom.

"Did Gabe send for you?"

The doctor nodded and started down the hall. "Came himself. He'll be along, but he's determined to take her back with him, Jon."

"Fool boy," Jonathan muttered as he led the doctor back inside the room. "Emma doesn't want to leave the island, Tom. Tell me honestly what you think." His voice wavered with doubt and fear.

"Well, now…"

The doctor's words trailed off as Jonathan shut the bedroom door. Lucie closed the front door, hung up the doctor's hat and coat and hurried to the Hunters' bedroom. When she stepped inside, Dr. Fulcrum was listening to Emma's heart and lungs and frowning. Lucie stood near Jonathan, resisting the urge to place one arm around the man, who looked as if he might wilt to the floor at any moment.

"Come and sit here while the doctor does his examination," she said, indicating a small upholstered chair between the bed and the window. Jonathan did not protest. She took up her place, standing just behind the chair as they both waited.

"It's not good, Jon," the doctor said as he put away his stethoscope, took out his pocket watch and lifted Emma's limp wrist to count her pulse.

"She overdid," Jonathan said weakly. "She just needs—"

"Jon, it could be pneumonia. She needs more than rest. She needs—"

"Proper care," Gabriel said from the open doorway. "I've made all the arrangements, Father."

At that Emma rallied. "Don't take that tone with your father, Gabriel," she rasped.

Gabe moved to the bed and sat on the side of it. "Mama, it's for the best," he said, his voice pleading like that of the boy he'd been rather than the man he was.

"Gabe is right," Jonathan said wearily. "Lucie, please get our things together. We can leave in the morning."

Gabe stood. "If you've agreed to go, then it will be tonight—immediately. Miss McNeil can follow with whatever you need tomorrow."

Emma tried to sit up, resulting in a fresh round of coughing that brought everyone to her side. "No," she protested, reaching through the tangle of hands and arms that were trying to keep her from further agitation, to grasp Jonathan's sleeve. "Don't let them," she pleaded as tears ran down her cheeks.

Gabe stood and stared down at his mother, his face a mask of shock and hurt. Lucie and the doctor both backed away, giving Jonathan room to gently ease Emma back onto the pillows. There was a long moment when an entire conversation passed between them without a word spoken, but then Jonathan nodded.

"Now, darling girl," he crooned, "I've thought this through and here's what we should do. You go and let Gabe's doctors have a look at you. I'll be right here taking care of everything until you can get back. It's for the best, darling."

Emma stared up at him, wild-eyed. "But it's not forever," she said.

Jonathan shook his head and chuckled. "No, darling girl, not forever."

Lucie swiped at the tears that ran down her cheeks.

"You keep Lucie with you," Emma said.

"Now, Emma, you know I can't do that. You take Lucie with you or else you'll have to…" He leaned forward and whispered something and to everyone's surprise, Emma smiled.

"That's not playing fair," she said.

Jonathan stroked her hair and shrugged. "Lucie goes with you, then?"

"You'll send for Adam?" she countered, before lapsing into a fresh bout of coughing.

Jonathan leaned forward and kissed her tenderly on each cheek, then stood and, without looking at his son, turned to Lucie. "Get your things together, Lucie. The doctor and I will see that Emma's ready for the trip." Finally he turned to Gabe. "A word," he said tersely, and led the way into the hall.

Lucie had to pass the two men on her way to her room at the top of the stairs. Jonathan was pacing while Gabe stood just outside the closed door of his parents' bedroom. "It's for the best," he began, but Jonathan stopped him with a look.

"Excuse me," Lucie murmured as she hurried past them.

From her room she heard the low murmur of their voices as she gathered clothes, toiletries and her prayer book into the worn, carpeted satchel she'd brought with her that day after the fire. It took her less than five minutes to pack and she paused to look around the spare room, which had been more home to her than any place she had ever lived. She wanted to be sure she was not missing anything she might need, for there was no telling how long she'd be gone. Or if she would ever return.

She set the satchel down and walked to the narrow bed. She ran her fingers over the soft cotton quilt that Emma and Jonathan had given her on her birthday just a few days after she'd come to work for them. She gathered it in her arms and buried her sobs in its folds.

A moment later she splashed water from the basin over her face and dried herself on a linen hand towel. Then she picked up her bag and, without a backward glance, left the room. But when she reached the top of the stairs, the voices of the two men engaged in serious debate made her pause.

"Be clear about your victory in this, Gabriel—it is not forever," Jonathan said as he paced the narrow hall, his hands locked behind his back as if inspecting his troops.

"I have never said that it was," Gabe replied.

Jonathan shot him a look. "Words are not always necessary. I want you to understand something that you are perhaps too young to appreciate."

Gabe stiffened and resisted the urge to remind his father that he was not too young to have made twice the fortune his father had, and in half the time. "I'm listening," he said.

Jonathan sighed and dropped his hands to his sides, and then he sat on the edge of one of Emma's prized rose velvet, tufted side chairs. "Your mother and I are coming to the end of our lives, son. Your instinct is to protect us and that is noble. But our instinct is to live every moment we have in the way that gives us the most joy and peace. This place does that for us."

"This place has become detrimental to Mother's health," Gabe argued. "Last winter alone…"

"This place is our home and we would rather have fewer days here than years in a place we neither know nor—"

"I am offering you a place in my home. Surely—"

"That mansion is the place where you reside and perhaps a symbol of all you have accomplished," Jonathan corrected. "You have not yet found your true home, Gabe, for you do not yet know love."

The two men were silent for a moment, and then Jonathan said, "As for Lucie—"

"There really is no need for Miss McNeil to go beyond accompanying Mother on the journey. Once we reach Boston, I will dispatch—"

Jonathan was on his feet and toe to toe with his taller, broader son. "You will not dispatch or otherwise give orders to Miss McNeil, Gabriel. She takes her directions from your mother and me—not you. She is to stay with and attend to your mother for the duration of her stay in Boston. Is that quite clear?"

"It's just that Mother seemed to think that you need her here," Gabe protested.

Jonathan smiled. "Well, I believe she's changed her mind on that score." He glanced toward the closed bedroom door.

Curious, Gabe followed his father's gaze. "And just how did you convince her?"

Jonathan locked eyes with Gabe and said, "I told her that either her care would be managed by Lucie or by your Miss Witherspoon."

There was half a second of silence, and then both men chuckled. Lucie decided it would be a good moment to make her presence known.

"Miss McNeil," Gabe said, stepping forward to relieve

her of the half-empty satchel as Lucie came down the stairs. "Allow me." He glanced at his father, who gave him a nod of approval and then went to bid farewell to his wife.

On the voyage to the mainland Emma held fast to Lucie's hand and called out for Jonathan, until Gabe motioned for Lucie to move and allow him to take her place. He sat on the side of the berth and took Emma's hand.

"Johnny?"

"Right here, darling girl," he murmured, and Emma smiled and fell into a fitful sleep for the rest of the voyage.

By the time they docked in Boston, disembarked and transferred Emma to a waiting carriage, it was nearly midnight and raining heavily. Emma's fever had worsened.

"We should have waited for morning," Lucie said, without realizing she had spoken aloud. She wiped Emma's forehead and pulled the covers tighter.

"Waited for what, Miss McNeil? For my mother to become so impaired that no one could help her?"

Lucie glanced at him. He had aged ten years in the last few hours. His eyes were wide with fear and when he looked at his mother, Lucie thought her heart would break for him. "Forgive me. I spoke out of concern," she said. "Of course, you know best."

The carriage rolled through the nearly deserted streets, where the streetlamps cast golden reflections on the wet pavement. The rain beat down on the leather carriage top. Gabe leaned forward, his hands clenched into tight fists, as if he could will the horses to move faster. Finally Lucie felt the carriage turn, and the beating rain stopped. The driver yelled out commands to unseen others as

Gabe leaped from the carriage and barked out orders of his own.

"You may go on into the house, Miss McNeil. Fraiser and Mrs. King will see to my mother."

Lucie emerged from the carriage to find herself stepping directly onto a stone portico fully protected from the pounding rain by arched columns supporting an ornately carved ceiling. She glanced toward the light spilling out from the house and saw a man and an older woman, both dressed in the black of servitude, rush forward. Behind them she saw three other people—an older woman who seemed quite distraught; a younger woman whose full attention was on Gabriel; and a man she had hoped never to see again—Thurgood Witherspoon. All three pushed forward and past her as if she did not exist.

Momentarily displaced, she moved away from the crowded vestibule and into the hall. A hall every bit as large as the Hunters' parlor. Matching carved and arched double pocket doors of a rich cherrywood led to a drawing room and library. Fires blazed in both rooms, but Lucie could not help but think that in spite of the inviting warmth of the fires, the rooms—the entire house—gave off an aura of superficiality and indifference.

"Miss McNeil?"

Lucie turned her attention back to the activities surrounding her—Emma being carried through the hall and into a small elevator housed just behind the grand staircase. The shutting of the outside door muffled the sounds of the carriage being pulled away. Finally her eyes came to rest on a tall, blond man standing at the foot of the stairway.

"Hello," he said.

"Hello," she replied, gathering her wits enough to start

the action of removing her own coat and hat in preparation for going to Emma.

"I'm Dr. Charles Booker. I understand from Mr. Hunter that you have attended his mother for these last several weeks."

"Yes." Automatically, Lucie's defenses went on alert. The young doctor seemed nice enough, but—

"Excellent. Please come with me while I examine the patient. I'll have questions." He waited for her to precede him up the curved and carpeted stairway.

Once they reached the second floor, the sound of voices—excited and solicitous—made asking directions completely unnecessary. Lucie stepped back and allowed the doctor to enter the room first. She liked the way he ignored everyone else and went directly to Emma.

"Thank you, Mrs. King," he said, and the older woman Lucie had seen taking charge of moving Emma when they arrived nodded and stepped away from the bed. "Miss McNeil, if you would," he called, and beckoned Lucie closer.

Thurgood Witherspoon frowned as he and the two grandly dressed women seemed to take in her presence for the first time. The two women exchanged whispers. Lucie held her breath, terrified that he would recognize her. But why would he? He had never truly seen any of the women who worked for him. She turned her eyes to Gabe and he nodded as if giving her permission to follow the doctor's request.

Emma seemed lost in the large bed with its pristine mound of cream-and-white covers and collection of lace-edged pillows. The doctor opened his bag and prepared to make his examination. Lucie remained standing opposite him, but when she saw Emma's eyes blink in confusion as she glanced at her surroundings, Lucie quietly reached forward and took her hand.

"Perhaps your guests would be more comfortable downstairs, Gabriel," Dr. Booker said, without taking his eyes off Emma.

Lucie saw Gabe glance around the room as if just now noticing the presence of anyone other than his mother and the doctor. "Yes," he said. "Mrs. King, would you—"

The younger woman rushed to his side. "Oh, Gabriel, you are not to concern yourself with us. Mother and I have seen to everything. Why, from the moment we received your wire telling us of your dear mother's illness, we simply could not rest until we were quite sure every possible detail had been—"

Gabe glanced down at the petite, full-figured girl clinging to his arm. "That's very kind, Jeanne," he said, then looked up at the older woman. "Thank you, Mrs. Witherspoon," he added.

"Well now, Gabe," Thurgood Witherspoon said, his voice thundering in the large room, "it's the least we can do, given everything you've done for us these last weeks—isn't it, my dears?"

"Forgive me," the doctor said quietly, "but it would really be best for Mrs. Hunter if you would all—"

"Of course, of course," Mr. Witherspoon bellowed as he took charge of herding the two women from the room.

"If there's nothing else, sir, I'll see to your houseguests," Mrs. King said.

"Thank you, Mrs. King. I'll be along directly."

Mrs. King nodded once and left the room, closing the door soundlessly behind her.

The doctor returned to his examination of Emma, asking questions of Lucie from time to time but making no comment on her replies.

Gabe paced the room, pausing now and then to straighten a photograph in one of the silver frames clustered on the dressing table or finger a fresh rose in the crystal vase filled with them on the lace-topped round table opposite the fireplace. Having made his tour of the room, he took up his post at the foot of the four-poster bed. Lucie could see his reflection in one of two gilt-framed floor-to-ceiling mirrors that hung on either side of the bed. He looked tired and worried and scared, and she had an urge to offer him words of comfort. But in the face of Emma's deteriorating condition and the doctor's tightly pressed lips and furrowed brow, there seemed to be little she could say.

The bedroom door opened and closed and through the mirror, Lucie saw the young Witherspoon woman tiptoe into the room and stand next to Gabe. She didn't take his arm or otherwise touch him, but played nervously with the ruffles at the neckline of her gown.

"Gabriel?" she said finally, when he had given no sign of seeing her.

He glanced her way.

"I've asked Mrs. King to have the room next door made up for me. I'll move there so that I can be near your dear mother should she have needs during the night. Mrs. King has arranged for a cot and one of the servants to sleep here in the room until—"

"I'll be here," Lucie said when she realized Gabe was simply acquiescing to this plan without giving it much thought.

Jeanne Witherspoon ignored Lucie, although she did

frown at the interruption. Lucie turned and took a step closer to Emma, who was in no condition to stand her ground in this matter. Lucie would have to do it for her.

"Your mother—" she began, speaking directly to Gabe.

Jeanne Witherspoon smiled tightly, her eyes alight with icy fury as she stepped between Lucie and Gabe. "I'm sure you've been a great help to Mrs. Hunter, however—"

Gabe placed his hand on Jeanne's shoulder. "My mother wouldn't want you to displace yourself in order to attend her, Jeanne. Miss McNeil is here for that purpose."

Jeanne turned her back on Lucie, effectively sending her back into the oblivion where servants dwelled. "Nevertheless, Gabriel, forgive me for saying so, but in spite of those attentions perhaps the woman is not trained—that is, your mother has not fared well. That is…"

Her voice trailed off under Gabe's probing, dark gaze.

"Of course, you must do what you think best," she murmured.

Dr. Booker cleared his throat, signaling that his examination was completed and he was ready to disclose his diagnosis and plan for treating Emma. Lucie gave the man her full attention, as did Gabe.

"It's her heart," he began.

By the time the doctor had finished delivering his assessment of Emma's condition—and her chances for recovery—Gabe had slumped onto a side chair, and Jeanne was stroking his shoulders as tears ran down her plump cheeks. Lucie remained standing, hearing the words, the prescribed course of treatment and the doctor's

final declaration: that in the end it would be up to Emma
and how much fight she had left.

"I'll send for my father," Gabe said.

"No," Lucie protested.

"Really, girl," Jeanne said disapprovingly.

"Forgive me, sir," Lucie said to Gabe, "but if your
mother is to fight, she must have something to fight for—
a return home."

"She is at home," Jeanne snapped, then softened her
tone as she knelt next to Gabe and took his hand in hers.
"Among people who love her. It's only fitting that your
father come, as well. How horrible it would be if—" Her
voice broke and she turned her face aside as she dabbed
at her eyes with a lace handkerchief she pulled from her
sleeve.

Gabe stood and looked down at his mother. "You're
right," he said, and Jeanne brightened, but Gabe was looking at Lucie. "Perhaps if we give it a few days and see if
she improves." He glanced at Dr. Booker for confirmation that he was not risking too much.

"A day or two will tell if the medicines and breathing
apparatus I'll have sent over are working."

"And prayer," Lucie added.

"And prayer," the doctor agreed. "Always the best
medicine."

It was just before dawn when Gabe, already dressed
for the day, knocked softly and then entered his mother's
room. The fire was banked and the drapes drawn. A single
lamp glowed on the small table next to the bed. The cot
that Fraiser had set up for Lucie was empty and had not
been used. Instead, she sat in a rocker she'd pulled close
to the side of the bed, her back to the door.

Her hair was down but otherwise she was still fully dressed. One hand and forearm rested on the coverlet of Emma's bed. Moving nearer Gabe saw that her hand rested on Emma's arm—a gesture no doubt meant to wake her if his mother should stir. He could not help but be impressed by her devotion. Her free hand rested on the small book of psalms he'd snatched from her that first morning. Her long, curly black hair framed her face, softening the features that seemed permanently frozen in an expression of alarm or defiance whenever she looked his way. One heavy curl had fallen across her left eye and he had the urge to tuck it behind her ear. He also had the urge to stroke her cheek.

Fighting such base instincts, he moved to the opposite side of the bed and cleared his throat as he focused his attention on his mother. As he had expected, Lucie immediately awoke.

"How did she do in the night?" he asked, never taking his eyes from his mother.

"She was restless for the first part, but about an hour ago her congestion seemed to ease and she fell into a calmer sleep. I thought it would be all right—as long as I stayed with her—if I—"

"Miss McNeil, we can hardly expect you to go without sleep," he said. "The medicine seems to have helped?"

"Yes," she replied as she pulled her hair back with one hand and tucked it inside the collar of her dress.

"And prayer?" he asked.

Lucie glanced down at the book of psalms, closed it quickly and set it on the table next to the lamp. "Yes, we prayed together, your mother and I."

Gabe looked directly at her for the first time since waking her. "My mother was lucid, then?"

"Your mother is almost always lucid."

"You know my meaning," he replied, and remained where he was, troubled blue eyes holding her violet ones as he waited for a response.

"When the fever eased, she asked me to read to her." Lucie glanced at the book of Psalms and then back to him. "I did as she wanted and then together we prayed—for her health, for the colonel and for you—as she has every day since I've known her."

Gabe turned away then and walked to the window. He lifted the curtain enough to allow him a view of the coming daylight. "Mrs. King will send someone to relieve you so that you can have your breakfast downstairs with the others—in the kitchen. Dr. Booker will be by midmorning to see Mother."

"Very well," Lucie said.

He remained at the window, and for the first time Lucie noticed the book he held at his side.

"Did you wish me to give that book to your mother?"

He looked at it as if it had perhaps magically appeared without his being aware. "I wasn't sure if you'd had time to bring along your own book, Miss McNeil, and I do appreciate the comfort my parents gather from reading Scripture." He passed her the book across the expanse of the bed.

*Holy Bible* was engraved in scripted gold lettering across the old but pristine leather cover. Lucie opened the volume to the frontispiece where, in Emma's firm hand, was written *To Gabriel Hunter on the occasion of his baptism.* She could not help but notice that the spine had been stretched as the Bible fell open of its own accord.

"It is well-used," Lucie noted, unable to completely disguise her surprise.

"It is well-traveled," Gabe replied. He stared at the book now in Lucie's hands and then shook his head as if to clear it. "I must go to my office and attend to some business. Fraiser can send for me should there be any change—any change at all. Is that understood?"

"Yes."

Gabe nodded, bent and kissed his mother's forehead and said, "Her fever *is* down."

"She's very strong and very determined," Lucie assured him, but her words went unanswered if not unheard, for Gabe had already left the room.

## Chapter Seven

Lucie liked Mrs. King immediately. She was a large woman given to laughing with abandon and stating her opinions openly. Her opinion of the Witherspoons was one Lucie was certain Emma would have delighted in hearing.

"They've been here three months now, living like royalty, ordering everyone about when Mr. Hunter's away—he travels so much for business. Mr. Witherspoon is supposed to be his partner but it's Mr. Hunter who does all the work."

Lucie opened her mouth to ask a question, but Mrs. King was not done.

"Mr. Hunter—bless him—is the soul of goodness. Takes care of others as if they were his own family. I can't tell you how folks who work for others up and down the street here would love to be in his employ."

Lucie wondered what Mrs. King would say if she told her about the conditions in the garment factory before it burned. "And the Witherspoons live here because of the partnership?" she asked instead.

"Oh, no. They had their own place but last autumn they suddenly decided to sell and find something grander. Silly people. Wouldn't you think you'd find the new place before selling the current one? Not to mention letting all their staff go in the bargain. Mr. Hunter was in Europe on business, so he suggested the Witherspoons stay here until they find another house. Of course, he had no idea it would be months instead of weeks."

Lucie carried her dishes to the sink and washed them. Mrs. King picked up a nearby dish towel and wiped them dry as she continued her tale.

"So they moved in and Mr. Hunter went to a hotel once he came back. Now, how ridiculous is that? Not that there's not plenty of room here for them all, but if you ask me, he stays at the hotel to get some peace and quiet. The reason he gave them was his concern for Miss Jeanne—living in the same house and all. After all, he has escorted her to several events in the last year and everybody expects them to announce their betrothal soon."

"I don't understand."

Mrs. King sighed. "Oh, for goodness' sake, Lucie, you simply cannot be that dense. The plan is to marry Jeanne to Mr. Hunter. In the circles these folks run in, it would be quite a coup to have your daughter marry Mr. Hunter. But as far as that goes, Mr. Hunter hasn't asked."

"Does she love him?" *Does he love her?*

"Love?" Mrs. King let out a hoot of laughter. "Folks with this kind of money don't marry for love, Lucie—except in the case of your Mr. and Mrs. Hunter." Her face went soft and her eyes dreamy. "Now, there's a match for the books. I've met Mr. Hunter's parents only twice, but what a joy they are—like seeing the world's grandest romance played out right there in real life. I told my mister that—"

The call bell chimed and a tiny light on a board labeled with room names showed that the call had come from Emma's bedroom. Lucie and Mrs. King both dropped their work and conversation and headed up the back stairs to the second floor.

"Mrs. Hunter has been abandoned," Jeanne Witherspoon announced dramatically when they entered the room. She was flitting around the bed, plumping pillows and layering on more covers, which Emma kept pushing aside. "I stopped by to see how she'd spent the night and found her here, unconscious and quite alone." She looked directly at Lucie. "Gabriel—Mr. Hunter—will not tolerate such negligence."

At that moment a young servant girl emerged from the dressing room that connected Emma's room to the next bedroom. She looked at Mrs. King and then backed away. "I— She asked me to— I was only away for a minute," she finally wailed.

"Shush, child," Mrs. King ordered before turning her attention back to Jeanne. "I am sure that Irina was only trying to do Mrs. Hunter's bidding," she said in a voice that on the surface was solicitous, but with an undercurrent of righteous indignation at the accusation.

"Mrs. Hunter—as I have said—was quite unconscious," Jeanne countered.

"I was dozing," Emma managed to rasp out as she held out one hand to Lucie.

"What do you need, Emma?" Lucie asked, ignoring the sucked-in breath of horror that came from Jeanne.

"My bed jacket—did you bring it?"

Lucie smiled and gently eased Emma back onto the stacked pillows. "I did," she assured her. "Are you feeling well enough to allow me to help you into it?"

"That young doctor…" Emma said, and then her voice trailed off into a fit of coughing. Jeanne pressed forward, but Emma waved her away as Lucie offered her a sip of water from the crystal glass on the bedside table.

"Perhaps a little tea with honey," Mrs. King suggested, and Emma's eyes brightened.

"Lovely," she managed.

One look from Mrs. King, and Irina scurried from the room.

"Now then," Lucie said quietly, taking charge of the situation, "the bed jacket can wait at least until you've had your tea."

Emma's hand flew to her disheveled hair. "I can't receive visitors looking like this," she croaked.

Lucie laughed. If Emma had one fault, it was vanity—especially when she might be in the company of a handsome young man like Dr. Charles Booker. Emma reached up and lightly pinched Lucie's cheek. "You could do with some color, as well, Lucie," she instructed.

"Well," Jeanne announced brightly, "thankfully you're doing ever so much better. Gabriel will be delighted. He was so worried, poor darling. He was quite beside himself last night—hardly touched his supper."

Emma frowned and looked pleadingly at Lucie.

"Perhaps, Miss Witherspoon, you would be so kind as to excuse Mrs. Hunter while I help her get ready for the doctor's visit?"

"Well, really," replied the young woman as she spun on her heel and left the room.

Mrs. King quietly closed the bedroom door, and when

she turned, she was smiling. "Is there anything I can do?" she asked Lucie.

"Just the tea, and perhaps one of those wonderful biscuits?"

Mrs. King beamed. "I'll go tell Irina to bring it at once, with two cups for the tea and a plate of biscuits."

"How are you, really?" Lucie asked as soon as she and Emma were alone. "You gave us all quite a scare."

Emma collapsed back onto the pillows and closed her eyes. Two large tears rolled down her cheeks.

"Oh, Emma, it's going to be all right," Lucie assured her.

Emma shook her head from side to side, then opened her eyes wide and clutched Lucie's hand. "If I— If the young doctor can't—"

"Sh-h-h," Lucie whispered as she stroked Emma's flattened curls away from her forehead. A light tap on the door followed by Irina's entrance with the tea tray forestalled any further discussion. Lucie turned to make room for the tray on the bedside table and saw the Bible that Gabe had left earlier.

"Emma," she said, "open your eyes and see what Gabriel left for you this morning." She handed the book to Emma, then took the tray from Irina, who immediately fled the room.

Once again Emma's eyes filled with tears, but these were tears of quiet joy. "He kept it all these years," she whispered as she fingered the cover.

"Shall I read something to you?" Lucie asked.

Emma nodded and handed her the Bible in exchange for the half-filled cup of tea.

Lucie allowed the Bible to fall open, and then smiled.

"Ah," she said, "it's one of your favorite psalms—the twenty-third."

"The Lord is my shepherd," Emma murmured, and it was as if the words were medicine enough to calm her. "Go on," she prompted as she sipped her tea.

Lucie read the rest of the psalm aloud, with Emma chorusing some of the lines with her. "…dwell in the house of the Lord forever and ever," they finished together.

"Amen," Emma added.

The two women finished their tea. Lucie broke off biscuit bits and fed them to Emma, all the while noticing how the sunlight played over the rich, burled surface of the headboard and intricately carved bedposts. She glanced up and gulped.

Emma's eyes followed her gaze until they were both looking at a painted mural of cherubs and angels floating on puffy clouds in an azure sky. Emma giggled. "When I first woke this morning and looked up and saw that, I thought I had died in the night and this was surely the heavenly choir come to greet me."

"It seems out of character for Gabe," Lucie murmured, and when Emma laughed, Lucie realized she had once again allowed her thoughts to become spoken words. "That is—it's just a little feminine, don't you think?"

Emma sighed. "Have you looked around this room? The lace doodads everywhere, the flowers, the crystals hanging from every light? *She's* done this. Or that mother of hers," Emma said. "I shudder to think what she's managed to do to the downstairs rooms."

"But surely—"

"Gabe has abdicated his home to these people while he lives in a hotel. I know my son and this is not his style." She waved her hand at the flying-cherub mural. "I just hope it isn't too late," she added as she allowed her arm to drop weakly back onto the covers.

*Too late for what?* Lucie wondered, but voices in the downstairs hall sent her to the dressing table for a hairbrush. "We'll save the bed jacket for Gabriel's visit when he returns from the office," she assured Emma as she fluffed the older woman's thin white curls. "Dr. Booker will understand."

There was a knock on the door and Mrs. King peeked in. "Dr. Booker," she announced, and at a nod from Lucie, she swung the door open to admit the doctor.

After the doctor had examined Emma and commented on her encouraging progress, Lucie sat with her through the afternoon. While Emma dozed, Lucie busied herself putting away the few personal items of Emma's that the colonel had packed for her. Lucie smiled as she unfolded the bed jacket, and fought back tears when she found the silver-framed photograph of the two of them in front of the house on Nantucket.

She placed the photograph where Emma was sure to see it, and then spent the remainder of the day tending the fire and checking often to be sure that Emma was resting comfortably, waking her only when another dose of medicine was due. Both of the elder Witherspoons stopped by, but Lucie assured them Emma was sleeping and that the doctor had advised rest as the best medicine of all. She could not help noticing that both of them seemed relieved to be excused.

Late that afternoon she heard Gabe's voice in the downstairs hall and wondered at the sense of happiness she felt that he was home. She waited for him to climb the stairs and come to visit his mother, but instead became aware of a raised voice—not his, but rather that of Thurgood Witherspoon.

"How much?" he boomed.

There was a low response.

"That's outlandish—impossible," the older man blustered. "Can this man be trusted?" Followed by, "Tell me how I can help, son."

The voices trailed off as both men evidently entered one of the downstairs rooms and slid shut the pocket doors to continue the discussion.

Lucie sat down with a book of poetry she'd borrowed from the shelf of volumes housed in the case above a writing desk in the bedroom. She settled into the rocking chair near the fire, positioned so she could watch Emma, but with the warmth of the fire and the setting sun, accompanied by the gentle snores signalling Emma's improved breathing, Lucie nodded off.

"Jonathan?" Emma called, and Lucie woke with a start.

The room was dark except for the glow of a single bedside lamp and the dying embers of the fire. The book had fallen to the carpet.

"No, Mama, it's me—Gabriel."

He was sitting on the side of the bed, holding Emma's hand.

Emma smiled and caressed his cheek with her palm. "You look tired," she said tenderly.

"And you look and sound much improved," he said.

"It's that handsome young Dr. Booker," Emma croaked.

Lucie moved to the foot of the bed. "She's slept much of the day," she reported, then, realizing he must have seen her sleeping when he entered the room, she took another tact. "Dr. Booker was quite encouraged."

"Yes, so Mrs. King told me." He did not look at her.

"Have you had your supper?" Emma asked.

"Not yet."

"Lucie hasn't eaten since breakfast," Emma reported.

"I'll see that she gets a tray," Gabe assured his mother.

"Nonsense. Have her sit with you. She can give you the full details of the doctor's visit."

"Mrs. King already—" Gabe began.

"Mrs. King was not present during the examination," Emma said irritably. "Don't be stubborn about this, Gabriel."

"Very well," he said, and turned his face slightly so that the words came from over his shoulder without his looking directly at Lucie. "Miss McNeil, would you be so kind as to join me downstairs in half an hour for supper?"

Lucie almost made an excuse, but Emma shot her a glance that was a demand. "Thank you, sir," she murmured. "And now, if you'll excuse me, I'll just step downstairs to the kitchen and see to Emma's—Mrs. Hunter's—tray while you visit."

As soon as Lucie left the room, Gabe felt the tension in his neck and shoulders ease slightly. When he'd entered the room, she'd been sitting by the fire, the last rays of the sunset golden on her face. As an employer he could be kind, but also demanding, and he expected those who worked for him to attend to their duties. And yet when he'd seen Lucie sleeping, he had felt only empathy. He hadn't slept much for the last two nights and he suspected the same was true for her. If he was bone-tired after doing very little, what must she be feeling? Instead of reprimanding her for sleeping, his instinct had been to cover her shoulders with the afghan draped over the foot of his mother's bed. Such behavior was out of character for him. He had mentally chastised himself for potentially falling into the trap of seeing Lucie McNeil as far more than a servant.

Instead he had gone to his mother's bedside and turned on a lamp. Then he'd sat on the side of the bed and watched his mother sleep, studying her color, her breathing and the odd smile that played across her face from time to time. When she woke, she had called out for his father, but this time he did not play into her fantasies. He wanted to see if the doctor's medicine had made a difference. Was she lucid? Had her health at least stabilized?

To his relief it seemed the answer to both questions was affirmative. She had no trouble making the transition from his father to him. Her voice was stronger and, given her insistence that he take his supper with Lucie and allow her to give him a full medical report, there was certainly no question of her lucidity.

"Gabriel, have you completely given over the running of your house to that Witherspoon girl and her mother?" Emma demanded in a surprisingly firm voice.

"The Witherspoons are my guests," Gabe replied.

"That girl has her cap set for you, young man—and if she hasn't, then her father surely has. Mark my words, if you continue to permit them to spend your hard-earned money on foolery like that…" Emma indicated the pastoral scene painted over the bed.

Gabe glanced up and his cheeks flushed. He could hardly admit that this was the first time he'd noticed the ridiculous mural. "Perhaps that is a bit excessive," he said.

His mother snorted.

"The Witherspoons are in the process of finding a new residence," he explained. "Jeanne and her mother were feeling quite displaced and asked if they might repay my hospitality by attending to furnishing and decorating the house—a task I had avoided and one that really had to be done at some point."

"If you truly felt at home here, you would have seen to such things yourself. This place is nothing more than…" A fresh bout of coughing interrupted her tirade.

Gabe gave her a sip of water and eased her back onto the pillows. "There now, Mama, calm yourself."

Emma smiled and reached up to brush back the lock of wavy hair that had fallen across his forehead. "You are such a handsome man—a younger image of your father." She sighed and closed her eyes, and Gabe waited for her to fall asleep. Instead she began to spin out a story, the way she had when he was a boy and she was the one sitting next to him, lulling him to sleep with her words.

"Your father and I came from such different worlds, Gabe," she said. "And yet those very differences have made us stronger and brought us a lifetime of love and blessings. You need someone who will challenge you by her very differences when it comes to how she views the world. Like your father—the Yankee, the colonel, the businessman," she murmured, her voice trailing off.

Gabe sat as still as possible, stroking her hand and waiting for the memories to take her into sleep. "And you—the belle of the South," he said softly, and she smiled.

"Like Lucie," she said, just before her face went slack and her breathing came in deep, even sighs.

Gabe eased her hand under the covers and thought, *Belle of the South and eternal romantic.* Then he turned to go, shaking his head at the ridiculous notion that he and Lucie McNeil had anything more in common than what even he had to admit was an unquestionable devotion to his parents.

Dr. Booker continued to come twice a day—morning and evening—to examine Emma and make adjustments to her medications and treatment routine. "I believe it might do you some good to sit up for a part of each day, Mrs. Hunter," he declared the morning of the third day. "For short periods, perhaps there at the table to take your meals," he added, directing these instructions to Lucie.

"And when might I take my meals downstairs?" Emma asked.

Dr. Booker smiled. "In time. These matters cannot be rushed. You don't want a setback."

"And when do y'all think I can return to my home?" Emma asked, her voice thick with her Southern accent—a sign, as Lucie had learned early on, that Emma was not above using charm to have her way.

This time the doctor laughed. "Now, Mrs. Hunter, why on earth would you want to leave this beautiful house and miss all the enjoyment of planning the surprise birthday party?"

Emma glanced at Lucie, who shrugged. "Whose birthday?" Lucie asked.

"Why, Gabriel's thirtieth," Dr. Booker said. "Miss Witherspoon is—"

"Ah." Emma grimaced, then looked at the doctor with a coquettish smile. "How right you are, doctor. I'm quite certain that Miss Witherspoon could use my help."

Lucie averted her eyes as the doctor glanced her way. "Well, as long as you don't overdo," he warned, and Lucie nodded solemnly, knowing full well that she would have her hands full trying to keep Emma from taking full command of the event.

"Do you have someone to escort to the festivities, Dr. Booker?" Emma asked.

The man's cheeks reddened as he busied himself packing his stethoscope and clamping shut his black bag. "Why, Mrs. Hunter, that is a very personal inquiry," he teased. Then he cleared his throat, all business as he turned to Lucie. "Miss McNeil, I wonder if I might have a word with you before I leave?"

Lucie led the way to the door. "I'll be right back," she assured Emma after waiting for the doctor to precede her.

"As long as you're out, Lucie, please find Miss Witherspoon and ask her to call on me at her convenience," Emma said.

Lucie was still working through how she might best keep Emma from getting too caught up in trying to plan a major social event as she followed Charles Booker down the hall and to the top of the curved stairway.

He paused and turned. "Miss McNeil, I do hope you won't see this as too forward of me, but I was wondering… That is, would you give some consideration to—" He swallowed hard, and his Adam's apple bobbed convulsively. "Would you consider accompanying me for a walk in the park after church on Sunday?"

Lucie could not have been more shocked if the man had suddenly suggested she slide down the highly polished curved banister. "I'm not sure I'll be attending church," she replied, stating the first thought to pop into her head.

The doctor blushed again and nodded. "It's just that on

the several occasions I've spent with you—and Mrs. Hunter—I've come to have a great deal of respect and admiration for you, Miss McNeil. I would like the opportunity to know you better, if that would be agreeable."

The floodgates of her repressed thoughts opened and she was startled at the order in which those thoughts spilled out, the very first being, *What would Gabriel think?* And the second being, *Perhaps I should—perhaps this is God's way of showing me a new direction.*

A flash of color caught her eye and she looked down to see Jeanne Witherspoon walk toward the drawing room, then stop at the foot of the stairs and stare up at them with interest. "Why, hello, Charles," she called gaily.

Charles Booker looked at Lucie and said quietly, "Please consider my invitation, Miss McNeil," then started down the stairs. "Ah, the fair Jeanne, I'm afraid I may have revealed your little secret."

Jeanne actually pouted. "How could you? Gabriel will never—"

"Gabriel is still in the dark, but I just assumed that his mother knew the plans."

Lucie watched Jeanne's reaction with interest. The first expression was a flash of abject horror, quickly covered over with a fawning smile as she took the doctor's arm and walked with him to the door. "Are you telling me that Gabe's dear mother will be well enough to attend?"

"More to the point, I'm telling you that the lady is delighted with your idea and cannot wait to assist you in the planning. I believe she has asked Miss McNeil to bring you to her room as soon as possible." He glanced back up the stairway to where Lucie stood, rooted to the spot where he'd left her.

He smiled and tipped his head to Lucie and then Jeanne, and left.

Jeanne kept her back to Lucie for a long moment, under the guise of watching him go. Finally she turned, and without looking up, started up the stairs. At the top she brushed past Lucie on her way to Emma's room as if Lucie were nothing more than an apparition. A moment later Lucie saw Thurgood Witherspoon emerge from Gabe's library and hurry out the front door.

They had been at Gabe's house for a little over two weeks when Lucie came down to the kitchen, bringing the dishes from hers and Emma's evening meal. Ever since Charles Booker had approved Emma's ability to sit at the round pedestal table in her room for meals, Emma had insisted that it simply wasn't civilized to dine alone. Therefore, if Gabe could not join her, she wanted Lucie to take her meal with her and not in the kitchen with the rest of the staff.

"Mr. Hunter asks that you join him in the library once his mother is settled for the night," Mrs. King said, with barely concealed curiosity.

Gabe had developed a regular routine of coming to the house in the late afternoon, spending an hour or so with his mother, then several hours in his library before returning to his hotel for the night.

"Very well," Lucie said, busying herself at the sink so that Mrs. King could not see her expression. She'd had very little contact with Gabriel over the last week. Whenever he came to sit with Emma, Lucie made some excuse to leave the room. Often she simply stepped into the adjoining dressing room on the pretext of attending to some mending, and left the door ajar in case Emma should

need her. The truth was that she found it increasingly difficult to be in the same room with him. He confused
her—rather, the way she felt when he was near confused
her. By all reason she should abhor the man, as she did
his partner. His very presence in the same room should
set her teeth on edge. Instead she found herself looking
forward to those times when she knew he would come to
the room—when he would be only a few feet from her.

Having taken care of any mending or other detail necessary for the care of Emma during the hours that Emma
slept each afternoon and evening, she would sit on the
single chair near the door and try to read. But she was
always distracted by the low murmur of Gabe's voice as
he read Emma a letter that had come that day from
Jonathan, or told her about his day and the people he had
encountered. His voice was always tender and tinged
with good humor, so very unlike the stern, impersonal
tone he often took with her. Emma's soft drawl usually
dominated the conversation, interrupted now and then by
Gabe's laughter and exclamations of, "Now, Mama…"

And because the sound of his laughter and the bass
tenderness of his voice touched her, she would sometimes pray for God to forgive her foolish heart. For she
could not deny that she was attracted to this gentle and
kind Gabriel Hunter in a way she had never been attracted
to any other man. She would sit in the dressing room with
her eyes shut tight, and pray that God would remind her
that there was another Gabriel Hunter. That man had
owned a garment factory and had done nothing to prevent
it from burning to the ground, leaving several girls dead
and the rest out of work and in the street, she'd remind
herself firmly.

"Lucie?" she'd heard him say one evening.

Immediately she'd stood, smoothed her skirts and run her palm over her tightly bound hair before stepping into the room. "Yes?"

He was standing on the opposite side of the bed, watching Emma sleep. "Mother would like to begin taking her meals downstairs. Please ask Dr. Booker if that's appropriate when he calls tomorrow morning."

Lucie moved to the other side of the bed and waited. He was looking at her, his face in shadow because of the dim bedside lighting. "Charles—Dr. Booker—has already suggested that if she continues to improve, she could begin coming down for her meals in another week."

"We can use the elevator," he said.

"Yes," Lucie replied.

Uncomfortable under his scrutiny, she reached to arrange the covers around Emma's shoulders. At that same moment he bent to perform the very same task. Their hands brushed and Lucie chastised herself for imagining that it had taken him longer than necessary to withdraw his fingers from hers.

She stood now at the kitchen sink, lost in the memory of the warmth and strength of his hand on hers, as Mrs. King babbled on.

"What do you suppose he wants with you?" Mrs. King asked, all pretense of subtlety gone.

Lucie forced herself back to the realities of her position as an employee of his family currently living in his household. She understood that for Gabriel Hunter, the line between her duty to his parents and his right to oversee that duty was so fine as to be nonexistent. "I'm sure I have no idea," Lucie replied.

## Chapter Eight

$G$abe paced the floor as he waited for Lucie's quiet knock. He knew it would be subtle—gentle. In spite of her inclination toward stating her mind, she was not forward or bold in the way of some females. Jeanne, for example, only pretended at delicacy, and was easily exposed when she did not get her way. The Witherspoons had spoiled her—especially Thurgood. The man talked of little other than making a proper match for his beloved child, and fretted constantly that she might end up with the "wrong sort."

"What is the right sort?" Gabe had asked.

"Why, someone like you, Gabriel," Thurgood had boomed. "In fact, nothing would make me happier than to have you as my son-in-law."

Thurgood was not a subtle man. More than once Gabe had been forced to temper his partner's rash promises or accusations with conciliatory words or even outright monetary concessions. But he could not forget that the man had orchestrated business deals that had given Gabe his start. In those early days Thurgood had been his mentor—mitigating Gabe's inclination toward being overly cautious with a reckless abandon that was both unnerving and thrilling. Together the two of them had amassed a fortune that far exceeded the one his father had lost, and yet...

The soft knock interrupted his thoughts. "Yes," he said, and moved behind his desk as Lucie entered the room.

"You wanted to see me?"

"Sit down, Miss McNeil." Gabe cleared his throat to soften the surprising gruffness of the command.

She perched on the edge of the straight-backed chair nearest the door.

"Over here, if you don't mind," he said, indicating the chair across from the desk.

He watched her walk the length of the large room. Had he never before noticed the grace with which she moved? The elegance of the tilt of her head? The proud set of her narrow shoulders? The thick black lashes that touched her cheeks when she lowered her gaze? The truth was that he had noticed all of that and more. In fact, it seemed that since she'd come to Boston to attend to his mother, Gabe had hardly thought of anything but Lucie.

She sat down in the chair he'd indicated, folded her hands in her lap and waited.

Gabe cleared his throat. "Miss McNeil—Lucie—I'd like to thank you for the care you've given my mother since she came here. Dr. Booker has been singing your praises. According to him, you have been most instrumental in Mother's recovery."

"Thank you—and Dr. Booker."

The following silence was unnerving. Gabe studied her hands, remembering the burns he'd seen there on that first meeting. He considered inquiring how she had sustained them, but thought better of it. He also realized that he was imagining stroking her palms—soothing them with his touch. He cleared his throat and spoke more loudly than he'd intended, startling her. "I trust that over these past few weeks you have come to a better understanding of the wisdom of having my parents come here to live permanently."

She swallowed. "Having your parents move in along with the Witherspoons would make the house quite full."

Gabe frowned. "The Witherspoons are houseguests, not permanent residents."

"Nevertheless, your parents are not interested in moving here. They respect what you are trying to do but—"

"Miss McNeil, please do not presume to tell me what my parents may—"

"With all due respect, I think I have a better grasp of their wishes than you do."

Gabe paced the room. "It may seem to you that I have neglected my parents. I assure you that nothing could be further from the truth. I have sent funds, supplies, even members of my staff, and all have been rebuffed. I can hardly—"

Lucie stood and faced him. "Of course. Emma—Mrs. Hunter—has spoken often of your generous nature. I apologize. It's just—" She moved a few steps toward him, forcing a halt to his pacing. She was near enough for him to touch, to observe the rise and fall of her breathing, to take her in his arms. He shook off the thought but did not move.

And neither did she.

They met each other's gaze, neither willing to be the first to glance away. Gabe inhaled the scent of her—like a summer morning on Nantucket. He lifted his hand to dismiss her with a gesture and instead found his fingers skimming her cheek. She leapt back as if burned.

She turned away and he reached for her, cupping her shoulders and turning her back to face him.

"Miss McNeil...Lucie, I—"

To his astonishment he noticed that her lowered lashes were damp with tears. "What?" he asked.

"Do not try and seduce me in order to get what you want, Gabriel Hunter," she whispered as she pulled away.

"I wasn't. I wouldn't," he protested, releasing her.

She took advantage of his action to distance herself from him, moving purposefully toward the door. "Emma's improved health has a price. She has begun to fret about Jonathan—the colonel. She's very concerned. You've brought no word from him these last three days. I believe it's best that I return to Nantucket and make sure he is all right. I'll leave tomorrow."

"I'll send someone else. Mother needs you here," Gabe replied, all business once again. *I need you here,* he thought, and was stunned at the truth of it as he imagined long evenings without her. He realized that however frustrating his day of business dealings might be, he looked forward to spending that hour or so in the company of his mother, with Lucie nearby.

"It's not the same," Lucie said quietly. "And you should consider what your mother would want."

He felt the beginnings of a smile. "You're a talented negotiator, Lucie," he said softly, not looking at her. "I've dealt with experienced businessmen who did not have your skill for finding the one thing I could not refuse."

She remained with her hand on the door and said nothing.

"I'll make the arrangements," Gabe said.

She nodded curtly and prepared to slide the door open.

"On one condition," Gabe added, and took some plea-sure in seeing her shoulders stiffen as she waited. "That you return with my father in time for this party Jeanne has planned for my birthday."

She half turned. "It's supposed to be a surprise," she replied.

"Yes, well, let's pretend I didn't say that. I wouldn't want to spoil things for Jeanne. She's a sweet girl."

"Of course," she replied, and her voice sounded strained. So much so that Gabe started toward her again, but before he could move beyond the massive desk, she was out the door and gone.

Throughout the rest of the evening and over the end-less, sleepless night, Lucie kept replaying the encounter with Gabe. His fingers warm and smooth against her cheek—as light as a butterfly. That, compared to his hands grasping her shoulders, when she had felt his heat seeping through her, heard his breath coming unevenly, stirring the fine hairs on the back of her neck. She had felt her neck tip unbidden toward his touch and resisted the urge to rest her cheek on his hand as it grasped her shoul-der.

In that moment she had seen clearly the temptation before her. Over the hours he had spent with Emma, the hours when she had sat listening to the sound of his voice, his laughter, his tenderness, she had been drawn ever more deeply under his spell. But how could there ever be a future for her with a man like Gabe Hunter?

Then he had touched her, and she had suddenly under-stood that her longings had been only the beginning. She had allowed herself to become vulnerable and, in the face of Gabe's touch, she had come so close to succumbing. It was that simple. It always surprised Lucie how easily temptation inveigled its way into the subconscious. It was just a small step from that to surrender, and then the deed was done.

Back upstairs she looked in on Emma, found her sleeping peacefully and then fell to her knees, using the rocking chair by the dying fire as her altar.

"Father, forgive me for my weakness. Show me Your way and keep me strong. Bless the Hunters—Emma, Jonathan…and yes, Gabriel. Deliver me from temptation and show me the way. Amen. Oh, and bless the Wither-spoons, and if it be Your will that Gabe marry Jeanne, then…"

"Lucie?"

Lucie quickly ended her prayer and hurried to Emma's bedside. "I'm here."

Emma smiled and reached out to her. Lucie sat on the side of the bed and took Emma's hand in hers. "I'm going back to Nantucket tomorrow," she said, and stroked Emma's hand when the older woman stiffened. "Gabriel has asked me to bring Jonathan here."

"No," Emma protested, so vehemently that she began to cough.

"Sh-h-h," Lucie soothed. "Gabe wants you both to be here for his party," she hastened to add.

Emma opened her eyes wide and stared at Lucie, then she smiled. "He knows."

"But Jeanne's not to know that he knows."

"Of course not," Emma said, and closed her eyes.

Lucie thought that Emma had fallen back asleep until the older woman started to speak, her voice soft with memory.

"Mother insisted that with the war over we should hold a ball. Our family was known for our balls. Guests would come from miles around and stay for two weeks. Father said no one would come—that there would be no one left to come. So many homes had been destroyed and so many young men had been lost on the battlefield."

"It probably was not the best time," Lucie said.

"I thought Mother had lost her mind," Emma announced in a strong, youthful voice. "Who would come, and what would we serve, and what would I wear?"

"How did it turn out?" Lucie asked, expecting a quick end to the story.

"They came," Emma said, her voice laced with wonder. "From miles away. The house was full of neighbors and family weary of war and anxious for something—anything that would remind them of better times."

"What did you wear?" Lucie asked, finding herself caught up in the story now that it had taken this surprising turn.

"My sky-blue pink satin," Emma said.

"Sky-blue pink?" Lucie asked softly.

"You know the unique violet color the sky is just after the sun sinks below the horizon and before darkness takes over?"

Lucie nodded and smiled. "And who did you dance with?"

"Jonathan," she whispered. "I was terribly attracted to him and yet it seemed such an unlikely match. In fact, I was quite certain that God was testing me, especially that evening."

Lucie straightened. The parallel with her feelings for Gabriel was too striking. "And yet you danced with him," she said.

Emma squinted at her and then closed her eyes again. "Well, wouldn't you? He was quite the handsomest man in the room."

"Still, so little time had passed since the war ended, and he was on the opposite side."

Emma waved her free hand in a gesture of nonchalance. "Wars—grown men trying to play at the games of their youth, if you ask me. The important thing was the future—my future and Jonathan's. The life we would embark upon and build through the years." She squeezed Lucie's fingers hard. "Family, Lucie. Family is everything. Of course, I didn't know that then, but God has His ways."

And with that pronouncement, Emma drifted back to sleep.

Lucie eased her fingers from Emma's grasp and pulled the covers high around the older woman's shoulders. In the quiet that followed she heard footfalls in the hall and recognized them as Gabe's. Her heart quickened and she closed her eyes and prayed for guidance. When she opened her eyes, she realized the footfalls had passed Emma's door. On the floor, just by the threshold, was a white envelope.

Lucie moved closer and saw that it bore her name in a large, firm male script. She eased her thumbnail under the sealed flap and removed the single sheet of linen paper.

*Fraiser has made the arrangements for our passage to Nantucket at seven tomorrow morning. Mrs. King will attend to Mother.*

*Our?* Surely he did not intend to go with her. She searched the note for more. No closing. No signature. No conciliatory words or even a mention of what had transpired between them in the library. She knelt to feed the note to the fire and then reconsidered, replacing it in its envelope and tucking it into the pocket of her dress.

The weather was gray and threatening as the yacht made its way toward Nantucket. Throughout the journey Gabe stayed on deck while Lucie sat on one of the tufted benches below, trying hard not to succumb to the roiling of her stomach, which echoed the pitching waters outside. Randolph offered her tea and crackers, advising that either or both might help settle her stomach.

Feeling slightly better after nibbling the crackers, Lucie decided to venture onto the deck to have her tea. Gabe was standing at the railing and, in spite of the unsteady seas, he appeared perfectly balanced and at ease. Lucie paused in the doorway, unsure of whether she should retrace her steps and stay below or face the fact that neither of them had spoken of the encounter in his library. She grasped the mug of tea with both hands and gingerly made her way across the rocking surface until she reached Gabe.

"Randolph made tea," she said, offering him the cup.

He accepted it as if it were a peace offering. "Thank you." After taking a long swallow, he balanced the mug on the railing and continued staring out into the mist of the bay. "I've sent word for Adam to meet us at the docks," he said.

"I'm sure that the colonel is all right," Lucie said, although she was not at all sure.

"I hope you're right. On the other hand, this is just the sort of circumstance that worries me the most. Can you not see that they are elderly and frail and alone over there?"

"Yes," she admitted. "They are getting up in years and their health is not the best, but they are hardly alone."

He glanced down at her, raising one skeptical eyebrow.

"They have each other and many friends in the village," she hurried to add. "And they have me."

"For how long, Lucie? You are still young enough to think of having a family of your own, certainly to have a life of your own."

"Do you not think of those things for yourself?" she asked, effectively turning the focus to him and away from herself.

"I have my life," he replied, but he did not look at her.

"Forgive me for saying so, Gabe—Mr. Hunter—but the life you have does not seem to make you happy."

"And how is it that you can judge whether or not I am happy?"

"Because I have seen you on Nantucket and I have seen you in Boston, and the difference is striking."

"On Nantucket I am on holiday. In Boston I have a business to manage."

"And does your work—your business—make you so unhappy?"

"Happiness—as you call it—is a romantic notion, Lucie."

"All right. Perhaps *content* is a better word. When I was a child, our minister used to say that the one question we are most likely to be asked in the afterlife is whether or not we have regrets."

"Everyone has regrets," Gabe said. He tossed back the rest of the tea. "You should go below. It's starting to rain, and Mother would never forgive me if you got ill, as well."

He turned to go, but Lucie put her hand on his arm to

detain him. "I wanted to tell you that—that is, last night—"

He looked out to sea but did not move. "You made your point."

"No," Lucie said. "I reacted badly. There was no reason to doubt your—sincerity. Yet it would be wrong for either of us to give in to those emotions."

He covered her hand with his. "Why?"

"Because it would be acting on impulse and without reason, and in time we would both come to see the folly of it. Your world and mine run on parallel tracks, like a train—both are necessary to keep the train in motion, but the tracks never meet, never cross paths, never connect."

"There was a time, Lucie, when I was every bit as poor and struggling as you are now. There was a time when—"

Lucie tightened her fingers on his forearm. "That was then, Gabriel." Then she slipped her hand free of his and took the tea mug from him. "I'll let Randolph know we are nearly there."

Jonathan was in a terrible state when they finally arrived at the cottage.

Adam had tried to forewarn Gabe on the ride from town. "Stubborn as the day is long," Adam fumed. "Caught himself the grippe not two days after you and Mrs. Hunter left, but refused to let me get Doc Fulcrum out there. This last week he's even refused to let me inside the house. I expect it's a mess you'll be facing there, Lucie."

"But the colonel is well now, is he not?" Lucie asked, glancing at Gabe's tight expression and trying hard to quell the alarm Adam's words were obviously causing him. "I mean, it's not serious—his illness."

Adam finally seemed to realize the impact of his rantings. "Now, don't you worry. He'll be fine. Just misses Emma, that's all. Once you let him know you've come to take him to her, he'll come around. You mark my words."

But the news brought Jonathan no pleasure.

"It's a trick," he grumbled to Lucie before turning on Gabe. "Your plan is to get us both off the island and into that crypt you call home. Well, I promised Emma I would stay put and I'm going to stay put," he fumed.

Lucie set a large bowl of hot fish chowder in front of him. "Eat your stew," she murmured. When he continued to sit motionless, staring out the window, she placed a napkin on his lap and handed him the spoon.

He looked terrible. He had aged ten years in the three weeks they'd been gone. He was unshaven and his hair was uncombed. He was wearing the same clothes he'd been wearing the day she'd left with Emma. From what she could tell he had attended to the outside chores—fed the animals, gathered eggs, milked the goat. Or had Adam attended to those things? Either way, the inside of the house was the mess that Adam had predicted. Fish, no doubt brought by Adam, had gone untouched for days, and the stench of it permeated the house.

Gabe stood up and looked around the messy kitchen. He seemed at a loss, stunned to find his father almost unrecognizable from the mild-mannered man he had known his entire life. "I'm going to check on the animals," he murmured as he grabbed his hat and left through the back door.

Lucie's heart went out to them both. "That wasn't very

nice," she said to Jonathan, deciding that a strong and direct approach was the best course.

Jonathan growled and blew on a spoonful of his soup.

Lucie moved through the downstairs rooms, throwing open every window and door in an effort to air out the house. "You'll need to bathe before we go," she said as Jonathan continued to slurp down the chowder as if it were his last meal on earth.

"I'm not going," he said firmly. "I promised Emma."

"It's Emma who wants you to come," Lucie replied.

That got his attention. "Is she worse?" His voice, as well as his hands, shook.

"On the contrary. She is much improved. She is planning a party."

"A party." He said the words as if they were foreign.

"Yes, for Gabe's birthday. It's to be a surprise, although your son already knows of it. He's promised Emma he won't spoil the surprise."

Jonathan's face softened and he smiled. "She does love a party."

"I'll pack your good suit," Lucie continued, as if he had not spoken. "And something for Emma. Her sky-blue pink, if I can find it."

"Attic," Jonathan muttered.

Surprised, Lucie turned and studied him. "You remember that gown?"

For the first time since she'd arrived Jonathan seemed to focus on her. He nodded and returned to eating. "She saves everything. It's bound to be up there somewhere."

"Would you help me look for it?" Lucie asked.

"After supper," Jonathan agreed, then glanced around. "Aren't you going to eat?"

Lucie put aside the food-encrusted plates she'd been

scrubbing and took down the last clean bowl from the cabinet. "I'm fine, but I'll serve up a bowl for Gabe. He's coming across the yard," she said as she ladled up chowder and set it on the table as Gabe came inside, slapping his hat at his thigh to shake off the rain.

"Things look fine, Papa," he said softly. Lucie nodded toward the soup bowl and Gabe took his place at the table across from his father, with Emma's chair between them.

"Emma wants me to come?" Jonathan asked.

Gabe glanced at Lucie, then blew on the hot soup. "Yes."

"She understands what it means if we both leave here?"

"She's excited about the party," Lucie replied. "I don't think she's considered what it might mean if you're both there." And suddenly she saw a solution—for Jonathan and Emma, as well as for herself. "But I could stay and care for everything."

Jonathan looked as if she had just thrown him a lifeline. "You'd do that?"

"Of course."

Then he shook his head. "No. You must be looking forward to the party as much as Emma is. You women love your parties."

Lucie burst out laughing. "Oh, Colonel Hunter, I won't be asked to the party—it wouldn't be proper, not in the world the Witherspoons live in. And it's Jeanne Witherspoon giving the party."

"You'll be at the party," Gabe said firmly. "Besides, we've more to celebrate than my birthday. There's Mama's health, isn't that right, Papa?"

"Exactly," Jonathan said as he got up from the table, and proceeded down the hall and up the stairs, muttering to himself. "…putting on airs…Emma's right… Witherspoon girl will be the…" The rest was lost in the thud of his boots on the wooden stairs that led to the attic.

Lucie spent the rest of that day, as well as the next and much of both nights, putting the house in order while Gabe performed the outside chores and took long walks around the property with his father. Lucie would see the two men through the windows as she went about her chores. Gabe, a full head taller, would incline his head toward his father, obviously listening as the old man talked. Jonathan became increasingly animated and more his old self as they walked the property together, but Lucie saw with relief that there was no tension between father and son. In fact, she often heard them laughing together, the sound carried on the wind through the open windows of the house. At meals she listened, fascinated, as Jonathan and Gabe discussed business ideas, including Jonathan's advice that Gabe should take advantage of any opportunity he might have to invest in business on Nantucket.

"This tourist business is bigger than whaling ever was. And it shows no sign of tapering off."

"I'll look into it," Gabe promised.

The night before they were to leave for Boston, Adam came for supper and Jonathan greeted him as if there had been no time when Adam hadn't been welcome. He told Adam about going to Boston for Gabe's birthday.

"The way I see it, if Emma's up to some fancy party, she's well enough for us to bring her home once the party's done. Right, Lucie?"

"I'm sure she'll be happy to get back to Nantucket and her quilting," Lucie assured him.

Gabe remained silent during these exchanges.

"Lucie offered to stay, but Emma would never give me a moment's peace if I didn't make sure Lucie was at that party. If I know my Emma, it's some matchmaking she's got in mind," Jonathan added. "She's got this idea that Lucie would be a good match for our Gabe here."

Adam grunted and concentrated on his supper. Gabe paused in the act of buttering a slice of bread and Lucie dropped her fork.

All three men turned to look at her. "You all right, Lucie?" Jonathan asked.

Lucie swallowed around the wad of meat stuck in her throat and bent to retrieve the fork. "Fine," she croaked as she reached for her water glass.

"Lucie?"

She blinked and realized Adam and Jonathan were standing on either side of her, worried frowns lining their aged faces. Gabe was half out of his chair, as well. "You all right?" Adam asked.

She nodded.

Reluctantly, the men went back to their places and resumed eating. "You gave us a fright there," Adam said. "Thought you might have caught a bone in your throat the way you went all red in the face and couldn't seem to say nothing."

"I just swallowed wrong," Lucie said, and mentally sent up a prayer for forgiveness of the small lie. "Did you gentlemen save room for pie?"

Jonathan grinned. "Is this girl a wonder? She's been cleaning and cooking ever since she set foot inside the door. Is it any wonder Emma wants to adopt her?"

"Emma always did pine for a daughter," Adam noted as Lucie busied herself with serving the pie.

\* \* \*

The following morning Lucie came downstairs to find both Jonathan and Gabe already up, bathed, shaved and dressed for traveling. On the porch were the two large steamer trunks Gabe and Adam had wrestled down from the attic the night before, under Jonathan's close supervision. When Lucie had suggested that she take a look at the contents and remove any items that might not be needed, Jonathan had waved a ring of keys and then pocketed them. "It's a surprise," he'd said mysteriously.

"I just hope Gabe's boat don't sink under the weight of them," Adam had commented before heading back to town. He had assured Gabe he would attend to the animals and make sure nothing was disturbed until the Hunters returned. Jonathan thanked him, apologizing profusely for his rebuffs earlier.

"I understand," Adam assured him. "You were worried. Any man in your position would be. But Lucie says Emma's on the mend and the two of you—the three of you—will be back here before you know it, full of stories about your high-society party-going."

Jonathan had laughed at that and clapped his old friend on the back as the two of them walked over to the barn where Adam had left his team of horses and wagon. Lucie noticed that once again Gabe made no comment when the subject of his parents' return to the island was introduced.

Relieved that Jonathan seemed to have revived himself and that Gabe had apparently decided to leave any decision about the future for another time, Lucie stood at the railing of Gabe's yacht as the crew navigated the calm waters off the mainland coast. She studied the buildings of the city, rising beyond the shacks and warehouses that lined the docks. There, between two buildings still blackened with the smoke from the fire, was where the garment factory had once stood. Two streets beyond that were the tenements where she had shared a room with her mother's cousins. And one floor above that was where her friends, the Gibson sisters, had shared a room with their parents, younger sister and four younger brothers.

Both sisters had died in the fire. In spite of everything Lucie had tried, they had died. She stared down at her palms, then closed her fingers over them, hiding the ugly marks of her failure to rescue her friends. She wondered what had become of Sarah, the youngest. Lucie did not know if Sarah had been in the factory that day—if she had, had she leapt to her death as her sisters had?

"Father is sleeping," Gabe said, coming to stand with her.

"That's best," Lucie said. She searched for a topic of conversation. "Judging from your discussions, it's evident that your father was an astute businessman in his day."

"He still is—one of the best I've ever known."

"But he suffered setbacks," she prompted, curious now that she had seen this other side of Jonathan to understand how he'd gone from business to farming.

Gabe gave her a wry smile. "He lost everything, Lucie—the house in Boston, his business, property he owned on Nantucket—everything."

"I don't understand. He's such a cautious man."

"He is that," Gabe agreed, "but there are times when business reversals are beyond a man's ability to control them. There are times when what had seemed to be going well with no end in sight quite suddenly is gone. Some sages believe that it is the cycle of things—the way that business has of not going off too far in one direction."

"And what do you say?"

Gabe looked out to sea and frowned. "I say that if you take your eye off what's yours for a single instant, it can be gone like that." He snapped his fingers, and the popping sound carried over the water.

They stood side by side in silence for several minutes, and then Gabe cleared his throat. "I wanted to thank you, Lucie, for everything you've done, everything that you are doing for my parents. I can see now that without you, they would not have fared so well over these last months."

*And yet you want to take them away,* she thought.

"It is easy to care for two such gentle and kind people," she replied. When he said nothing more, but continued standing with her, Lucie searched her mind for some comment. "You and the colonel appear to have a great deal in common—more than I or perhaps even you would have imagined."

"My father is a wise man," Gabe said. "He is still a businessman at heart—an entrepreneur always able to see the possibilities in undeveloped ideas."

"Forgive me for saying so, Gabe," Lucie ventured, "but it was difficult not to notice that your own business ventures seem to be causing you considerable worry."

She waited for the reprimand, the brusque statement that his business ventures were none of her concern. So she was taken aback when he smiled.

"You could say that," he replied.

Emboldened by his response, Lucie decided to risk yet another comment. "Perhaps while your father is in Boston, he might provide some counsel."

Gabe looked down at her as if she had just suggested a solution for all his worries. "That's a wonderful idea, Lucie," he said, and for the first time since she'd known him, the full power of his smile was turned on her. Her heart skipped a beat and she grasped the railing more tightly to maintain her balance as Gabe continued. "He'll be bored senseless staying in the house all day. You packed his good suit and for the time being that will suffice. I can order him additional business clothes and provide him with his own desk and secretary."

Lucie could see that he was ticking off the details of the plan as they came to mind. "I'll look into that idea he had of investing in something on Nantucket. Perhaps our young violin maker would be a good place to start." He laughed. "It would certainly be more stable and practical than my father's idea."

"Which is?" Lucie asked.

"He was talking about the idea he once had to build an additional cottage on the Nantucket property and open it to tourists. When he first mentioned it, I thought it was ridiculous. But then he kept bringing it up, and the more he talked about it, the more it seemed that maybe, down the road…"

"It may be exactly what is needed to get him back in the role he was born to play in life—that of an entrepreneur and businessman," Lucie ventured.

"Possibly. Certainly if my father becomes a partner in the firm, he and Mama are bound to see that remaining in Boston—with perhaps a holiday now and then on Nantucket—is the only practical course."

He was beaming. Lucie was horrified. What had she done? By opening her mouth she had unintentionally provided Gabe with the very plan he needed to bring his parents to Boston.

Charles Booker was at the house when Lucie and Jonathan arrived. Gabe had gone on to the office, anxious to get everything in place before asking his father to accompany him the following morning.

Jeanne Witherspoon waited with Charles to receive them as soon as the carriage pulled up to the portico. Charles was obviously pleased at Lucie's return. But Jeanne disguised her true feelings under the cloak of fawning over Jonathan.

"Why, Colonel Hunter," she exclaimed, "Gabriel never told us how handsome his father was."

Lucie covered a smile when Jonathan looked at Jeanne as if she might have dropped out of the sky from another planet. "I'd like to see my wife, Miss," he said, and glanced nervously at the young doctor. "Has she had a relapse?"

Lucie liked the way Charles took a step closer, setting down his bag on the large marble-topped table in the foyer as he did so. "On the contrary, sir, Mrs. Hunter appears quite improved. Perhaps anticipation of your arrival has been the best medicine."

Jonathan smiled and grasped the doctor's hand, shaking it vigorously. "Thank you, Dr. Booker, for everything. Lucie tells me that you've been here twice daily, monitoring my wife's condition."

Charles turned his attention to Lucie. "Why, Miss McNeil, have you been singing my praises?" he asked with a smile.

Before Lucie could reply, Jeanne inserted herself physically between Jonathan and Charles, taking Jonathan's arm in the process. "Now, we mustn't keep your dear wife waiting a moment longer," she said, turning to lead Jonathan up the stairs. Her chatter about Emma and Gabriel and the plans for the party continued all the way up the grand staircase and along the long hallway that led to Emma's room.

Lucie and Charles were left alone in the foyer. Charles picked up his hat and doctor's bag, but did not move toward the door.

"Did you have time to consider my invitation, Lucie?" On their second Sunday-afternoon walk, Charles had asked her to allow him to escort her to the party for Gabe. Lucie understood that for the young doctor to appear at a social function of this caliber with her on his arm would be sending a message to everyone: he was seriously courting the Hunters' hired woman.

"About the party," she replied, and there was no question in it. "I'll be at the party if the Hunters want me there—to attend to Emma and make certain that she doesn't overdo."

"But you won't allow me to escort you?"

Lucie stared down at her hands and then hid them in the folds of her skirt. "I shall be on duty, Dr. B— Charles. My time is really not my own."

Booker nodded. "Mrs. Hunter will be well enough soon to return to Nantucket."

Lucie was surprised at this news. "Have you told her?"

Charles laughed. "I'm afraid she forced it out of me. She's talked of nothing else, and apparently is determined that the three of you will be back on the island the day after the party."

"And you agree that she's well enough?"

He released a long sigh. "Unfortunately, I do."

"Why 'unfortunately'?"

His eyes locked on hers. "Because I don't have many occasions to get to Nantucket, Lucie, and if you go back…"

"*When* we go back," she corrected softly.

"Precisely." He took two steps toward the door and, without turning, asked, "Is there someone else, Lucie?"

Gabe's face flashed through Lucie's mind and she could feel his fingers on her cheek. "It's not that," she said, hoping Charles would not turn, for surely the truth was written on her flushed face.

Rebuffed, he said nothing more and let himself out just as Lucie heard Fraiser's soft footfalls coming along the hall from the kitchen.

"Ah, Miss McNeil, you're back," he said with what for him was an exclamation of delight, although his stoic expression was more appropriate for a funeral.

"Yes. How have you been?" It was a rote question, one said as a nicety while she gathered her thoughts.

"Why, quite well, Miss. And you?"

Lucie glanced at Fraiser and realized how seldom anyone inquired after the health of servants. "It's good to be back," she answered. "Is Mrs. King in the kitchen?"

"She is. Miss Witherspoon hired a new girl to attend to Mrs. Hunter."

"But I…"

Fraiser's expression said it all. And Lucie's posture, as she marched up the stairs toward the sound of Jeanne's pealing laughter, left no doubt that she was less than pleased about this turn of events.

The last thing Gabe needed was a surprise birthday party. As usual Jeanne and her mother had gone overboard in deciding the guest list and arranging for the flowers and food and entertainment. It was to be a costume party. Gabe hated costume parties. They were silly and pretentious.

Thurgood Witherspoon had been drafted into the

scheme. He had told Gabe that his family had been invited to this event—a costume party—and Jeanne really needed an escort, since he and her mother would hardly be able to decipher who was a proper suitor and who was not when all were wearing masks. Unstated was the fact that if Jeanne appeared on Gabe's arm, the message would be clear—Gabriel Hunter and Jeanne Witherspoon were an item, and in time, there would no doubt be an announcement regarding their betrothal.

For a week or so Gabe had taken some pleasure in saying he could not be there. He could hardly miss the urgent whispers and visual signals from Mrs. Witherspoon and Jeanne, prodding Thurgood to keep at him. Finally he had agreed. Now he had not been back in the house an hour before Jeanne knocked on the door of his study and bounced in to discuss what costumes the two of them should wear.

She was partial to Marie Antoinette for herself and King Louis for him, but Gabe drew the line at donning a wig and short pants with stockings.

"We don't have to match," he observed, and Jeanne pouted. "What if I dress as a sea captain?" he added, hoping to soothe her hurt feelings and shorten this discussion.

She gave a derisive sniff at that idea. "What about a pirate," she said, "and I could be your captive." She brushed against him, batting her eyelashes as she stroked his arm.

Gabe moved a step away. "We don't have to match," he said again, "so choose whatever costume suits you. Marie Antoinette sounds like a perfect idea."

"Very well, and you shall make such a dashing pirate. A sea captain is so—mundane."

"If I agree, will you leave me to my work?"

She reached up and kissed his cheek. "Thank you, darling Gabe."

If he had reached for her she would not have resisted. He knew that. But he had no interest. Since when? She was beautiful, and what's more she was charming, wanting to please him. He was genuinely fond of her, having watched her blossom from the sweet young daughter of his business partner into a true beauty with a real talent for painting and the arts. Until a few weeks ago he had believed that they would probably wed. It was not a priority for him, but there was no one else, and Jeanne had all the qualities a man of his standing might want in a wife.

Except he did not love her.

The image of Lucie McNeil caught him off guard. She had made it clear that whatever they might feel for each other, there was no future in it for either of them. He had wanted to explain that what he felt for Lucie was as great a mystery to him as it was to her, and wasn't such an obvious connection worthy of exploration?

"I have work to finish," he said, moving past Jeanne to his desk. "Have Mrs. King send for the dressmaker and whatever materials you need for this party and charge it to my account."

He had quickly learned that the one thing that could heal any wound Jeanne might suffer was the opportunity to shop. She blew him a kiss and fairly danced from the room. Certain that he had successfully given her and her mother enough to keep them occupied for several days, he rang for Fraiser.

Silent as a cat, the ageless man glided into the room. "Sir," he said quietly.

"Has my father settled in?"

"He has, sir."

Gabe ran through the files again, more slowly this time. "And Miss McNeil?"

"She has moved to one of the bedrooms on the third floor. I suspect she wishes to give your parents their privacy."

Gabe paused, but did not look up until Fraiser gently cleared his throat. "Pardon me, sir, but Mrs. King would like to know if the new girl can be let go now that Lu— Miss McNeil is back."

"What new girl?"

"The one hired by Miss Witherspoon to attend to your mother."

Now Fraiser had Gabe's full attention. "I thought Miss Witherspoon had insisted on attending to my mother with Mrs. King's help," he said, and realized that with everything going awry in his office downtown, he'd hardly had time to meet with either Fraiser or Mrs. King about the household accounts or management. "Yes, dismiss her at once."

Fraiser turned to go.

"But see that she has two weeks' pay," Gabe added. "And, if Mrs. King agrees, a reference for future employment."

Fraiser slipped out of the room. Gabe stood, staring down at the stacks of files. "There are limits," he muttered, and vowed to have a talk with Thurgood the following day about the liberties his wife and daughter had assumed.

# Chapter Nine

In spite of the fact that she didn't really care for the Witherspoons and the way they had taken charge of the household, Mrs. King was thrilled at the idea of an actual party. She had launched a thorough cleaning of the mansion's downstairs rooms, and when Fraiser delivered the message that the new girl was to be let go, Mrs. King was beside herself.

"I should think that she can stay on until after the party," she protested. "She's quite inadequate as a nurse but she follows instructions to the letter and she's proficient with a brush and bucket."

"I'll ask Mr. Hunter if she might stay the two weeks he already plans to pay her," Fraiser replied with a long-suffering sigh.

"Surely he'd rather get some return on his money," Mrs. King fumed as she and Lucie shared a cup of tea. "Why the man would just hand over two weeks' pay is beyond me, but that's the way of him." She clicked her tongue disapprovingly but then brightened. "A party, Lucie—imagine it."

"I take it that Gabe—Mr. Hunter—has not entertained much?"

Mrs. King snorted. "He's never entertained. Oh, now and then he'll bring home some business acquaintance to have dinner and stay the night, but that's business. Mr. Hunter is always thinking about business, talking about business, shutting himself up in that library and working on business. Why, I suspect the man dreams of nothing but business."

She smiled the way Emma often did when she was lost in thought. Lucie sipped her tea and gave her the moment's pleasure.

"It's to be a costume party, you know, so what to wear for the colonel and his missus is less of a problem now that you've got those beautiful old clothes of theirs."

"I just don't want them to feel out of place," Lucie said, thinking about the contents of the trunks Jonathan had insisted on bringing. The two steamers had been packed with ballgowns and formal wear—all at least two decades old.

"I'm sure there's something we can put together, Lucie. What about your costume?"

"Mine?" Lucie laughed. "Oh, Mrs. King, I shall go as myself—the Hunters' nurse and companion."

Mrs. King raised her eyebrows. "And disappoint the good doctor? I think not, young miss."

Lucie blushed and was thankful for the distraction afforded by an outburst of tears and wails in the hallway.

"But it's our party," Jeanne Witherspoon wailed. "How can Madame Colette have failed to allow for that?"

"The dressmaker," Mrs. King explained to Lucie as she hurried out to the foyer to rescue Fraiser. "Is there anything I can do to help?" she asked.

"I do apologize, Miss Witherspoon," he began, but was cut off by a fresh set of tears and wails.

"I assumed the gown would be the easy part," she cried. "I have the wig—I even have the shepherd's crook and a stuffed lamb to carry."

"I'm not sure I understand," Fraiser said, becoming more flustered by the moment.

Jeanne's tears dried instantly. "Marie Antoinette," she shouted. "She used to entertain by dressing herself as a young shepherdess. I will attend this party as Marie Antoinette or there will simply be no party."

She flounced away.

Lucie had moved to the pantry door and saw the look that Fraiser exchanged with Mrs. King. "When I sent for the dressmaker to come around with a selection of fabrics and designs, I was told that she is fully booked for the next two weeks. It would appear that all of Boston society is excited about the opportunity to attend a function at the Hunter mansion."

Lucie thought of the piles of beautiful gowns upstairs in Emma's room—and of Emma. How delighted she would be to play designer.

"I may have a solution," she said. "No promises," she added when both Fraiser and Mrs. King looked as if they might actually embrace her.

As Lucie had expected, Emma was thrilled with her idea. She had taken to sitting on the silk damask chaise lounge in her room as she worked on a new quilt—a beautiful white-on-white design of interlocking circles. Emma had been working on it for hours each day. Lucie had soon realized that with Jonathan going off to work with Gabe each day, Emma—feeling stronger every day—was at loose ends. Once again she had to accept that

Gabe had surprised her with his thoughtfulness when it came to his mother. For while they'd been in Nantucket to get Jonathan, Emma reported, Gabe had arranged for a local fabric merchant to call.

The man had presented Emma with literally dozens of fabric samples from which to choose. The merchant would not tell her prices, but she knew fabric and she had deliberately dismissed the expensive silks and embroidered goods he'd shown. Instead she had selected six or seven serviceable cottons and given the man yardage amounts. The following morning the fabrics arrived, and inside the box were the fabrics she had chosen along with yards of every one of the precious silks and satins and damasks that she had coveted but declined to order.

"And look at this," Emma had gushed almost before Lucie could unpack. She displayed a smaller box bursting with lace trim and colorful ribbons and beads.

Now it was that box of trimmings along with one rose-colored gown she pulled from Emma's collection of gowns that Lucie brought from the dressing room for Emma to examine.

"It's ideal," Emma exclaimed. "Mrs. King, go find that silly girl and send her to see me at once."

Mrs. King looked anxiously at Lucie.

"Jeanne Witherspoon," Emma said with exasperation when Mrs. King failed to move quickly enough. "I need to see Jeanne, and tell Fraiser we shall need a sewing machine and pins and needles and— Oh, never mind. Just get the girl and I'll make a list. And ask Fraiser to send up the new girl. I think you mentioned that she sews, and Lucie is going to need help."

"She's been let go," Mrs. King reported. "She left an hour ago."

"What's her name? Where does she live?" Emma asked.

Lucie could not have been more shocked when the girl Mrs. King had spoken of turned out to be Sarah Gibson— the younger sister of Lucie's friends who had died in the factory fire.

"I know her," Lucie said.

"Well, go fetch her," Emma pleaded. "We need to get started at once."

"But Mrs. Hunter," Mrs. King protested, "your son has—"

"My son will surely allow me to hire this young woman back. After all, he would do as much for the Witherspoon women, and I am his mother."

"Yes, ma'am."

Emma turned her attention to Lucie. "Lucie will need the carriage," she said.

"I'm afraid it's not available," Mrs. King said, her voice trembling slightly.

"Why not?" Emma asked.

"Mrs. Witherspoon—"

"Oh, bother," Emma huffed, and began coughing.

Lucie hurried to her side, but was immediately rebuffed. "I am perfectly fine," Emma managed in a croak. "Well, hire a carriage, then."

"I can walk," Lucie said. "In fact, I prefer to walk. It's been days since I had the opportunity, and—"

Emma's tense expression softened. "Very well. You go, and I shall meet with Miss Witherspoon. I'll be on my very best behavior," she assured both Lucie and Mrs. King. "Now, go, shoo!"

Lucie took a streetcar at Mrs. King's insistence. When she got off, she realized she was only a few blocks from where the factory had stood. In fact, she was standing in the very spot where her dream always began. Lucie began to walk, her footsteps seeming to take their own direction in spite of her intent to go directly to the tenement and find Sarah.

"Are you all right, Miss?" a woman asked, coming alongside her and staring up at her with concern.

"Yes, thank you."

She pressed on until she came to the corner where she had first seen the flames, heard the screams and watched helplessly as the bodies had fallen. She shut her eyes and prayed for strength, then opened them and stepped around the corner.

There, where the original factory had once stood, was a barren lot littered with charred wood and twisted metal. It was as if it had never existed—as if *they* had never existed. Lucie felt as if she might be sick. She staggered back and nearly fell into the path of a passing dray. "Watch it there, girlie," the driver shouted, gesturing rudely at her.

Lucie recovered her wits and turned away from the de- filed space—the devastated remains that gave no sign that her friends and coworkers had ever existed. She hur- ried down the nearest street—the same way she had that day after realizing there was nothing to be done. And almost without remembering how she arrived there, she found herself standing at the foot of the chipped and broken steps that led to the tenement where she had once lived.

A For Rent sign in the lower apartment window told her she would not find her mother's cousin living there. She hoped this was a sign that the family had found a better life. She opened the peeling exterior door and stepped into the dimly lit foyer. A stairway stretched up into darkness, and as she placed her hand on the loose banister and started to climb, she heard a rat scurry over the side of the stairway and down the back hall.

"Oh, Lucie, it is you," Sarah squealed with genuine delight when she opened the door to the dank and tiny apartment and saw Lucie standing on the threshold. "When Mrs. King spoke of Lucie McNeil, I hardly dared to hope. After all, there are many McNeils, and Lucie is a common enough—"

She stopped in midsentence and stared at Lucie, horror-struck. "Why are you here? Have they let you go, as well? Come in, come in."

"I've come to hire you back," Lucie hurried to explain as soon as she had stepped into the single room that made up the apartment, and Sarah had shut the door.

"Truly?" Sarah's eyes went wide. "But, how— That is—"

"There is to be a costume party," Lucie began.

"Oh, I know. The whole of the time I was there Miss Jeanne was beside herself about it."

Lucie told Sarah about Madame Colette. "And now we have all these costumes to make. Sarah, I do hope you are as handy with a needle as your sisters."

"Better, some say," Sarah said meekly.

"Then you have a position—at least for the next two weeks. And if you prove yourself, perhaps there will be more work for you."

Sarah wrapped her arms around Lucie and hugged her hard. "Oh, Lucie, you are an answer to prayer. Papa is ill and can't find steady work, and Mama—well, she's never quite recovered after—"

"Can you come now?" Lucie asked, wanting nothing

so much as to escape the apartment and the memories that assailed her from every corner.

"Of course," Sarah said. She stepped to a curtained area of the single room and pulled the curtain aside. "Mama? I have to go back to work. I made some cabbage."

There was the weak murmur of an answer and Sarah allowed the curtain to drop back into place. "Let's go," she said, her face once again wreathed in a smile.

Sarah was still chattering away when she and Lucie stepped off the streetcar and walked the half block to the Hunter mansion. When they entered the kitchen, it was obvious that Mrs. King had been watching from the window and was curious about the connection.

"Sarah and I knew each other when I lived in Boston," Lucie explained. She glanced at Sarah, hoping the girl would understand that she did not wish to reveal any more information.

"Oh, yes," Sarah gushed, emboldened by Lucie's directness with Mrs. King. "Lucie lived in the apartment just below ours and—" She paused, having finally grasped Lucie's signal. "She and my sisters were friends," she finished.

"But you lost contact?" prompted Mrs. King, a master at ferreting out more information than was offered.

"Well, I went to Nantucket and the winter was harsh, so three months passed and we simply lost touch. Sarah, shall we go upstairs? Mrs. Hunter is expecting us."

With the arrival of Jonathan, and especially once he began spending his days in the office with Gabe, Jeanne Witherspoon and her mother seemed genuinely delighted to be in the presence of Gabe's parents. They were even civil to Lucie once they realized it was she who would be filling in for the dressmaker.

"How marvelous," Jeanne exclaimed, clapping her hands with delight when Lucie held up the rose satin gown. "We can lower the neckline and puff the sleeves and— Oh, could we use this lace trim, Mrs. Hunter?"

"Of course, my dear. You'll be the belle of the ball."

Jeanne preened with pleasure, and her mother beamed at Emma.

"And now for your costume, Mrs. Witherspoon," Emma said.

"Oh, please call me Dolly," Mrs. Witherspoon said. "After all, I feel we've become such good friends already, and one day we might be family."

"Mother." Jeanne sounded a warning, but it was too late. Dolly Witherspoon had provided Emma with an opening, and she took full advantage.

"Family?" She looked mystified while the Witherspoon women shifted uncomfortably.

Dolly smiled uncertainly as Emma continued. "Oh, I see. Yes, Gabe's quite fond of Jeanne. He never had a sister, you know." And without seeming to notice Dolly's crestfallen face, she turned her attention to Lucie. "The lavender faille, Lucie. Let's start with that for Dolly's costume."

For the next two weeks, Lucie and Sarah spent hours together, sewing and pinning and altering costumes for the Witherspoons. Sarah was indeed even more gifted as a seamstress than her sisters had been. Furthermore she seemed to genuinely love the work. By the second day the women were singing her praises. Lucie could not fathom how Sarah could be so civil to the wife and daughter of the man whose neglect of basic human safety had resulted in the deaths of Sarah's sisters.

Every night Lucie prayed for the strength to find a way to forgive Thurgood Witherspoon—and Gabe—for putting profit ahead of human welfare. That was the heart of it for her. On the one hand she was deeply drawn to Gabriel Hunter—attracted on an emotional level she had never experienced before. But on the other, she could not forget the day that Mr. Witherspoon had come to the factory with Gabe—the day when Sarah's sister, Ellie, had identified the two men as partners and owners of the business.

Whenever Gabe stopped by to visit with his mother, Sarah was a bundle of nerves. In fact, had she not been nearly as tall as Lucie was, Lucie was quite certain the girl would have hidden like a child, clinging to Lucie's skirts for protection. So it remained a mystery how she could be so talkative and lighthearted with the Witherspoon women.

"You recognize Mr. Hunter, don't you?" Lucie asked one afternoon as the two of them shopped for additional trimmings to complete the costumes.

Sarah nodded. "I had no idea, but I desperately needed the job that Mrs. King was offering. Mama hasn't been herself since the fire and Papa barely leaves the apartment these days. The boys are grown with families of their own. Someone has to come up with the rent and food, and it seemed that working in a fine house like this one was a good idea."

"But then?"

"Well, of course, I saw Mr. Hunter and then I saw that other man—Mr. Witherspoon. Oh, Lucie, it was all I could do to keep myself from scratching his eyes out. He was the one who was always down there, always adding to the work, always demanding more and more and paying less and less."

Sarah was right, of course. "And yet you stayed."

"How could I not? The job brings us the rent money, and Mrs. King may be strict, but she's a good soul."

She let the words trail off as Lucie followed Mrs. King's instructions and charged their purchases to the household account. Twenty dollars in beads and lace and ribbon, she thought. Twenty dollars that could probably pay the rent and feed Sarah's family for a month.

"Why do you stay?" Sarah asked once they were out of the shop.

"I don't work for him," Lucie said. "I work for his parents, and they are the dearest people I have ever known."

"Still, you're there—in his house."

"That's temporary," Lucie assured her. But was it? In spite of Emma's improved spirits, Charles Booker had warned Lucie that Emma might not survive another winter on Nantucket—even one milder than the last. Lucie understood that Charles was also reminding her of her own need to make plans for her future.

"Dr. Booker is so handsome, isn't he?" Sarah sighed, and Lucie wondered if somehow the girl had read her thoughts.

"He's a good man," she replied.

"He's quite attracted to you, Lucie," Sarah teased. "More than once I've heard him ask Mrs. King about you when he came to call. First question was always, 'Has Miss McNeil returned?'" Sarah giggled. "You could be a doctor's wife, Lucie. Imagine that."

"Oh, Sarah, you are such a dreamer," Lucie chided, but she smiled as she said it.

* * *

"How are the costumes coming along?" Gabe asked Emma one night when he stopped by after work to bid his parents a good night. On such occasions he asked Mrs. King to deliver a tray with chamomile tea and cakes for him to share with his parents as they sat together around the fire in the large bedroom. Even though Emma was now well enough to spend her evenings in the parlor after dining with Gabe and the Witherspoons, she and Jonathan usually chose to retire to their room.

"Now, Gabriel, keep in mind that this is a surprise for you."

"I understand that, but there's no surprise in the costumes, remember? I'm supposedly escorting Jeanne to a party at some other location."

"Then you'll have to ask Lucie, for I am only the designer," Emma said with a dramatic sigh, then she laughed. "Pass me another of those lemon cakes, will you, dear?"

"Well, Miss McNeil," Gabe said, turning to where Lucie sat near the light, altering some handwork on Dolly's costume.

Lucie had been seeking some opportunity to speak up for Sarah. Perhaps this was that moment. "I could not have completed half the work without the help of Sarah."

"Sarah?" Gabe was clearly at a loss.

"The young girl Jeanne hired, who you dismissed with two weeks' pay," Emma said. Was he truly so unaware of what went on under his own roof?

"If I dismissed her then why is she still here?"

"I asked Mrs. King to send her up to help Lucie," Emma announced. "If you were going to pay her anyway, the girl might as well earn her wages."

Gabe stared at the banked fire. "She does good work, this Sarah?"

"Gibson," Lucie added. "Sarah Gibson—and yes, she is an artist."

"Jeanne and her mother are pleased, then?"

Emma snorted in disgust.

"They are pleased," Lucie assured him.

Gabe nodded. "Very well." He bent and kissed Emma's cheek. "I've some work to do, so I'll say good-night."

"You work too much," Emma huffed. "You should take some time for yourself. Are there no plays or concerts you could attend?"

Gabe laughed. "Yes, Mama, there are plays and concerts. Perhaps you would attend one with me once Dr. Booker says you're up to it."

"I'm up to it now," Emma snapped, "but we have this surprise party coming up, and shortly after that your father and I—and Lucie—must get home. The garden will be coming up and the house will need airing after being closed up these last weeks and…"

"We'll talk about it another time," Gabe said gently, his eyes locked on his father. Jonathan looked away.

Gabe walked to the table and examined the fabric Lucie was working on. "Do you have everything you need?" he asked.

"Yes, thank you."

"Then I'll say good-night." But he lingered, still fingering one end of the fabric she held, and Lucie had the strange feeling they were connected by that sheer strip of silk. Her breath quickened and she pricked her finger with the needle.

"Please make certain that Mrs. King understands that this girl— Sarah, is it?"

Lucie nodded.

"Make sure that we are all clear that once the costumes are completed…that is, I do not need another person on the household staff. The Witherspoons will be moving into their new home soon. Perhaps she could work for them."

An hour later Gabe was surprised by a tentative knock on the library door. He glanced at the mantel clock that had just struck eleven.

"Yes?"

Lucie slid back one side of the double pocket doors and slipped into the room. As before, she remained near the door, her fingers pressing down nonexistent wrinkles in her skirt. Given their last encounter in this very room, Gabe could not have been more surprised to see her.

"Has something happened to my mother?" he asked, thinking that surely only Emma's health could bring Lucie back to him.

"No. She's sleeping, and your father, as well." She inched a foot farther into the room and paused.

"Then what is it that brings you down here at this hour, Lucie?" His heart beat double time. He actually dared to hope that she might have reconsidered the idea of exploring the energy that flowed between them whenever they were in the same room.

"It's about Sarah Gibson," she said.

Gabe shook his head to clear away the fog his hopes had created. "The new hired girl?"

"She needs this job."

Gabe blew out a sigh of weariness. "I was told that Mrs. King was less than satisfied with her work." Then the light dawned. "Is she a friend of yours?"

Lucie paused, and he knew he'd struck the truth. "I know her family."

"I see. Well, as I mentioned earlier, I'm sure that the Witherspoons could take her on. They're going to need a full staff when they move into their own home."

"She cannot work for them."

"Why on earth not?"

The nervous fidgeting continued. "I can't explain that."

"That's unacceptable," Gabe said, and turned back to his desk.

Lucie's head snapped up and her eyes flickered with defiance. "Why won't you at least consider keeping her?"

He saw immediately that she regretted her outburst. "Because that's not the way I do business, Lucie. And although it may seem to you, and others, that my funds are limitless, I assure you they are not, and I cannot take on this girl for charity's sake."

He turned away, essentially dismissing her, but there was no sound of the door sliding open and shut. He waited.

After a long moment she spoke, and this time he realized she had moved all the way into the room and was standing on the opposite side of his desk.

"What if I agreed to support you in your cause to have your parents come here to live with you?"

"You would do that?"

"I can see now, based on Charles—Dr. Booker's—assessment of Emma's condition, that the move is inevitable," she said. "I am simply offering my support in helping you persuade them."

The room was in shadow beyond the lamp on his desk. He came around and stood in front of her, as close as he'd been that other night. He searched her face. She did not flinch or back away.

"It's business," she said softly, her eyes defiant and her stance immovable.

"And what of you, Lucie?" he asked. "If my parents come here to live, shall I make room for you, as well?"

The question caused the first crack in her determined stance. "I will not work for you—or the Witherspoons," she said, but her voice shook. "In my heart I know that God has a plan for each of us. The events of these last weeks have convinced me that His plan for your parents and you is that you should be together as much as you can. That's only possible if you are willing to see that it's best if Emma and the colonel stay on Nantucket for the summer and autumn. You can visit often, take them for sails on your yacht and go out for drives with them." She hurried her words, lest she lose her nerve. "Then the rest of the year they would live here with you."

"And what is God's plan for you?"

She shrugged. "All will be revealed in God's own time," she murmured, her eyes cast down.

Gabe placed one finger under her chin and urged her face up to meet his. "You would do this for me?"

"Not for you," she whispered. "It's what is best for everyone—your mother, the colonel, Sarah…"

He realized she had not stepped away from his touch. He moved his forefinger along the line of her cheek. "Lucie," he murmured as he lowered his mouth to hers and hesitated. When she did not resist he covered her mouth with his.

She gave in to his kiss, her lips pliant and willing beneath his, but when he went to deepen the contact, she stepped away.

"So, we have a bargain—you will keep Sarah in your employ and I will help persuade your parents to move permanently to Boston in the fall."

Gabe fought the flood of emotions that threatened to engulf him—desire mixed with confusion and disbelief. Had she actually just allowed him to kiss her as a seal to a business deal? Had his touch meant no more than the price she must pay to gain her goal?

She turned and headed for the door, but he caught her arm and pulled her back into his arms. This time his mouth demanded and took, and he held her so tight against him that he could feel the beat of her heart against his chest. When he released her, he took some satisfaction in noticing that she was now as stunned as he had been a moment earlier. Now it was he who had the upper hand. "Yes," he said. "We have a bargain. Good night, Miss McNeil."

Lucie walked stiff-legged to the door and slid it open. When she turned to shut it, Gabe was standing with his back to her. She closed the door and ran up the stairs, down the hall and on to the third floor. When she finally reached her room, she was barely inside before the floodgates opened and she threw herself onto the single bed and sobbed.

*Dear Father in Heaven,* she prayed silently, *please help me. I don't know what to do. I don't understand what You want of me. Surely it is You that brought me to the Hunters. But then there is Gabe, and I am so drawn to him. Give me the strength to resist, and forgive me for my weakness just now. I wanted him to kiss me. Oh, God, forgive me. I wanted so much for him to love me.*

* * *

It rained for the entire day of the party, and Dolly Witherspoon was beside herself. She fretted over the late delivery from the florist and then decided there wasn't nearly enough food to feed the three dozen guests they'd invited. Then she panicked that those guests might decide not to come because of the weather. When the sky blackened and thunder rolled over the house like the crash of the sea against the shore in a sou'wester, Dolly Witherspoon threw up her hands and took to her bed, claiming a headache.

"You'll just have to manage," she screamed at Mrs. King. "After all, this is not even my house."

"Not her house, indeed," Mrs. King huffed.

"Where are your lists?" Lucie asked, knowing Mrs. King was inordinately well organized and had kept detailed planning lists for every aspect of the party.

"There," Mrs. King replied, casting a baleful eye at the papers on the table. "I can't make heads or tails of them now. She's thrown everything and everyone into a panic."

"Is there a problem, Mrs. King?" Neither woman had noticed Gabe's arrival.

"Oh, no, sir," Mrs. King stuttered.

He walked to the table and stood near enough to Lucie that, had she moved her arm, it would brush his coat sleeve. It was the first time they had been in the same room since the kiss.

"What's all this?" he asked, indicating the papers.

Mrs. King looked as if she might burst into tears at any moment, so Lucie took charge. She stood up, steeling herself against the rush of pleasure that was inevitable at the nearness of him.

"Mrs. Witherspoon has doubled the orders for the food and flowers," she said.

"On whose authority?" Gabe asked, and Lucie recognized that same quiet yet dangerous tone that she had observed when he'd been told Jeanne had hired Sarah.

"Mr. Witherspoon's," Mrs. King replied, wringing her hands. "Oh, Mr. Hunter, it was all to be a surprise, and now I've spoiled it."

Gabe collected the stacks of papers. "Please don't concern yourself, Mrs. King. I've known of the party for some time now." He flipped through the papers. "Are these the new orders?"

"Those are Mrs. King's lists for the details of the party," Lucie explained.

"Mrs. King, please ring for Fraiser and have him come to the library. We'll have this matter straightened out immediately."

"Yes, sir," Mrs. King said as she hurried to do his bidding.

"It's neither the fault of Fraiser nor Mrs. King," Lucie said.

"I'm aware of that, Miss McNeil, but if the duplicate orders are to be canceled then I'll need to send word." He started from the room, but paused at the doorway. "I assume you will be at the party in case my mother should need you?"

"Of course."

"Then I assume that you have chosen a costume, as well?"

"I shall be dressed as myself."

"Given that the event is in honor of my birthday, perhaps you would do me the courtesy of not being the only guest to arrive without proper dress," he said.

"Perhaps you would prefer I not attend," she replied, lifting her chin.

He considered this for a long moment. "I would prefer that you attend to your duties. I'll arrange for a costume for you to be delivered this afternoon."

"It's already nearly four," Lucie protested, but Gabe had left the room.

Just before six, Fraiser brought a package to Lucie's room.

"Thank you, Fraiser," she murmured as she examined the large white box tied with a wide, lavender satin ribbon.

"Shall I have Mrs. King send someone to assist you in dressing?" Fraiser asked.

"Absolutely not," Lucie replied, and then smiled at him. "That is, thank you, Fraiser—but no, I'll manage." She turned her back on the box and followed him to the door. "As a matter of fact, I should help the colonel and Mrs. Hunter."

Fraiser held the door and waited for her to precede him down the back stairway to the second floor.

"And Mrs. Hunter is to attend as the Southern belle?" he asked conversationally as they walked down the long hallway.

"Yes, and wait until you see how lovely she is, Fraiser. The gown had to practically be remade to fit her tiny frame, but Sarah has done the job."

"Then everything is in order," Fraiser said, more to himself than to her.

"And Mrs. Witherspoon?" Lucie asked the obvious question.

"Mrs. King has sent Sarah to assist the Witherspoons. The girl seems to have a way with them."

*And Gabe?* Lucie thought.

"Young Mr. Hunter, however, is still in his library working." Fraiser sighed heavily. "I'm just on my way to remind him of the hour."

# *Chapter Ten*

$\smallfrown$

$G$abe played his part, feigning concern when the carriage arrived at the mansion where the decoy party was supposedly to be held and the place was as dark as a tomb.

"What on earth?" Thurgood boomed, a bit louder than usual—even for him.

"There's no one home, sir," the driver reported after following Thurgood's order to ring the front doorbell. "The butler says that the party is tomorrow evening and that the family has gone out this evening."

Thurgood turned to his wife. "Did you confuse the date, Dolly?" he asked.

Dolly nervously toyed with the feathers that framed her headdress.

"Well, there's nothing to be done but to go home," Thurgood fumed. "Driver!" He knocked on the roof of the carriage with the gold knob of his walking stick. "We can get out of these silly costumes and have Mrs. King lay out a supper for us. I'm famished."

Gabe understood this was all a ruse to get him away

from the house so the guests could arrive and wait for his return. But he deeply resented Thurgood's proprietary manner. He saw Jeanne cast a look first at him and then at her father. For all her flightiness, he would give her one thing. She was a keen observer of the human expression. It was one reason she was a more than passable portrait artist.

Once they'd arrived back at his mansion, Gabe pretended shock and delight at the assemblage of business associates and members of his social circle, all gathered to surprise him on his thirtieth birthday. Gabe scanned the room, searching for Lucie.

He had selected her costume himself, calling on an old friend at the opera house where Gabe served on the board. He'd seen Fraiser's expression of surprise—the slightest raise of his thick eyebrows—when Gabe had returned just before six and handed the butler a large white box tied with satin ribbon, to deliver to Lucie.

He saw his parents first. His mother sat primly on a white silk damask chair, the skirts of her multilayered gown billowing around her as she flirted with his father from behind her fan. His father looked every inch the commander he had been, standing tall and proud in his uniform, with its double row of gleaming gold buttons and his sash and saber at his side.

Jeanne had required everyone to wear a mask, and Gabe saw that his mother's was a work of art of pink plumes and crystal beading surrounding the slope of the cutouts for her eyes. His father's was a simple, deep blue satin with gold nautical braiding. Gabe had given in to the idea of a pirate's eye patch, but had adamantly refused to wear a mask.

But where was Lucie?

Then he saw her, and his breath caught. He and his friend at the opera had gone through several racks of costumes before Gabe had seen the perfect one. It was a green silk kimono used in the company's production of *Madame Butterfly*. He had chosen the costume because of her masses of black hair and the unblemished porcelain of her face. And now he saw that he had chosen well. He started toward her, but stopped when he saw Charles Booker step to her side.

The doctor, dressed as a desert sheikh, said something, and Lucie smiled. Gabe's breath caught. She had smiled that same smile the day he'd gone to church on the island. It had been the first time he had really seen her beauty, and since that day he had often wondered if he might ever be the fortunate recipient of her smile—the one that was carefree and without restraint. The one she offered Charles Booker now.

Gabe felt the rise of jealousy like bile in his throat. Charles Booker had been his friend for years. Yet at that moment Gabe hated his friend. He hated him for the ease with which he and Lucie spoke. He hated him because, in spite of Gabe having easily tenfold the wealth and power Charles had, it appeared to Gabe that Charles was by far the richer man.

As if she'd felt his gaze on her, Lucie looked up and across the crowded room. She was not wearing a mask, although he had included one in the box. It was a ridiculous affectation, as were the costumes—as was the entire party, for that matter. Gabe felt a sudden irritation that Jeanne would for one minute think he might enjoy such foolishness as a way to mark his thirtieth year.

He heard the clink of a fork against a crystal goblet, and glanced toward the doorway, where Thurgood Witherspoon was calling for attention. "Ladies and gentlemen," he boomed, "thank you all for coming."

Gradually a few guests shushed the others until Thurgood had everyone's full attention. "I believe we can all agree that my beautiful daughter has indeed managed to surprise a man who we all know takes a special pride in not permitting himself to be surprised—at least in business."

There was a murmur of appreciative laughter throughout the room. Gabe shifted uncomfortably. He did not enjoy being put on display. That was more to Thurgood's taste. He smiled tightly as several guests looked his way, a nightmare of familiar faces hidden behind half masks. He glanced at his parents—and Lucie. Her gaze was undisguised. She was studying him, and in her eyes he read empathy and understanding. Of everyone in the room only she seemed to realize his discomfort.

Thurgood drew in a breath, clearly prepared to continue his oration. "Gabriel Hunter is not only the guest of honor at his own party," he bellowed. "Gabriel Hunter is like my own son." His voice broke on cue.

"A toast," Gabe heard his father call in a strong voice that matched his costume as a commander. "A toast to our son." He placed one hand on Emma's shoulder as he and she raised their glasses to Gabe. "Happy birthday, Gabriel," Jonathan said.

"Happy birthday," the guests echoed in unison as they raised their glasses and turned away from Thurgood Witherspoon to face Gabe.

The string quartet hired for the evening struck up the birthday song, and everyone sang. Gabe smiled and nodded and then waved them off when they would have repeated the chorus.

"Enough," he said, removing his eye patch and stepping forward to perform his duty as guest of honor.

To his surprise, many others in the room took this as their cue to remove their masks, and set them aside. Jeanne appeared at his side, her mask still firmly in place along with her shepherd's crook and the ridiculous stuffed lamb.

"Shall we go in for dinner?" she asked, and did not wait for an answer as she led Gabe the length of the room and out into the grand hall, where a long table had been set for what Gabe could see would be a multi-coursed feast. He could not help but wonder what all this was costing him.

Jeanne led him to the foot of the table and prepared to take her place at his right.

"Should I not be at the head?" he asked, watching as Thurgood and Dolly made their way along the length of the grand table with the obvious intent of taking their places as hosts.

"Father thought—" Jeanne began uncertainly.

"And my parents?" Gabe continued, as if she had not spoken. All the while he moved along the opposite side of the table, his long strides quickly outdistancing Thurgood's shorter ones.

The two partners met at the head of the table after Gabe had paused to ask Fraiser to be sure his parents were seated on either side of him, with Miss Witherspoon next to his father and Miss McNeil next to his mother.

Thurgood was clearly flustered, and Dolly was frantic. "We just thought—" she hastened to explain.

"I appreciate everything you've done, Mrs. Witherspoon," Gabe said without taking his eyes off Thurgood, "but as this is my home I believe it only fitting…"

"Of course. Our intent all along," Thurgood blustered.

Gabe pulled back the chair for Jeanne, as Charles did the same for Lucie.

It seemed to Lucie as if every time she looked up, Gabe was watching her, his eyes disapproving. Well, he was the one who had insisted she be there. He was the one who had chosen her costume. He was the one...

"Lucie?" Emma was staring at her with a quizzical expression. She lifted her glass slightly higher and nodded toward Mr. Witherspoon.

"To my beautiful daughter, Jeanne," he boomed.

"Hear, hear," said several of Thurgood's contemporaries as Thurgood's toast continued.

"What a lovely party, my dear. You are a natural hostess and—forgive me, Gabriel—but it seems to me that Jeanne is quite an asset to this beautiful house."

Several guests sucked in their breath and murmured to each other from behind gloved hands at this brazenness. But when Thurgood raised his glass to his lips, courtesy demanded that everyone follow suit. Lucie glanced at Gabe over the top of her goblet as she sipped the water. She could not help noticing the way his fingers tightened around the stem of the goblet before he replaced it on the table without taking a sip. She risked a glance at Mr. Witherspoon and was shocked to see that he was unnerved by Gabe's action.

Throughout dinner, and afterward during the entertainment—a puppet show more suited to a child's birthday than a thirty-year-old business tycoon's—Gabe remained close to his parents. When he saw that Emma took delight in the puppet show, he smiled and even laughed at the antics of the clownish figures.

Lucie was aware that Gabe often glanced her way. Was it to see if she was enjoying the show? Was it because he was displeased that she had elected to remain standing on the fringes, not more than three steps away from Emma and Jonathan? Was it because they could not seem to take their eyes off each other?

Surely not that. Lucie silently prayed for strength to resist the temptation of imagining attentions that were clearly impossible. She asked God to give her the wisdom to decipher Gabe's wordless communications, spoken through his eyes, his half smile, his frown.

As the puppet show came to an end, Emma applauded by tapping her fan enthusiastically against her gloved hand, and Jonathan actually stood and shouted, "Bravo!"

Lucie did not miss the smirk Thurgood Witherspoon sent his colleagues at Jonathan's enthusiastic response to such simple entertainment. Nor did Gabe. And seeing it, Gabe leapt to his feet and echoed his father's ovation, at which point several of the other guests joined in.

Dessert was served in the great hall, which had magically been cleared of the long dining table and chairs while the guests enjoyed the entertainment in the drawing room. Now, there was a feast, which included sweets and cheeses and exotic fruits, all served by men standing at attention like so many soldiers at each station.

For the remainder of the evening, Lucie stayed close to Emma and Jonathan. She could see that Emma was exhausted, and yet nothing she or Jonathan said could lure Emma away from the party.

Charles Booker continued to be attentive to Lucie's needs—sometimes even before she knew she had a need. He brought Emma and Jonathan small china plates filled with a selection of desserts and fruits. He shared a third plate, delivered by one of the hired staff, with Lucie while he made conversation with the Hunters. He was so kind and easy to be around that Lucie wondered why her gaze kept drifting away, seeking Gabe. And why, when she found him, Gabe seemed always to be watching her.

"And now, as your doctor, Mrs. Hunter," Charles announced, "I really must insist that you call it a night."

"The good doctor is right, my dear," Jonathan said. "You mustn't overdo."

Having seen both his father and the doctor leaning over his mother, Gabe hurried toward them. "What is it?" he asked anxiously.

Emma waved an impatient hand at all three men. "It's nothing. A matter of these two being tired and assuming that I am, as well. Well, Jonathan Hunter, in case you have forgotten, at the ball my parents gave, I was the last to leave—except for you." Her eyes misted as she stared at Jonathan. Then she reached out and touched his cheek. "You waited to see me, remember?"

"I did," Jonathan murmured.

"You were leaving the following day—the war was truly over and I thought I would never see you again."

"Ah, love, try and get rid of me so easily," Jonathan said as he nodded to Lucie, who brought the wheelchair from its place near the wall and pulled it close to Emma's chair.

"One more of those luscious petit fours," Emma declared as she popped one into her mouth, then smiled up at the three men. "Well, Lucie, look at us surrounded by the three most handsome men at this party."

All three men chuckled as they helped her into the wheelchair. Belatedly, all three Witherspoons gathered around them.

"Oh, dear," Dolly whined, wringing her hands. "I knew it would be too much. I told Thurgood that…."

"Yes," Emma replied. "It was perhaps a bit much, especially for someone as reserved as my Gabriel. But nevertheless, it was a lovely party."

Lucie took that as her signal to wheel Emma to the elevator, and was surprised when all three men plus the Witherspoons followed.

"I hardly think we need a parade," Gabe said quietly when they reached the end of the hall. He bent and kissed his mother's cheek, touched his father's shoulder and then turned back to the Witherspoons. "We have guests," he said, and walked back into the crowded party.

Lucie got Emma settled for the night and assured Jonathan that should either of them need anything they were to call for her immediately. But she was still wide-awake, and too many memories of the evening tumbled through her brain to allow her to sleep anytime soon.

The truth was she felt different dressed in the simple but elegant costume, and she was reluctant to take it off and return it to its box. She thought there would be no harm in sitting for a while in the upstairs sitting area—at least until she heard the others start up the stairs. As she passed through the upper hallway she could hear Jeanne's gay laughter and Thurgood Witherspoon's booming voice as the last of the guests said their good-nights. She assumed Gabe was standing at the door, graciously seeing everyone off before returning to his hotel for the night. She fingered the beautiful, heavy silk skirt of her costume as she wound her way among the half-dozen chintz-covered chairs and sofas that furnished the informal family sitting room.

It occurred to her that Gabe had gone out of his way

to show her a kindness. She had never worn anything so fine as the beautiful jade kimono. Dressed in her own clothes, she surely would have been out of place—even at a costume party. Dressed as she was, the other guests had barely noticed her. Of course, a great deal of the credit for that belonged to Charles. He had been so attentive throughout the evening that there had never been a time when Lucie had felt out of place. But the costume had made the real difference. Lucie realized she should thank Gabe for it.

She stopped at the small desk stocked with notepaper and pens for the use of Gabe's houseguests. Surely it would be all right if she used a sheet of paper to pen a note of gratitude.

She sat on the edge of the cane-bottomed desk chair and pulled a piece of the heavy vellum paper onto the blotter. Uncapping the pen, she mentally composed the note.

*Thank you for…*

*Please accept my…*

"Dolly, go to bed," she heard Thurgood boom. "And Jeanne, you, as well." He sounded angry, and Lucie had a sudden memory of him standing on the walkway above the factory floor, yelling at the factory manager.

"Yes, dear," she heard Dolly murmur, and then she heard the muffled sounds of the two women hurrying up the grand stairway and along the hall in the opposite direction to where she sat. The Witherspoons had taken over the master suite of the house, and Jeanne had the large room next to theirs.

Lucie heard the low rumble of Gabe's voice at the same time as two doors closed at the end of the upstairs hall.

"Don't you presume to tell me to calm down," Thurgood raged. "How dare you embarrass me and my family after all we have done for you? You think you are so high and mighty, young man? You would be nothing—nothing—without me."

Again the quiet rumble, like distant thunder, of Gabe's answer.

"Well, you've a strange way of showing gratitude, then. Perhaps it's your upbringing, perhaps—"

Gabe's voice interrupted, and Lucie heard him clearly. "Don't ever suggest that my parents are any less than you or yours, Thurgood. Do not mistake their choice to live a simpler life for a lack of breeding."

Lucie realized she was holding her breath. Were the two men about to come to fisticuffs? Then she heard Gabe speak again.

"As for my debt to you, Thurgood, you're right. I owe you a great deal, but I have also repaid a great deal. I have taken you and your family in when you ran into... When you faced some difficult financial times of your own. I would say that we are even."

"Oh, we are far from even, Gabriel. You have given every indication that you will one day marry my daughter, and yet—"

"I'm sorry if I have given you any such impression, Thurgood. Jeanne is a lovely young woman, but I do not have feelings for her that would be the basis of a loving marriage."

"You may not love her, but you care for her. That's the reason you took us in, isn't it? For Jeanne's sake?"

"It's one reason," Gabe admitted.

"But ever since you brought your father here and practically set him up as a third partner in the firm, I've felt left out."

"I wonder why that should make any difference to you at all. These last several years we've been partners in name only—each making our own investments."

"Don't get me wrong," Thurgood hastened to assure Gabe. "The colonel is an asset to the firm. He has a wealth of experience and I appreciate his counsel."

"He'll be glad to know that," Gabe said. "It's late," he added, "and we've both been under a great deal of strain. Perhaps it would be best if we said our good-nights."

There was another gruff murmur, and Lucie heard Thurgood Witherspoon trudge up the stairs. He stopped first at Jeanne's room to compliment her on the party and then Lucie heard him open the door next to Jeanne's room, followed by Mrs. Witherspoon's worried inquiry and the soft click of the door shutting.

Quickly, Lucie scrawled the rest of her note, writing the first thing that came to mind. After all, it was the gesture, not the words, that mattered. A man like Gabe would no doubt open the note, read it quickly and form his reaction on the fact that she had taken the time to write it. She slipped the folded paper into one of the envelopes, sealed it and ran down the stairway to slip it under the door of the library.

Exhausted, she took the back stairs to her bedroom on the third floor. Left open on the bed, the large white box with its mounds of white tissue that had contained her costume glimmered in the moonlight, and she realized the storm had finally passed and the skies had cleared. To-morrow would be a beautiful day, and the day after, Charles had said they could leave for Nantucket.

Lucie dropped to her knees by the small window that

overlooked the garden and folded her hands in prayer. But her head spun with memories of the evening, and every memory included Gabe—his eyes on her, his nearness at dinner and during the entertainment, his half smiles and deeply furrowed frowns of disapproval, which made her want to run to him and ask what he saw that displeased him so. She shut her eyes tight and prayed for guidance and forgiveness for feelings she could not seem to control when it came to Gabriel Hunter. She was falling in love with him and she desperately needed God's patience and help to see her through this impossible situation.

## Chapter Eleven

Gabe asked Fraiser to prepare the room next to his parents for him. He was physically and mentally exhausted. The last thing he wanted to do was go back to an impersonal hotel suite, no matter how luxurious.

He worked for over an hour at his desk, going over the files and documents that he'd already gone over a dozen times. It was well after midnight when he stood and stretched. That's when he spotted the envelope. He sighed. Jeanne, no doubt—her insecurities spilling out in reams of the thin sheets of stationery she preferred. Apologies and self-recrimination for being so silly, for failing to deliver a proper birthday celebration, for…

He was tempted to shove the envelope into his coat pocket and read it in the morning when he would be better suited to respond, to reassure her that everything had been lovely and that he'd been delighted. But he recognized the paper as his own.

He turned the envelope over and, finding no inscription on the front that would give a clue to its author or contents, he slid his thumb under the seal.

Lucie's handwriting was exactly as he would have expected—as bold, simple and straightforward as the woman herself. The message was likewise simple and direct—in essence thanking him for the costume. And yet there was so much more, because in the simple gesture of writing the note, she was surely trying to tell him— what? His heartbeat quickened.

His instinct was to go to her. He imagined racing up the stairway and opening her door. He imagined her sitting on her bed, waiting for him, still dressed in the silk kimono, her eyes wide with the disbelief they shared that two such different souls should connect. He would take her in his arms and pour out his feelings for her, because the one thing that had been more clear than anything during the long hours of the party tonight was that he was falling in love. For the first time in his life he had met a woman he could not take his eyes off, that he could not bear to be separated from, that he could see himself spending the rest of his life with. For the first time in his life he finally understood what his parents had found in each other, and he wanted that for himself.

Gabe reached the foot of the stairway leading to the third floor and hesitated. Surely he had allowed his fantasies to overpower his common sense. This was Lucie, and she would never welcome his barging into her room uninvited. He would see her in the morning, and in the light of a new day she would be unable to deny the truth of his declaration of feelings for her. He turned to retrace his steps down the hall, past the room his parents occupied.

He smiled as he recalled how excited his mother had been at the party. More than once he had seen her eyes alight with joy and her head tossed to one side as she gave

Charles Booker one of her patented Southern belle smiles. Other than her need for the wheelchair, she had seemed in the best of health, and Lucie and Booker were to be thanked for that.

The clock in the great hall struck one and Gabe resisted the urge to look in on his parents. He had moved on to his own room when Fraiser came rushing up the stairs.

"Your father rang," the butler said by way of explanation as he tapped lightly before opening the door. Gabe brushed past him and saw his father sitting on the side of the bed, holding his mother's hand as she gasped for breath.

"Send for Dr. Booker," Gabe said tersely. "And get Lucie," he added as Fraiser exited the room.

"Papa, what happened?" he asked.

"She was asleep. We both were, and then a few minutes ago she started to choke and…"

Emma grabbed Gabe's hand, her face pink and contorted with the effort to breathe.

"Sh-h-h," he said, stroking her thin arm and willing her to breathe by mimicking his own slow, deep breaths as he had seen Lucie do. "There," he whispered. "That's it."

She fell back against the pillows, and although her breath still came in quick gasps, she seemed at least to be getting some air.

"I've sent for the doctor," Gabe assured her. "And Lucie."

At that moment Lucie appeared. She had changed out of the costume, but her long, thick hair was still in a braid that fell to her waist. She moved with purpose to Emma's bedside, and Jonathan stood to give her his place.

"Bother," Emma croaked.

"Not at all," Lucie assured her. "Who could sleep after

such an evening?" She smiled at Emma even as she efficiently readjusted pillows to better support the woman in an upright position.

"You were quite the belle of the evening," she said. She glanced at Gabe. "Help me lift her a little higher," she said in a low voice that had nothing to do with the casual words she'd spoken to his mother.

He followed her lead as she hooked her forearm under Emma's left arm and waited for him to do the same on the right. "One, two, three," she counted, and on three they lifted, and Emma gave a sigh of relief.

"Better," Emma whispered. "You make a good team," she managed to add.

"We do at that," Gabe agreed as he continued to stare at Lucie.

Lucie did not meet his gaze, but continued to comfort Emma. "I'm sure that Dr. Booker will be here as soon as possible. I do believe that the colonel may have a rival for your affections, Emma," she teased gently as she fitted Emma with the breathing apparatus Charles had ordered after her first attack.

She glanced over at Jonathan, who smiled uncertainly. "Are you feeling better, love?" he asked, his face contorted with worry.

Emma nodded and stretched out her hand to him. Lucie stepped away from the bed and waited by the fireplace, giving them some privacy. Once again Gabe followed her lead.

"Charles is on the way," he said. "The party was too much for her."

"The party was wonderful for her," Lucie corrected. "It gave her such pleasure—all of it, from the planning to the making of the costumes to the event itself. It's been some time since I have seen her so…alive."

"And yet…"

Lucie faced him directly. "Your mother is in frail health, Gabe. Charles says that she could survive any number of episodes such as this one, or suffer massive heart failure, and she could do so whether she is dancing an Irish jig or sitting quietly at her quilting. The party is not to blame for this any more than the sail we took when you came to Nantucket brought on that attack."

"What are you suggesting?"

She hesitated. "It is not my place to suggest anything. Charles can offer his counsel."

"I'd like to hear what you think," Gabe pressed.

Lucie started to speak, then pinched her lips together as if to keep the words from escaping. Then she took a deep breath. "I think that if Emma were my mother, with such an uncertain future I would do anything I could to ensure that whatever time she had left—be that days or years—was spent living her life rather than trying to keep from dying. We shall all die, Gabe. The question is, how well will we have lived when that last moment is at hand?"

There was a light knock at the bedroom door, and then Fraiser ushered Charles Booker into the room. He nodded at Lucie and Gabe, but went straight to Emma's side, opening his bag and removing his stethoscope as he went.

"Well, now, Mrs. Hunter, to what do I owe the pleasure of being in your company twice in one evening?"

Emma gave a snort that ended in a cough and rasped out, "It's nearly dawn."

"Not quite," Booker replied, and pressed his stethoscope to her chest. "Take a deep breath," he instructed. "That's right. Now let it go. Again."

No one moved, and the room was silent except for the sound of Emma's labored breathing and the doctor's quiet instructions. One glance at Lucie and she moved immediately to his side to help Emma lean forward so he could listen through her back.

In that instant Gabe saw what a team *they* made. Dr. Charles Booker would never find a more proficient nurse than Lucie McNeil. Furthermore, his friend was in love with Lucie. Gabe had not missed the way Charles had literally followed Lucie wherever she'd moved during the party. He had been at her side constantly. They had laughed together, talked quietly together, shared dessert from the same plate. The intimacy of that last act had been almost more than Gabe could stand as he had watched as Lucie coaxed Charles to try one sweet, and when he'd rejected it, had finished it herself.

If Gabe loved her, then shouldn't he do what was in her best interest rather than selfishly consider his own? With Charles she would have security and love and a future filled with happiness. What did he have to offer her other than a fortune that at the moment he seemed incapable of protecting? He was not as strong as his father had been under similar circumstances. Without his money and power, Gabe had no identity—no friends, no pleasures, no real purpose. What was that to offer a woman like Lucie?

"Gabe? Colonel? A word," Booker said as he led the way to the far end of the room. Gabe and his father followed while Lucie attended to Emma.

The news was not good, and yet Charles was quick to

point out that Emma had been through worse episodes and come out fine.

"What do you suggest?" Jonathan asked, and Gabe had new respect for the way his father had remained strong in the face of this latest crisis.

"Rest and time," Charles replied. "Let the medicine have whatever effect it's going to have, and then we'll have a better idea of the future."

"And our return to Nantucket?" Jonathan asked.

"Father, that's impossible," Gabe said gently.

Jonathan ignored him and kept his attention focused on the doctor. Charles looked from one man to the other and took his time choosing his words.

"She should remain in bed for the next day or so—to allow her to rebuild some stamina. After that I see no reason why she should not return to her home. In fact, given her anxiety that she may never see Nantucket again, that may be the best of all medicines." This last comment was directed at Gabe.

Torn between wanting to provide the best possible care for his mother and his understanding that what the doctor said was undeniably true, Gabe was suddenly reminded of Lucie's words. Everyone lived and died. The question was, how well. Gabe stared at his father for a long moment, and for the first time since leaving home he realized that his father had been far more successful at achieving a life well lived than Gabe had for all his money and power.

Jonathan met his gaze, and his eyes were pleading. "She wants to go home, son," he said softly. "And so do I."

Gabe nodded. "All right, but she remains here for the next two days while I make the arrangements for both of you to return to Nantucket."

"And Lucie," Jonathan reminded him.

"And Lucie," Gabe agreed.

Booker cleared his throat and turned to Jonathan. "If you like, once you return to Nantucket, I could come over once or twice a week to check on Mrs. Hunter."

"That would be greatly appreciated," Jonathan replied before Gabe could fashion the words to deny the necessity of such an inconvenience. He had no doubt that the offer was sincere, but he also had no doubt that the underlying motive was the chance to maintain a connection with Lucie.

"Then it's settled," Jonathan said, shaking the doctor's hand vigorously. "I'll let Emma know, and I've no doubt that you'll see an improvement by morning." He crossed the room quickly and sat by Emma, quietly laying out the plan. "No, Gabe has agreed," Gabe heard him assure her, and Gabe saw his mother smile as she closed her eyes.

By the time Charles had given Lucie her instructions and packed his equipment, the first rays of morning light were beginning to filter through the closed draperies.

"Thank you, Charles," Gabe said. "I'll see you out." When the two men reached the door, Gabe turned back. "Will you stay with them, Miss McNeil?"

"Of course," she said. The thick plait of her hair had fallen over one shoulder, and she fingered it nervously without meeting his gaze. Earlier he had called her by her given name, but now he had reverted to the more formal—the more class-distinctive—*Miss McNeil.*

Lucie used the time it took for Gabe to usher Charles out to pin her hair up into its usual tight chignon. She retrieved an apron from the dressing room and tied it in place. When she returned to the bedroom, Jonathan was snoring softly as he leaned against the massive carved headboard, with Emma's head resting on his shoulder. Satisfied that they were both resting and that she was appropriately garbed for her role, she waited.

Gabe returned and, without looking directly at her, went to check on his parents. Then he turned to her.

"Thank you for your note, Lucie," he said.

It was the last thing she had expected to hear. She nodded and fingered the edges of her apron.

"Will you sit with me?" He indicated the door and she followed him to the family sitting area. He waited for her to choose one of two chairs to either side of the fireplace and then sat opposite her in the other. Their knees were only inches from touching.

"I have agreed that my parents are to return to Nantucket," he began, and this got Lucie's immediate attention.

"I see," she said.

He smiled wearily and ran one hand through his thick hair. "No, I doubt that you see at all. The truth is that as much as I want to protect them and give them everything they lost all those years ago, that is not the life they would choose. It is rather what I would choose for them—or would have until this evening."

Lucie held her breath, not daring to believe what she thought he was telling her.

"And that is your fault, Lucie McNeil," he added sternly.

"I hardly think that…"

"You reminded me that the time of our death is not our choice. And that we also do not get to choose what kind of life is best for those we love. Take you, for example."

Lucie's heart thundered in her ears. "I don't understand," she whispered.

"Charles Booker is in love with you. Surely you see that. And yet, the question is not whether he is in love with you but whether or not you return those feelings."

Lucie swallowed around the sudden lump in her throat. This was Gabe the way he was with Jeanne. The older brother, the friendly advisor—but never the beloved.

"I don't believe that this is a matter for your concern," she said stiffly.

"Exactly," he replied. "And yet..."

Lucie stood and bent to stir the last of the embers. "You are confusing me, sir. This is not a conversation that..."

"And yet," Gabe continued as if she had not spoken, "it is human nature to want to do what seems best for others." His voice trailed off. "I have a great many people for whom I feel responsible, Lucie. Some of them I love deeply. Some of them I owe a debt of gratitude for the success I have enjoyed. Some of them are simply innocent bystanders."

Lucie tried to sort through the names of those who might fit into each class. She wondered if her name might be included in any of those categories. And then she found herself wondering if the nameless girls and women who had toiled for him in the garment factory had made his list.

"Then perhaps you might reconsider keeping Sarah Gibson in your employ," she said, retreating to the safer ground of an impersonal business matter.

Gabe looked at her as if she had suddenly begun to speak in a foreign tongue.

"What has Sarah Gibson to do with this?" he asked, standing in frustration.

"She needs this job," Lucie replied, once again facing him.

Gabe shook his head in confusion. "We are not discussing business here, Lucie," he said irritably. "I am talking about my parents and you and…"

"If you have agreed that your parents may return to Nantucket and live out their days as they wish, that's kind and generous of you," she allowed.

"Yes, it is, because it goes against everything I know to be in their best interests. The cottage there has been in need of major renovation for years. It is drafty and damp, and Mother's health will suffer needlessly for being there."

"And yet, you have agreed," she reminded him, and stood.

"I have given my word." He moved a step closer to her. "You are very clever at turning the topic away from yourself, Lucie. Why is that?"

"There are far more important matters to be discussed."

"Like Sarah Gibson?"

"Yes."

"But you still won't tell me why she is so important to you?"

"I cannot."

They looked at each other wordlessly communicating through eyes that spoke of longing and fingers that twitched nervously to restrain the desire to touch.

"I have to change," Gabe said, looking down at his costume. "I have a business meeting this morning." He sighed heavily. "Please do not hesitate to interrupt that meeting should there be any change in my mother's condition."

Lucie nodded. "Of course." She stepped aside to allow him to pass, but he remained where he was. "Lucie, I have— There are things I would like to ask, to tell—" He shook off his babbling and began again. "There are business matters that I cannot allow my personal feelings to distort, but I ask that you believe that I will have only the best interests of my parents—and you—in mind in whatever I may do going forward."

She replayed the conversation she'd overheard between Gabe and Thurgood Witherspoon earlier. For whatever reason, he remained loyal to Thurgood Witherspoon, and yet she could not help but think there was some connection between Gabe's business problems and Mr. Witherspoon. After weeks under his roof, Lucie understood that the one thing Gabe could never abide was personal failure. If he lost everything the way Jonathan had, he could never be happy.

"I'm afraid I don't understand," she said.

"I am in love with you, Lucie McNeil, and yet I cannot—" He swallowed hard and she rushed to save him from having to find the words.

"As you have said, Charles Booker has feelings for me. I count myself most fortunate," she replied, and lowered her eyes. "And Miss Witherspoon seems devoted to you, so we are both blessed."

"Perhaps in time—" Gabe bowed his head but it was a gesture of defeat rather than one of reverence.

Her heart went out to him, for he was a man in such mental and emotional anguish that it was almost physically painful to watch him suffer. Lucie placed her hand on his forearm. "Gabe? You should know that the matter of Sarah—the reason it is so important to me is because of the fire that destroyed the factory. She is the sole supporter for her parents. If you cannot see a place for her on your staff here, perhaps if you would consider rebuilding—not just for Sarah, but because it could help so many others."

His eyes were wide with astonishment, but she pressed her fingers tighter on his arm. "I believe that if you will only take responsibility for what happened there and find a way to seek God's forgiveness, then you will find the peace and contentment you seem to want in this life."

Gabe stared at her. "What are you talking about? What factory? What have I done to need forgiveness from God or anyone else?"

Surely he understood. Surely he knew. How could he profess his love for her and still deny what had happened? "The garment factory near the wharves. The one that burned last January. The one that took the lives of Sarah Gibson's dear sisters and countless others. The one that you and Mr. Witherspoon owned, Gabe."

She felt as if she were shouting the words at him, but realized they were being delivered in a hoarse whisper. She had raised her fists and pounded them into his chest with each point.

Gabe caught her wrists and held them. "We sold that factory last summer, right before I left for Europe," Gabe said. "I heard of the fire, and it was a tragedy, but it had been under new ownership for months. You cannot blame…"

Her head was spinning. How could he pretend not to know the truth of what she was saying? "I worked there, Gabe. I saw you, Witherspoon, the fire—everything. You must face that."

"You have no right to preach to me, Lucie McNeil."

She wrenched her hands away and stepped back. "Then stop lying to me—and to yourself," she rasped out, and ran down the stairway and out the front door.

## Chapter Twelve

Once she reached the sidewalk, Lucie started to run with no direction or purpose other than to get as far away as possible from Gabriel Hunter. She ran through the dark and empty streets as fast as she could. Tears streamed down her cheeks, and her mind raged like the sea in a storm.

How was it possible that she had fallen in love with a man estranged from God and unwilling to admit his own failings? Surely this could not be God's will for her. Surely it was a test, and one she had failed. For in spite of everything, whenever she thought of Gabriel Hunter, she thought only of his goodness and his undeniable love and devotion to his parents. She thought of the stories both Emma and Jonathan had told her—stories of their beloved son and his devastation when the family lost everything, and his determination to make it all right again. Surely that was the mark of a good and decent soul.

Her side aching and her breath coming in desperate gulps, Lucie collapsed onto a park bench, which was damp with the predawn dew. Silently she prayed for a sign, for guidance, for forgiveness for her weakness. Hours passed without her noticing, and the sun came up. Spent from crying and berating herself for her shortcomings, she leaned back against the metal slats of the park bench and considered the budding trees, the fragrance of the flowers, the songs of the birds come home from their winter travels.

Calmer, she walked up one block and down the other, oblivious to her surroundings as she tried to reason out the events of the last several hours. She was convinced that confronting Gabe about the factory had not been a mistake. She had shown him the error of his ways and now it would be up to him to find a way to redeem himself. He was at his core a decent man. She was certain God would lead him to that redemption. In fact, perhaps this had been God's plan all along. Through her knowledge of what had happened at the factory that day, she held the key to bringing Gabe to face his guilt and come back to his faith.

Confident now of God's purpose, she squared her shoulders and started toward the house, ignoring the passing streetcars that might have shortened her journey. When she was finally in sight of the mansion that had once seemed an impenetrable fortress, a clock from a nearby church tolled ten times. She ran the last half block, aware that she had been gone for hours and that Emma might have needed her.

When she reached the house, she found everything in a state of chaos. Mrs. Witherspoon hovered nervously in the front hallway, wringing her hands. Fraiser was just coming out of the library with a tray containing a silver coffee service, two used cups and a full plate of untouched breakfast pastries. Beyond the partially open door, Lucie could see Mr. Witherspoon standing at the window, his shoulders slumped and his head bowed.

Lucie followed Fraiser to the pantry, and she could hear Mrs. King muttering to herself in the kitchen beyond. Knowing she was more likely to get details from Mrs. King than from Fraiser, she hurried into the kitchen, certain that Emma had suffered a setback.

"What has happened?"

"He's lost his mind, that's what's happened," Mrs. King huffed, then peered closely at Lucie. "Where have you been?"

"I— Oh, never mind that. Is it Mrs. Hunter? Has she…"

"She's up and brighter than ever. Had herself a full breakfast—her and the colonel. Though she might well drop over once she hears the news."

"What news?"

"Mr. Hunter has asked Miss Witherspoon to marry him." She waited a beat for that to sink in before continuing. "Out of the blue, he walks into the parlor not a quarter of an hour ago and says, 'Jeanne, I have asked your father for permission to marry you and he has given us his blessing.' I was in the room at the time, or I wouldn't have believed a word of it."

"And what did Jeanne—Miss Witherspoon—say?" Lucie asked, feeling as if the very breath had been sucked from her.

"That was the strange part. She just sat there, looking down at her sketching. It was her mother who leapt to her feet and threw her arms around Mr. Hunter."

"And how did he…seem? Mr. Hunter?"

"You'd have thought he'd just announced that he was

about to leap off a high bridge," Mrs. King blurted. "Oh, it's a crime, it is. He don't love that girl."

"I don't understand."

Mrs. King's brow furrowed. "It's all mixed up in his business with Mr. Witherspoon. First thing this morning, Mr. Hunter tells Fraiser that he and Mr. Witherspoon will have breakfast in the library. So the two of them are in that library with the door closed. Words were spoken, I'll tell you that for passing by you could tell that this was a spirited conversation. Next thing you know, there's Mr. Hunter standing just inside the door to the parlor, speaking his piece."

Suddenly Lucie thought of Gabe's parents. The one thing Emma wanted for her only child was for him to find true love and a happy marriage. She was bound to be saddened by this news. Would it be enough to cause her a relapse?

"Have the elder Hunters been told?"

"By now, no doubt. Mr. Hunter took Miss Witherspoon to the upstairs sitting room just now, like he was on some sort of crusade or something. Mrs. Witherspoon started to follow but, polite as you please, he asked her not to come."

Unwilling to hear more, Lucie hurried up the back stairway. But she slowed her steps when she reached the top. What was she thinking? She could not stop this, and her presence might only make things worse. She made her way down the hall until she could see the four of them. Emma was sitting in her wheelchair with Jonathan standing close beside her, one hand on her shoulder. Gabe and Jeanne were seated on a sofa facing the elder Hunters, their backs to Lucie.

Emma sighed heavily, and Lucie knew she had just

heard Gabe's news. The beautiful white quilt she'd started slipped to the floor unnoticed.

"Mother—Mama—will you wish us well?" Gabe asked.

Emma stretched her hand out to him, and he took it in both of his. "Of course I do, Gabe. It's just that—"

Lucie saw Jonathan's fingers tighten ever so slightly on Emma's shoulder. Emma sat back, pulling her hand free of Gabe's. "It's just so sudden," she said, and it was obvious to everyone that this was not at all what she had intended to say.

"Yes," Jeanne agreed. "Very." She cast a sidelong glance at Gabe and then looked back at her hands, folded primly in her lap. Lucie had never seen Jeanne so reserved.

"Do you love him?" Emma asked.

"Well, of course she does," Jonathan said with a too-hearty laugh. "That's the way of it for these young people, Emma." He stepped forward and offered his hand to Gabe. "Allow me to offer my congratulations, son."

Gabe stood, and what passed between the two men behind the forced smile and the businesslike handshake was the worried frown of a concerned parent for the future happiness of his only child. And then Jonathan turned to Jeanne. Offering her both his hands, he pulled her to her feet and kissed her lightly on each cheek. "You'll make a lovely bride," he said, and the tension in Jeanne's narrow shoulders appeared to ease slightly with the compliment.

"We shall marry in December," Gabe said without a glance at Jeanne.

"In church?" Emma asked quietly.

Gabe hesitated, and it was Jeanne who answered, "Of course." Then she knelt next to Emma's chair. "Mrs.

Hunter, I would very much appreciate it if you would agree to help Mother and me plan the ceremony and reception."

Emma glanced at Jeanne and then stared up at Gabe. "I'll do whatever Gabe asks of me," she said, "as long as it can be done from Nantucket."

"Nothing has changed there, Mother," he said quietly. "I'll ask Fraiser to see to the arrangements, and you and Father may leave for the island tomorrow if you wish."

"And Lucie," Emma added.

Every eye was on Gabe as he swallowed hard and murmured, "That has nothing to do with me. It is between you and Miss McNeil." He offered his hand to help Jeanne stand and added, "Now, if you'll excuse me, I have business to attend to."

"Will you be home for dinner?" Jeanne asked, already sounding like a wife.

"No." The single word was a simple reply and not the reprimand Jeanne clearly took it to be. "Father, may I see you in the library?" Gabe asked, without looking back as he preceded his bride-to-be down the stairs.

"Of course," Jonathan agreed, his eyebrows raised in surprise at the unusual request. "As soon as I help your mother back to our room."

"Go," Emma said irritably, waving a hand at him. "I'm perfectly capable of managing, and Lucie should return soon."

Lucie watched as Jonathan, Gabe and Jeanne went down the curved stairway like soldiers on their way to a hanging. The men went into the library while Jeanne returned to the parlor, where her mother waited anxiously by the door. As soon as they were all gone, Lucie stepped out of the shadows.

"Well, obviously you heard," Emma said, her voice petulant and thick with her South Carolina drawl, the way it became whenever she was upset.

"You should be happy for them," Lucie replied, keeping her voice steady by sheer force of will.

"Why on earth should I be happy for two young people who are about to throw away their lives?" Emma demanded. "Three, if I count you. And believe me, I am every bit as saddened for that twit of a girl as I am for my son. They will make each other miserable inside of six months. And you…"

"Now, you can't know that," Lucie chided. "Perhaps it is God's will that—"

"God's will," Emma huffed. "It is an aberration, Lucie McNeil, and you and I both know it." She pinned Lucie with a look that defied disagreement. "My son is in love with you and you are in love with him, no matter how much you try and make yourself believe that you are not."

"Emma," Lucie warned, "don't go upsetting yourself. The last thing you want is to have a relapse and not be able to return to Nantucket."

"Nothing is going to stop me from that," Emma declared firmly. "My only regret is that my son will not be coming home, as well." Then she sighed heavily. "I'm tired, Lucie. Take me back to my room, please."

Lucie nodded and wheeled her employer down the hall. As they passed the railings that overlooked the foyer, she saw the library door open, and Thurgood Witherspoon stepped into the foyer. He glanced around for a moment, as if not quite sure what he should do next. Then, shaking his head as if he had just learned of a death, he went into the parlor where his wife and daughter sat. After that the library doors remained shut, and Lucie could not help but wonder what Gabe was saying to Jonathan behind those closed doors.

"What is all this?" Jonathan asked as he studied the documents Gabe had placed before him.

"I am signing over certain assets to you and Mama," Gabe said. "I had hoped the two of you would agree to remain here in Boston, but circumstances have changed and perhaps you can use this money to build that new house on the island—the one you want to turn into an inn."

"I can persuade Emma to spend winters here in Boston," Jonathan replied, watching his son closely.

Gabe laughed. "There may not be a place for any of us here in Boston."

Jonathan let the papers fall to the embossed leather top of Gabe's desk and leaned back in his chair, facing his son. "What's happened, Gabriel?" he asked quietly.

Gabe buried his head in his hands as he rested his elbows on the cluttered desk. His long fingers burrowed into his thick hair as he shook his head from side to side. Finally he looked up at his father. "It's hard to explain."

"Try."

"Recently Thurgood and I decided to go our own ways, although we have kept the firm intact. Thurgood suggested that with each of us seeking investments and new opportunities we could double the profits."

"But his business deals have not been as successful as yours," Jonathan ventured.

Gabe nodded. "That's part of it."

"What else?"

"The last of the assets we held in common was a garment factory. I had never been comfortable with conditions that seem acceptable to others in that business. Last August, before I left for Europe, I told Thurgood I wanted to shut it down, but he protested and said that if I was so worried about the women working there, shutting it down would surely put them in greater hardship. I couldn't argue that."

"So you sold it," Jonathan said, having heard that from Gabe himself.

"I thought we'd sold it," Gabe said. "Thurgood saw the opportunity for one grand profit. He thought that if he could build the business to its maximum and then sell it, the return would be far greater. So he borrowed money from other business accounts, canceled the insurance and anything else that cost money and poured everything into the factory. He hired more workers and added more machines and made impossible promises to customers willing to front him more money."

"I see."

"No, Papa, I doubt that anyone can imagine the rest. The factory caught fire right after Christmas and burned to the ground, killing several women in the process. My factory…my workers…my responsibility." The last three phrases came out in a single breath that reminded Jonathan of Emma when her lungs had filled and she could not sustain air.

Jonathan gave his son a minute to compose himself. "What does all this have to do with Jeanne and with this?" he asked indicating the documents before him.

"I have to make things right. The easy part was to start with Thurgood. He begged me to protect Jeanne from the scandal of his financial ruin. He has agreed to 'retire' to some property his brother owns in Delaware in return for my willingness to marry Jeanne so that she will have a secure future."

"But you don't love her," Jonathan reminded him.

"I am fond of her."

"Still, you are in love with another woman—you are in love with Lucie McNeil."

Gabe hung his head at the bold truth of that. "She won't have me. She worked at the factory and she thinks that I knew—that I condoned..."

Jonathan placed a hand on Gabe's shoulder. "I wish you had come to me before you proposed marriage, Gabe."

"Well, it's done now, and so I move on to the next step—trying to find some way to pay off the creditors Thurgood owes—we owe. I'll sell this house, and there are other assets I can liquidate. Thurgood has already sold everything he could—his house, Dolly's jewelry, their furniture and art collection. He has nothing left."

"He has your loyalty," Jonathan said. "In spite of everything, he has that."

Gabe shrugged. "I can start over once this is all cleared up."

He stopped talking, but his father remained standing by his side. "You could have Thurgood arrested for theft and fraud, Gabe," Jonathan said. "Why are you letting him off the hook?"

"And what good would that do? He's already ruined financially—and unless I stand by him, the family will be ruined socially. Everything will go to pay off his creditors. I can't do that to Jeanne."

"So you'll marry a woman you don't love to keep her from suffering the scandal of her father's lost fortune?"

Jonathan opened the first of several documents Gabe had handed him. "Let me help you find another solution."

Gabe let go a choked laugh with no mirth in it. "You can't. You have no resources. The only thing you can do is accept what I'm signing over to you—at least that much can be protected. You can use it to build the inn. The place will provide you and Mama with some security."

Jonathan smiled. "That idea was nothing more than a ruse to try and get you to come home, son. I figured if I could get you involved in some business venture on Nantucket, you might see that it's your home—it's always been your home."

"Still, it's a sound investment—we both know that. After all, that was always the point of all this." Gabe waved a hand to include the lavish furnishings of the large library. "All I ever wanted was to get back what you lost."

Jonathan looked directly at his son. "No, son, that's what you started out wanting, but the more you got the more you needed. It was never enough to simply replace what you thought I had lost. You were always chasing after what you thought you had lost—opportunities, a certain lifestyle."

Gabe swiveled his chair to avoid meeting his father's gaze. He stared out at a cloudless day and saw a robin—the harbinger of new beginnings—perched just outside his window.

"How did you do it, Papa?"

"Do what?"

"How did you find the strength to keep going after you'd lost everything?"

"I didn't lose it all, son."

"I know. Even when you understood that you and

Mama would end up with very little, you gave most of it away. Why?"

"Because others would truly end up with nothing— Adam and others who had worked so hard for me their entire lives. I still had so much. I had your mother—and you. That's fortune enough for any man, and I had even more."

"A cottage that today is practically falling down around you, and a piece of land that grows rocks like weeds," Gabe said.

"I had friends. I had faith. I had my dignity."

The two men sat in silence for a long moment and then Gabe said, "I have no friends," as if the idea had just occurred to him.

"You have many people who admire and respect you, son, and that's a starting point. You have a chance to make it up to those who lost their livelihood when the factory burned and to the families of those who lost their lives."

Gabe continued to stare out the window. "Don't you think I want that? But by the time I pay off the debt Thurgood has created for the firm, what's left?"

"You'll have this," Jonathan said.

Gabe slowly turned until he was looking at the slim bankbook his father had just laid on the desk. "What's this?"

Jonathan smiled. "Your mother calls it your rainy-day fund, and although the sun is shining today, I would say it is appropriately named."

Gabe flipped through the pages, noting the deposits and no withdrawals. "This money is yours," he said. "I gave it to you."

"And I am giving it back. You need it. We don't." He tapped the documents before him. "With these assets you've managed to secure, plus the bank account, we can do this—together."

Gabe continued to study the bankbook. "For so many years I thought of you as weak because I thought you gave up after you lost it all. And I could never understand how Mama could forgive you. Now I know that you were the strong ones."

"You have that strength, Gabe. You've just lost your way," Jonathan said. He reached for the pen in the ornately gilded penholder on Gabe's desk and signed the documents.

Gabe watched as his father took possession of the only assets Thurgood Witherspoon had been unable to access. Then Jonathan stood up, replaced the pen in its holder and handed Gabe the papers.

"Could I offer one piece of advice, son?"

"Please," Gabe said, his eyes alive with hunger for any words that might save him from himself.

"Don't compound the mistakes of the father by marrying the daughter. There's only one reason to marry, and that's for love. Jeanne is young. She'll have other proposals."

"Not once others learn that she has no fortune," Gabe said wearily. "I remember what it felt like when we suddenly went from wealth to veritable poverty, Papa. But a man can take steps to overcome that. Jeanne won't have that chance unless I provide it."

On the voyage back to Nantucket, the Hunters spent most of the trip in Gabe's stateroom. Emma agreed to rest in bed for the duration, and Jonathan would not leave her side. "Go up on deck and enjoy the day," Jonathan told Lucie. "We're fine here."

"We're going home, Lucie. What could be better than that?" Emma added with a beaming smile.

Reassured that Emma did seem to have weathered yet another attack, Lucie accepted Jonathan's invitation. Once on deck, she stood at the railing in almost the exact spot where she had stood that Sunday afternoon when Gabe had sailed with them. How very long ago that seemed now. First they had looked at each other with skepticism and curiosity. Then they could barely look at one another at all for fear that the longing they felt might be exposed to others. Or perhaps it was more that the longing they felt might have to be acknowledged and affirmed. And now they could not bear to be in the same room with one another.

Lucie closed her eyes and filled her lungs with the salty sea air. It was a new day and another new beginning for her. Ever since Gabe had walked across the dunes and into her life, so much had changed. Ironically she felt more sure of her future now than she had before he'd come into her life. She had won his trust through her love of and devotion to his parents, and if nothing else, that in itself had brought her a measure of security related to her employment.

She still was not certain what lay behind his sudden decision to marry Jeanne. A part of her wanted to believe he had acted impetuously after realizing he could never have Lucie, but those were the sins of vanity and pride, and she sent a silent prayer to God for forgiveness.

In the distance she could see the shoreline of Nantucket, and the very sight of it gave her a sense of peace and homecoming. In so many ways the Hunter cottage had been more home to her than anyplace she had ever lived before. She looked forward to getting back to the familiar kitchen, using the ostrich-feather duster on Emma's beautiful collections and sweeping the porch, which wrapped around the house as if holding it in a hug. Most of all she looked forward to being back in her room at the top of the stairs, with its large windows and morning view of the rising sun over the bay.

They were going to be all right, she thought. For however long Emma had, Lucie would care for her and Jonathan, and when one or both were gone, she would stay on the island, finding work and perhaps a small house in town to rent. She would be alone—but never lonely. For here she was a part of something—a community of friends and people she knew from church, as well as the family she had found with Emma and Jonathan. And if one day, in God's own time, she found love again, that would be a gift too rare to contemplate. For now, her life was full enough.

Charles Booker came to check on Emma the following week. He arrived on the ferry that ran daily between Nantucket and New Bedford throughout the summer, and rode his bicycle to the cottage. In his knickers and newsboy cap, he made quite a sight coming along the road that wound its way up to the Hunter property. And Lucie could not help but smile when she saw him.

"Emma," she called, and Emma glanced up from the quilt she'd been working on every day since their return. "Look," Lucie said, "I think you have a gentleman caller."

"I think it's you who has the caller, Lucie McNeil," Emma huffed, and to Lucie's surprise Emma frowned and then turned her attention back to her quilting.

Charles brought the bicycle to a halt and leaned it against the porch. "Hello," he said in a voice that was a little too loud for the proximity between them.

"Hello, Charles," Lucie replied.

"How's our patient?" he asked, and this time his voice was normal.

"See for yourself," Lucie said, and stepped down from the porch to lead him across the yard to where Emma continued working without looking up.

"I'm just fine," she muttered around a mouth filled with pins. "Did Gabe send you?"

"Now, you know I promised the colonel that I would stop in and see how you're doing." He opened his bag and took out his stethoscope. "Shall we have a listen?"

Emma squinted up at him. "Is that the sole reason for this visit?"

Charles colored slightly, but he grinned down at her. "Well, now, when else do I have the opportunity to take a boat ride on a summer day, ride my bicycle through some of the most beautiful country known to man and end up here, in the company of two lovely ladies?"

"You'll be staying for lunch, I suppose," Emma said, softening a little.

Charles shifted from one foot to the other. "I thought I would ask Miss McNeil to accompany me on a picnic— if that would be all right," he added quickly.

"It's perfectly all right with me," Emma replied. "Miss McNeil will have to speak for herself."

In the flash of a heartbeat, Lucie considered the invitation. If she accepted, she was raising false hopes. If she declined, she was in danger of appearing haughty and rude. "Perhaps we could all go," she suggested. "We have

cheese and bread and fruit that could be added to whatever you brought, Charles."

"No," Emma said almost before the flash of disappointment had had time to skitter across the doctor's face.
"Colonel Hunter and I are expecting the minister for
lunch—or did you forget, Lucie?"

She hadn't known. In fact, she was certain Emma had
never mentioned it. Besides, they had only been back a
few days and the minister had not called, nor had they
attended church, so how… She saw Emma watching the
road, and turned to see the minister's carriage turning in
and approaching the house. "I'll just set three places for
lunch then—that is, Charles, if you can wait?"

"Of course," Charles replied. "Take your time. I'll sit
here with Mrs. Hunter and the minister until you're
ready."

After she had laid out a luncheon for the Hunters and
Reverend Ashford, Lucie walked with Charles to a spot
on the bluff overlooking the bay, but within sight of
the house where the others were enjoying their lunch on
the porch. He spread the blanket she'd brought while she
unpacked the contents of the picnic basket he had
strapped onto the back of his bicycle.

"This is quite a surprise, Charles," she said.

"I said I would come," he reminded her.

"Yes, to check on Emma's health."

He sat down on the blanket, and she could feel him
watching her. "It is more than my duty as a physician that
brought me here."

Lucie forced herself to continue the tasks of slicing
the bread and cheese and then filling the cups with the
lemonade from the flask. "I know," she admitted.

"But?" Charles accepted the cup of lemonade but did not drink.

Lucie was kneeling next to the basket. She closed the lid and then turned to look at this man who cared for her, who could give her a life filled with security and even happiness. "Charles," she began, but he held up his hand to stop any further comment.

"I know," he said. "I just had to be sure. That's why I came—I mean, besides to look in on the Hunters. It's all right, Lucie. I do understand."

"I would like to be your friend," Lucie said softly.

He raised his glass. "To friendship," he said, and the smile he gave her was so genuine that she sighed with relief.

"To friendship," she agreed, and sipped her lemonade. "You aren't angry?"

"Disappointed would be a closer description, but I'll get past that." He nibbled a piece of cheese and reached for a hunk of the bread. "Gabe will be relieved," he added.

"I can't think why," Lucie said primly.

This time Charles laughed loud and long. "Oh, the two of you do make a pair, Lucie McNeil. The man is desperately in love with you and unless I am the worst diagnostician to ever take the Hippocratic oath, you feel the same for him."

"That's utter nonsense," she protested, and turned her attention once again to fussing with the food, picking crumbs off the blanket, rearranging the fresh fruit slices on the plate and refilling his cup with lemonade.

"Now, Lucie, if we are to be friends, then I'll have to insist we be honest with one another. Are you saying you don't love him?"

Lucie felt her cheeks grow hot and her eyes fill with tears. *Yes, I love him,* she wanted to scream, *but it's not to be, so please stop talking about it.*

"Lucie?" Charles's face had gone sober and he reached for her hand. "Ah, Lucie, if it helps, the man is every bit as miserable as you appear to be."

Lucie blotted her wet lashes with the back of her hand. "How would you know that?"

"Because he's my friend, as well, and he was the one who suggested the picnic and had Mrs. King prepare the food."

Willing herself to regain control of her emotions, Lucie smiled. "Then you must thank Mrs. King for her kindness. And now, couldn't we just enjoy the day and the food and not spoil it by discussing matters that have already been decided?"

"If you wish," Charles replied, but she felt him watching her, and after they had spent the rest of the hour enjoying the food and discussing how well Emma was doing now that she was back on Nantucket, Charles said, "Lucie? All you need do is send word that you will have him."

"That's not true," she said. "He would never go back on his promise."

"He would abandon everyone and everything if it meant he could have you," Charles said as they walked back across the lawn together.

"And eventually he would regret that," Lucie replied. "Come on, Reverend Ashford is leaving." She quickened her step and called out to the minister as Charles hurried to catch up to her.

# Chapter Thirteen

Dear Gabe,

Mother and I are fine—as is Lucie. We all miss you, of course.

I've looked over the plans the architect you recommended sent. It's a splendid design, much larger than our present cottage, with rooms enough to house perhaps a dozen guests plus living space for us and Lucie. We've selected a site that is closer to the road but has a better view of the harbor and beach below. The best news is that I have secured a loan through the Pacific Bank here in town, and construction will begin next week.

On another, more personal matter, it's clear to your mother and me that Lucie has rejected the young doctor's proposal of marriage. Although he continues to call on her (under the guise of checking up on your mother) and the two of them seem to have remained friends. But your mother is concerned about Lucie's future security. Her idea is that I could train Lucie to manage the inn, and *when the day comes that Emma and I have passed on, Lucie would inherit and have a secure home and business.*

*Your mother and I are quite excited about the whole idea. We haven't broached the topic with Lucie yet. We wanted to discuss it with you first, for it is your money that is making all of this possible.*

*Your mother asks that I remind you of how therapeutic the sea air on Nantucket can be—especially effective in clearing the mind, she notes. We would be most happy if you came for a visit—and of course, bring Miss Witherspoon.*
*With love,*
*Papa*

Gabe paced his library as he reviewed the steps he had taken to correct the many wrongs Thurgood's actions had created. But always under it all was the accusation that Lucie had thrown at him that evening—the accusation he had called a lie. The accusation he now knew to be true.

He and Witherspoon had owned the garment factory, where Lucie and dozens of other women and girls had toiled and where eventually some of them had died. He hadn't known—he couldn't have known that Thurgood would lie, that he would go to the lengths he had in an effort to take this one, grand shot at recouping his financial reversals. No one would hold him accountable if they knew the details. But Gabe was a man who took full responsibility for his actions—or in this case, his inaction.

He understood his partner very well. Thurgood had always looked for the fastest way to a dollar. Gabe had always been the conscience of their partnership. But in this case he had left it all to Thurgood—and never questioned, never checked, never given it another thought. In the scheme of things his feelings about running a "sweatshop" had been a small matter—one easily corrected by selling the business. He'd had no more thought about what he was condemning those women and girls to than Thurgood had every time he'd added another machine or promised another order.

Gabe folded his father's letter and placed it in the brass letter rack with the rest of his mail. In the slot in front was the bankbook his father had given him. It had been Gabe's intent to find a way to return these funds to his parents, but perhaps there was a better use for this money.

"Fraiser," Gabe called as he opened the library doors and stepped out into the foyer. The sound of his voice was hollow against the hard surface of the marble floor, the intricately curved wrought iron stair railing and the empty rooms at the top of those stairs. The day after Gabe's parents and Lucie had returned to Nantucket, the Witherspoons had moved out. Thurgood had made some excuse about it not being appropriate for Jeanne to live under the same roof as Gabe until they were properly married.

"Where will you go?" Gabe had asked.

"We have other options, Gabe," Thurgood had blustered, but he was immediately contrite. "It's time we let you have your peace."

It was Fraiser who had reported to Gabe later that evening that the Witherspoons had taken up residence in the home of the Van Heusens. "Mr. and Mrs. Van Heusen are visiting friends on the continent for the next several months. I believe that Mrs. Van Heusen and Mrs. Witherspoon are first cousins."

"Fraiser!" Gabe now called out again, and he heard the click of the butler's leather soles coming from the pantry.

"Yes, sir?"

"I'm going out and I may be quite late."

"Shall I have the carriage brought around?"

"No. I'll walk."

"It's raining, sir."

Gabe pulled a caped raincoat from the front closet and put it on. He smiled at Fraiser. "The weather suits my mood this evening."

Fraiser actually seemed about to protest, but thought better of it and smothered a frown as he said, "Very good, sir."

"Don't wait up," Gabe called over his shoulder as he pulled open the front door and stepped out into the storm.

He walked with purpose through the driving rain that soaked through his coat in minutes and flattened his hair against his forehead and cheeks. Block after block he kept on walking. Mansions gave way to storefronts. Storefronts became tenements. Streets narrowed. Shadows huddled in doorways, faceless voices called out to him, begging for a handout. Gabe kept walking.

The rain tapered off into a fine mist that coated his face and hands. He turned the final corner, remembering how the last time he had made this journey it had been in the automobile that Thurgood had just bought. The day had been hot, and the wind rushing by as Thurgood drove the open-air sedan through the slums of Boston had offered little relief on that stifling August afternoon.

Now Gabe stood under a streetlamp and looked across at the ruins of a building that had once provided employment for dozens of faceless women and girls. Some of them had been the sole supporters of their families, others were—like Lucie—immigrants trying to find a toehold on their climb to the American dream.

He thought about Lucie and wondered if he had seen her that day as he'd looked down at the women hunched over their machines, their eyes riveted on their work. If any of them had happened to glance up and catch his eye, they had quickly looked away and concentrated all the harder on their work. The sound had been a roar and the building had vibrated with the constant whine of the machines.

Lucie had been there that day. She had worked for him then and he'd never known it. And on the day of the fire, she had worked for him, as well. He thought about the burns on her palms. What had she gone through that day? What had she witnessed? What losses had she suffered that had changed her life forever and sent her running for her very life? And how, through it all, had she managed to hold on to her faith—her trust that this, too, was part of God's greater plan?

Gabe crossed the street and walked across the littered lot to where the remnants of the factory lay in a charred pile of broken glass, twisted metal and blackened wood. The building had stood three stories tall—taller than the center mast on his yacht. Gabe closed his eyes and thought of escape, and could not help but imagine the screams, see the flames, feel the heat. For the first time he began to face the horror that Lucie could not forget—or forgive. It was then that he understood. If he was going to make amends for this tragedy, he had to know everything, and the one person who could tell him what had really happened that day was Lucie.

Life on the island settled into a routine that suited Lucie, mostly because she was so busy that there was little time to think about Gabriel Hunter. Not that thoughts of him didn't pop into her mind at the oddest moments. She'd be at the stove, and turn, and the memory of him sitting at the kitchen table with Jonathan—the two men deep in conversation about some new business idea— would spring to mind. Or she'd be hanging laundry on the line to dry in the gentle summer breeze and hear the sound of hammers and saws as the workers Jonathan had hired from town worked day after day on the new inn. It was hard to watch the progress of that inn and not think of Gabe, for it was at his order that the building supplies needed to create the beautiful inn arrived.

Lucie was fully informed about how the inn had come to be. Emma and Jonathan kept nothing from her as they freely discussed the way Thurgood Witherspoon had practically ruined Gabe, as well as himself. Their pride in Gabe for refusing to abandon the man who had taught him much of what he knew about business was bound- less. And Emma had even begun to express some sympathy for young Jeanne Witherspoon.

"An innocent bystander to her father's greed," she an- nounced one evening. "I'll tell you one thing," she added, "the minute I met that girl I understood that she was liv- ing her life for one purpose and one purpose only—to please her father."

"Now, Emma," Jonathan said, "Witherspoon dotes on her, as well."

"It's not the same thing at all. That girl has every right to her father's love without feeling she needs to sell her soul in the bargain. I've asked Gabe to bring her with him when he comes to check on the progress of the inn this Sunday." She ignored Lucie's sudden intake of breath at the news that Gabe was expected. "Perhaps I can get her alone and talk some sense into her."

"Emma," Jonathan warned, and neither of them noticed the way Lucie's hands had begun to shake so badly that she had to abandon her darning.

That was the night the dream came back so unexpectedly and clearly that Lucie thought it was her life since the fire that had been a dream. It started the same way it always did. The air was clear and the sun was out. The trees were just beginning to push forth their brown buds. And then smoke was blackening everything like night, filling her lungs and stinging her eyes as she ran. Usually the dream ended there. Startled awake by the realization that it was the fire, she would bolt upright in bed, her breath ragged, her side aching and the covers a tangled mess. But not this night. Try as she might, she could not wake herself up.

*She fought her way through the smoke only to step back into a clear day—a summer day, hot and humid outside, meaning that inside it would be worse, the air dead and stifling, the machines packed together so close they were almost touching, creating even more heat. She turned a corner and there it was—the factory. Had it always been so big, so ugly? An eyesore, really, in a landscape of eyesores—empty lots filled with trash, tenements with their paper-thin walls, dark, dank hallways and the stench of cabbage and onions permeating everything. Streets that were little more than alleys and alleys that were sewers.*

*She walked quickly but reluctantly toward the entrance, but she wasn't alone. Ellie and Hannah Gibson were on either side of her. The three of them were laughing as they hurried toward the door where the foreman held his pocketwatch in one hand and scowled at them. Then she was at her machine, running fabric through in an endless ribbon. Yards and yards and yards of it, knowing she couldn't rest until she reached the end. But there was no end.*

*She glanced up and saw two men step out of the office with the manager, who looked anxious and overly eager to please. One of the two strangers was stocky and loud, his voice audible if not comprehensible above the din of a hundred sewing machines. He was talking a lot and gesturing wildly. The other man was tall and it was hard not to admire the cut of his clothes and the perfect way they fit his broad shoulders. He was quiet, his eyes scanning the workers. That man was Gabe, and she dreamed that when his eyes finally came to rest on a single worker, that worker was her.*

Lucie forced herself to wake. She lay there willing her breath to steady and wiping the perspiration from her neck and face with the sleeve of her nightgown. The window was open and she could hear the distant sound of waves hitting the beach. *He's coming,* they seemed to chant. *Sunday. Sunday. Sunday.*

Lucie shut her eyes tight and prayed for guidance and strength. And then she prayed for forgiveness, because as much as she knew Emma and Jonathan were looking forward to Gabe's visit, Lucie did not want him here. She knew that seeing him again would rekindle all of the turmoil of emotions she had thought she had finally put to rest. She had been fooling herself, of course, for with the mere news that Gabe was coming to Nantucket, everything had come flooding back—the dream, the fire and, most of all, her love for a man she could not possibly love.

On Sunday Lucie helped Emma get ready and then put on her Sunday dress and a straw hat while Jonathan brought the carriage around. At the church Adam waited as usual with Emma's wheelchair. Lucie greeted neighbors and people from town as she wheeled Emma to her place at the end of the third pew. As Reverend Ashford announced the first hymn, Lucie felt her tension ease. Gabe would be at the house for lunch but Lucie was not going to let her apprehension over seeing him spoil this hour in church.

She opened the hymnal and began to sing with all the joy and solace that the music and words gave her. She would be all right. She would get through this day. She would...

There was a hushed murmur of voices behind her and the titter of one of the Bushnell sisters' laughter. Lucie frowned. Arriving late for services was rude, but creating a stir was inexcusable. She sang louder and fought the urge to glance to her left to see who was causing such interest.

Then Gabe came down the side aisle and slid into the pew next to her. He nodded to his parents and then took one side of the hymnal Lucie held and gently pulled it so that he could see the words.

"I need to speak with you," he murmured.

She decided to ignore him, and kept singing.

"After the service," he added. And then she felt his gaze on her and glanced up.

He looked terrible. There were dark circles under his eyes and his hair was badly in need of a trim. "Please," he whispered as the congregation held the last note of the hymn.

Lucie nodded, shut the hymnal and sat down with everyone else at the minister's instruction. Gabe sat a beat later, his broad shoulders grazing hers in the narrow pew. Throughout the sermon he sat still as a stone, his face riveted on Reverend Ashford, whose topic was forgiveness.

As soon as the service ended, Lucie made some excuse and quickly crossed the aisle to speak to a group of young women gathered there. "I'll be along," she assured Emma and Jonathan without looking at Gabe.

"I thought we were to have the pleasure of Miss Witherspoon's company," Jonathan said as Gabe wheeled Emma up the aisle toward the exit.

"She wanted to come, but I asked her to postpone her visit," Gabe explained. They had reached the vestibule and Gabe stepped forward to shake the minister's hand. "Thank you for your words today, Reverend," he said humbly.

The minister quickly covered his surprise at Gabe's compliment and returned his handshake. "God's words, my son, and if they have touched you, then I have done good work."

"I wonder if you would mind if Miss McNeil and I remained here a while longer."

The minister's eyebrows shot up at this strange request, and Jonathan also seemed taken aback. Only Emma had no reaction—other than to smile.

"I assure you that there is nothing improper in my request," Gabe hastened to add. "If you like, I'll ask my parents to remain here, as well."

Reverend Ashford looked down at Emma. "No, that won't be necessary, but since you have chosen to speak with Miss McNeil here in the church, is there something I could do to be of help?"

"It's a topic that could cause Miss McNeil some distress, and I thought that—in case she needed—"

"Of course. I shall be next door at the parsonage if you need me."

Gabe could see that he had aroused considerable interest as to what he might have to say to Lucie that could be so upsetting, but he made no attempt to explain further. Instead he turned to his parents and said, "I have left Randolph from my crew at the cottage to prepare lunch for you."

"But you have to eat—and Lucie," Jonathan protested.

"We'll wait to dine with you," Emma said.

"No, please, let Randolph serve you, and by the time you've eaten and rested, I'll be there and we can have a nice visit. I'm anxious to see how the inn is coming."

Jonathan beamed. "Construction is right on schedule."

Lucie saw the Hunters getting into their carriage and hurried over to join them.

"I'm sorry but—" she began, but Emma placed one translucent hand on Lucie's.

"Now, Gabe has taken care of everything. And, Lucie?"

Lucie raised her eyes to look directly at Emma.

"Think carefully before you make any hasty decisions." Her eyes twinkled with delight. "It would make us so happy to welcome you into our family as our real daughter," she added.

"Oh, Emma," Lucie said, "he hasn't come to— He hasn't come for that."

"Then what could it possibly be?" Emma asked, still certain she had seen through her son's plan. "We'll see the two of you at home later, dear."

Lucie stood rooted to the spot until the carriage was

out of sight. It was the last carriage to leave the church-yard and as she turned back to the church she saw Reverend Ashford making his way across the yard to the small white parsonage. He raised a hand in her direction and Lucie could not help but wonder if he was offering her his blessing.

Taking a deep breath, she stepped inside the church. Sunlight streamed through the window behind the altar, casting a rainbow of colors on the empty pews. Gabe was sitting in the front row. He sat on the edge of the pew, his hands resting on his knees, as if poised for flight. She moved down the aisle and took a seat at the far end of that same pew.

"Thank you for seeing me, Lucie," he began.

"I cannot think what could possibly be so urgent that it could not be discussed over lunch with your parents."

"I need to know about the fire. I need for you to tell me every detail that you can recall about who was there and what happened."

Lucie put one gloved hand to her mouth. "I cannot," she whispered. "Please, you don't know what you're asking."

He slid a few inches closer and she backed away until she felt the hard wood at the end of the pew press against her back. "I want to make things right. I am trying to—"

"You cannot make this right, Gabe," she said, finding her voice and the strength to tell him the truth.

He stared down at the floor and nodded. "Perhaps not, but I have to try, and I can't do that if you won't tell me what happened."

Lucie closed her eyes tight and immediately the horror of that day flashed into her mind. She shook her head from side to side and nervously pulled at the fingers of her gloves, unconsciously removing them and allowing them to fall to the floor. Suddenly Gabe was beside her, holding her hands in his.

"Lucie, you need this as much as I do. You have held the memory of that day inside all these months, never telling anyone. I'm asking you to tell me and I promise I will never ask another thing of you."

Lucie felt his warmth and strength seeping into her as he held her folded hands between both of his. She looked at his face, ravaged by the guilt she had exposed for him, and knew he was right. She had to relive that day if she was to have any hope of moving forward with her life. And Gabe had to relive it with her so that he would finally know the full extent of the devastation Thurgood's greed and his own neglect had wrought.

"All right," she said, and started at the very place where her dream always began. "I was on my way to the factory. It was an unseasonably warm day for December. Everyone was speaking of it. Cold but not frigid, and without the usual wind. The sun was out and the air felt fresh and clean and then—"

"Why were you on your way? It was afternoon, wasn't it?"

Lucie nodded. "But we were working in shifts round the clock, and I had been assigned the later shift."

"Go on."

"I was late and in a hurry so I was not really paying attention, except to regret that I could not enjoy such an unusual day. But then everything changed. The air was thick and pungent with the smell of smoke. Around me people were running, shouting, but I couldn't make out what they were saying. I heard the clang of the fire wagons and the pounding of the horses' hooves as they pulled the wagons down the narrow streets. I turned the corner, and through thick black smoke I saw the factory." Her breath came in quick gasps as she relived every detail of that day.

"What did you do?"

"I ran toward it. I could hear the sound of breaking glass and screams from those trapped inside. I looked up and saw my friends at a window. I screamed at them not to jump but they shouted back that it was the only way because the door to the fire escape was blocked."

"Blocked?"

Lucie nodded. "With several large bolts of fabric we were to use for the new order and an entire row of new sewing machines all bolted to the floor."

Gabe shut his eyes and then opened them again as if he needed to face whatever she might say next. "What did you do then?"

"I ran toward the fire escape. I thought maybe if I could open the door from the outside somehow that would help. One of the firemen saw me and ran after me. He grabbed me, but I fought and held on to the railing, trying to get to the door."

Gabe turned her palms up. "That's how you burned your hands." He thought of the twisted remnants of melted metal he had seen at the site. "It must have been like laying your palm flat on a hot stove."

But Lucie was not listening to him. She was caught up in playing out the memory that even in her dreams she had never allowed herself to relive to the end. "I begged them to wait. I begged the fireman to help them. But then they jumped," she said. "And once they did, others followed their lead. I remember the fireman loosening his hold on me as the bodies started falling around us. He swore and I prayed."

Gabe was still holding her hands, but his head was bent and suddenly she realized he was crying, his tears splashing onto her scarred palms. She touched his hair as she watched his shoulders heave with fresh sobs.

She was so moved by his sorrow that it was a moment before she realized her own eyes were dry. She had cried every time the dream had come to her, waking her as she sobbed out her grief. But not this time. This time, when she had told Gabe the whole horror of that day, she did not cry. She felt only relief that at last she had spoken aloud the pain she had carried inside all these months.

"Can you ever forgive what I've done, Lucie?" he asked.

"It is not for me to forgive, Gabe. It is between you and God. If you truly never knew, then how could you have prevented it?"

"But in so many ways I should have known, Lucie. Thurgood was always pressing me to bring in more machines, more workers. Finally I told him I was uncomfortable with the entire business and I wanted to sell. So you see, I turned a blind eye." He looked up at her for a second and then immediately he bowed his head again.

Lucie drew him to her, holding him as he sobbed out his confession.

"I never asked. I heard about the fire but I never asked. I knew Thurgood well enough to know that he might change the plan we had agreed upon, but I never asked." He raised his face to hers. "I killed them, Lucie. God forgive me, I'm every bit as much to blame as Thurgood."

Lucie cupped his face in her palms. "It's never too late, Gabe. God will forgive."

Gabe pulled himself away from her and took her hands once again. "But can you forgive me, Lucie? For these marks that will remind you every day of your lost friends?"

"We make choices, Gabe. God gives us choices. Sometimes we act in haste, as I did. It was foolish to imagine I could open that door or save them, but that's the choice I made. My friends chose to jump because it seemed the only possible escape."

"And I chose, as well," Gabe said miserably. "Inaction is also a choice."

They sat in silence for a moment. Every now and then Gabe would utter a dry sob of pure grief and mourning. Lucie had no more words to console him. She wanted to hold him and reassure him. She wanted to tell him that knowing that he had thought Thurgood had sold the factory and that he had truly thought the fire had happened under the new ownership, she could forgive him. She wanted so very much to open her heart to him and pour out all the love she had suppressed for weeks. But he was betrothed to Jeanne, and it did not matter whether Lucie forgave him or not.

"Gabe?" She bent and retrieved her gloves from the floor. "I'm going to walk back to the cottage. Your parents will be wondering where we are. You stay here until you're ready. I'll explain."

He nodded.

Lucie walked back up the aisle. At the door she turned and looked back at him. What she saw was a broken man sitting before a stained-glass portrait of a dove ascending into a blue sky. "Shall I ask Reverend Ashford to come over here?"

He hesitated, and she saw his shoulders stiffen slightly, but then he hunched forward once again and nodded. "Please, forgive me," he whispered, and Lucie could not have said whether this was an entreaty to her or the prayer of a lost soul.

## Chapter Fourteen

It was dusk when Lucie finally saw Gabe and Reverend Ashford coming up the road. The minister had his arm around Gabe's shoulder and she heard Gabe's rare but familiar laughter.

"He's back," she hurried to tell Emma and Jonathan, who had taken up their vigil in the parlor when Gabe still had not returned after supper. Lucie had assured them both that Gabe was all right and that the minister was with him. Emma took comfort in that.

"He's coming back to us, Johnny," she said with tears in her eyes.

"And maybe to God, as well," Jonathan said.

As soon as Lucie delivered the news that Gabe was on his way, Jonathan took charge of moving Emma's wheel-chair through the hall and onto the porch.

"The prodigal son returns," Gabe joked nervously when he saw his parents.

Emma held out her arms to him, and when he knelt to receive her embrace, Jonathan placed a hand on Gabe's head as he looked up at the minister. "Thank you, Reverend," he said, his voice breaking.

"Not at all. It's God's work and we are but His messengers."

Gabe got to his feet and turned to the minister. "I must tell you that when we first met, I thought… That is, I judged you to be…"

"You are a businessman, Gabriel, and it is perfectly understandable that you form your first impressions of others based on that experience. All I ask is that you keep in mind that God's business is one of touching the hearts and souls of His creatures—regardless of their financial condition."

Gabe looked confused and stumbled for words to further explain himself.

Reverend Ashford put his hand on Gabe's forearm. "What I am trying to say, son, is that working for God often requires a quieter, more gentle approach. In business I expect that you are more accustomed to going after what you want or need to succeed. God prefers to wait for you to come to Him."

Gabe smiled.

"And have you?" Emma asked, and everyone laughed at her directness.

"I've started on the path," Gabe assured her as his eyes settled on Lucie, who had remained standing in the front hall on the other side of the screened door.

"Well, hallelujah," Emma whispered as she dabbed at her eyes.

Jonathan took out a handkerchief and blew his nose and wiped his eyes, as well, then turned to the minister. "Have you eaten? Lucie, do we have any of that lamb left?"

"No, thank you," Reverend Ashford said, before Lucie could reply. "I must be going." He turned to Gabe. "You'll be all right?"

"Yes. Thank you for everything—for listening and for—"

Again the minister stopped him with a touch. "Give your thanks to God, Gabriel. It occurs to me that you are well named for singing His praises."

After they had watched the minister until he was through the gate and back on the road again, Emma said, "I suppose you need to be getting back to Boston, Gabe."

"I thought I would stay the night. After all, I haven't yet had the grand tour of the inn," he added.

Jonathan beamed. "I can show you around first thing tomorrow," he assured Gabe. "In the meantime let me show you the plans. You may have some additional ideas, and it's not too late to make changes."

Gabe and Jonathan talked about the inn well into the night while Lucie went about her usual routine of getting Emma in bed and then attending to evening chores. Through it all, she felt a lightness of heart that was new and confusing to her. The murmur of Gabe's voice as he and his father talked gave her such comfort. Ever since he'd come back to the cottage from the church, his laugh seemed to come more readily and with abandon. Indeed his entire posture had changed. Gone was the tension she was used to seeing in the set of his shoulders and his furrowed brow.

And yet she could not allow herself to forget that he was betrothed to another. Nothing had changed there. If anything, Gabe's return to his faith assured that he would honor the promise he had made to Jeanne and her father.

"May I get either of you anything?" Lucie asked when

the clock had struck eleven and there still seemed to be no sign the two men were done talking.

They looked up at her and then at the clock. Jonathan rolled up the plans for the inn. "I had no idea it had gotten so late," he said. "Gabe, let's continue this in the morning—once you've seen the place."

"I've prepared your room for you," Lucie said, unable to meet Gabe's eyes.

"I thought I would stay on the yacht tonight," he replied, and turned to his father. "May I borrow one of your horses, Papa?"

"Of course, but why go to all that bother? Why not stay…" He glanced from Gabe to Lucie and said, "Ah. Perhaps staying the night on your yacht would be best."

Lucie felt her cheeks flush and covered her dismay by taking a sudden interest in straightening the lace doilies Emma liked on the arms and backs of every chair.

"May I take those plans with me, Papa? I'd like to study them more."

Jonathan placed the rolled blueprints into a leather container and handed them to Gabe. "Have a good night, Lucie," he said as he left the room.

"Thank you," she murmured, and could not for the life of her think why she didn't take advantage of Jonathan's exit to make one of her own. Gabe remained standing near the sofa his father had just vacated. He shifted from one foot to the other.

"Will you be having breakfast with your parents?" Lucie asked. "I need to know so that I may be sure to set…"

"Don't play the servant, Lucie," he said. Then in a softer tone he added, "I will be here for breakfast with my parents—and you."

Lucie swallowed. "Then I'll say good-night," she said, and turned to go.

She hadn't heard him cross the thick Persian carpet that covered the wood floor and was startled when he touched her arm. "Stay," he said as his fingers closed around her forearm.

"I am tired," she said, when her mind was screaming, *Don't you understand that I cannot?*

"I am going to break it off with Jeanne, and after that…"

She turned to him, her eyes flashing like violet crystals. "Please do not put me in that position, Gabe. If you care for me at all…"

"I love you," he said, and stepped closer, his fingers stroking her cheek. "Don't you understand, Lucie? I love you—not Jeanne."

"Then do not make me the cause of your failed engagement." She pulled her arm free of his hold and walked tall and proud up the stairs to her room.

Gabe returned to Boston the following afternoon. He had gone to the cottage for breakfast but Lucie had not been there.

"Something about a sick friend in town," Jonathan said, looking at Gabe with a frown. "It's the first she's spoken of this friend," he added.

"Oh, do stop beating about the bush, Johnny. Did you do something to upset our Lucie, Gabriel?" she demanded.

*I told her that I loved her.* "Now, Mama, why would you assume such a thing?"

"Because your father certainly upset me before we

were finally married," she snapped as she glared from Jonathan to Gabe and back again.

"Now, darling girl, that was all a misunderstanding and you know it."

"You left without a word. You declared your love and then—*poof*—off you went. I was devastated."

Gabe risked a glance at his father.

"I explained," he argued, but Emma was having none of it, so he turned his entreaty to Gabe. "Your mother and I had declared our love for each other and—"

"Your father had promised matrimony," she said primly.

"I went to her father to ask permission." He turned to Emma. "You know very well that it was your father who required that I be well established with a solid future. He was not about to permit you to marry anyone who could not assure that you would never again—"

"Oh, bother," Emma challenged. "My father was determined that I should not marry a Yankee. He sent you on a wild-goose chase and you went, and that was the real story."

"But I came back, darling girl," Jonathan reminded her as he reached across the table and took her hand in his.

"Took you long enough," she huffed, although Gabe noticed she did not pull her hand away. "Three long months," she reminded her husband.

"But you waited," he said gently, and this time Emma smiled.

"Of course I waited. I had no other prospects."

The three of them laughed at that, knowing that if Emma had set her mind to it she would have had suitors lined up outside her door.

*And what of Lucie?* Gabe thought later that day as he

sailed back to Boston. Did she not have another suitor in Charles Booker? It didn't matter that Charles had let him know that there was no chance for a romance between Charles and Lucie. She might change her mind. Gabe thought he could not abide seeing Lucie with another man, even his good friend. But she had made it equally clear that she would not have Gabriel as long as he was engaged to Jeanne. Further, if she had any reason to believe she was the cause of the end of that engagement, she still would refuse him.

Gabe stood at the railing as the buildings outlining Boston Harbor and a life he did not want closed in on him. The prayer he uttered was unspoken, but so clear that he closed his eyes and raised his face to the sky as the words came.

*Dear God, I love her and if that is wrong, then I beg Your forgiveness. I have been on my own for so long that now it is hard to fathom what Your plan for my life might be. But surely—*

Gabe opened his eyes in dismay that he would challenge God the way he might any business associate.

*Forgive me,* he prayed, closing his eyes once again, and this time bowing his head. *Thy will be done, and if it be Your will that I marry Jeanne, then I pray that in time she and I will find a bond that will sustain us throughout our life together.*

He felt the yacht slow and heard his crew preparing to dock.

"Amen," he murmured.

The following Sunday Gabe once again came to Nantucket. As before, he came down the side aisle of the church and took the seat next to Lucie. And as she had observed the previous Sunday, there was a faint murmur of speculation among the congregation at his presence.

"Is this to be your habit?" she asked on the third Sunday of visits, when the two of them were alone for a moment as Emma and Jonathan bid farewell to the minister, who had come for Sunday dinner. "Do you plan to come every Sunday?"

"Yes," he admitted. "Is that a problem for you?"

"Not at all. It's good that you are making regular visits to the island—your parents are delighted."

"And you?"

"I am happy for your parents," she replied, and went outside to shake out the tablecloth. She hated that she sounded so prim, but it was best. She was annoyed. He was an intelligent man but he couldn't seem to apply that common sense when it came to managing his own life.

To her relief, Jonathan kept Gabe busy the whole afternoon. They discussed the progress on the inn and Gabe examined the workmanship, declaring it to be of a higher quality than he could get in the city. Over supper Jonathan began telling Gabe about his ideas for furnishing the inn.

"Now, you men just leave that to Lucie and me," Emma interrupted. "What do the two of you know of properly furnishing a home?" She looked directly at Gabe. "Cherubs on the ceiling, of all things."

Even Gabe chuckled at that.

"Would it be all right if I sent over some vendors with samples for you to consider?" Gabe asked.

"I suppose that would be best," Emma agreed. "What do you think, Lucie?"

"That would be very nice," she said, but her mind was not on the conversation at hand. It was on the discussion she'd had with Gabe earlier. He planned to continue these visits on a regular basis—every Sunday, weather permitting, according to a delighted Emma.

And while Lucie was happy for the Hunters, she was quite sure she could not endure these weekly reminders that she was in love with a man she could never have. She had to do something, and after several restless nights and daily prayers for a solution, she was sure she had found one.

"Emma," she said one day when the two women were sitting together working on the beautiful white quilt. "I was thinking. Now that you are feeling so much better and the colonel is doing so well, would it be possible for me to take one day a week off?"

Emma's eyebrows shot up and she looked positively distressed. "Oh, dear Lucie, we have grown so used to having you with us—as a member of our family and household. Well, it simply never occurred to us that— But of course, you can't be spending all your time with two old people like us. How is your friend in town, by the way?"

Lucie blinked and then blushed at the small lie she had told them. "There is no friend," she admitted. "Actually, that is the point. I would like to have a day to myself and perhaps over time—"

"Of course, Lucie dear. How does Saturday suit you?"

Lucie hesitated. "I was hoping that perhaps Sundays might—"

Emma frowned as she clipped a thread. "Is this about Gabe?"

"No," Lucie hurried to protest, but then faltered. "Not entirely," she added. "It's just that Sunday seems to be the perfect choice simply because he is here and you wouldn't be alone. I could make sure you have breakfast and are ready for church and leave dinner for you and a cold supper and—"

Emma studied her for a long moment. "You would not attend services?"

"I thought I might try one of the churches in town," Lucie said.

The two women continued sewing, and Lucie wondered if Emma was going to give her an answer.

"You love him, do you not?" Emma asked.

"Yes," Lucie admitted, "but—"

Emma held up one finger—a command to stop talking. "There are no *buts* when two people are as deeply and clearly in love as you and Gabe are," she instructed. "God will find a way, Lucie. You must simply give Him time."

"Yes, ma'am," Lucie replied, but there was no sarcasm in her tone, just acquiescence.

"On the other hand," Emma continued, "I can see the problem Gabe has created for you. The congregation— at least the female part of it—is buzzing with speculation, and that is not at all good for you or your reputation. Jonathan has this idea that you shall manage the inn, and it simply will not do for there to be any question at all about your character. It's Gabe's fault, of course. Men do not see the fine points when it comes to a proper courtship, especially one as delicate as this."

And then Emma launched into the story of Jonathan's courtship of her, telling Lucie the familiar tale of how horrified her family and friends had been and how cautious she had had to be to protect her standing in the community. Just when Lucie was sure Emma had lost track of the original question, Emma gazed at Lucie and said, "Yes, I believe that Sundays off is an excellent idea."

* * *

Gabe was not happy when he learned of the new arrangement.

"The woman deserves some time for herself," Jonathan said.

"I know," Gabe replied. "It's just that—"

"Gabriel, it's perfectly obvious to your mother and me, as well as others, that your weekly visits here are only partly to fulfill your role as the dutiful son."

"I come to see you and Mama because I wish to be with you," Gabe protested.

"And to keep an eye on your investment in the inn and—more than you may be willing to admit—to be with Lucie."

Gabe took a sudden interest in running his hands over the smooth stone of the enclosure that ran the perimeter of the inn's wide porch.

Jonathan placed a hand on his son's shoulder. "You have to put matters in order, son. You are engaged to Miss Witherspoon. Break that off and then come calling on Lucie."

"She still won't have me," Gabe said miserably.

"How do you know?"

"She told me that she would not be the cause of my breaking it off with Jeanne." He slumped down on the top step of the porch. "I don't know what to do."

Jonathan sat next to him. "Perhaps there are other ways you can prove yourself to her so that in time she might see that in breaking it off with Miss Witherspoon you are actually doing the honorable thing. But right now, son, she knows one side of you—the side that goes after what he wants regardless of the consequences."

"But she knows that I've come back to the church," Gabe protested.

Jonathan frowned. "Did you do that to impress her or because you truly realized the need for God's guidance for your life?"

"You know it's the latter," Gabe snapped.

Jonathan stood. "Then, son, here is my advice—if you need God's guidance, all you have to do is ask and then listen for the answer. You may not like it, but in time you will see that whatever way He leads you will be for the best—for you and for Lucie."

All the following week, Gabe replayed his father's advice. He took long walks after leaving the office each day and more often than not he found that his walks led him to the site of the burned factory and the neighborhood where Lucie had lived. Something kept drawing him back to this place. Without it Lucie would never have gone to Nantucket. They would never have met. And yet the place reeked of horror and death and catastrophe.

One evening, as he stood across the street from the factory site, he thought of the two sisters who had leapt to their deaths. He could not recall their given names, but the last name, Gibson, had stayed in his mind. A common enough name, and yet it seemed too familiar to him to be a coincidence.

"Gibson," he muttered, and then it came to him. "Sarah Gibson," he said aloud, and a passing woman glanced his way.

"No, sir," she said, obviously thinking he had called out to her. "The Gibson family lives there." She pointed to a run-down building at the end of the alley. "Sarah's their daughter—the only one left," she added sadly.

"Thank you," Gabe said, and reached in his pocket for money.

"No," the woman said proudly. "You give that money to the Gibsons if you're of a mind. Since Sarah lost her housemaid's position there's been no work for them."

Gabe thanked the woman again and hurried down the alley. It would soon be dark, but day or night did not seem to matter once he stepped inside the tiny entrance to the building and the door shut behind him.

A single gas light flickered weakly, and he could make out a stairway. He started up, unsure of why he was here and what he would do if he found the right apartment. He reached a landing and a door, and knocked.

He recognized the girl, as soon as she opened the door, as the one who had worked on the costumes with Lucie. And she obviously recognized him, for the minute she saw him, she drew in her breath and moved to protect herself with the door.

"Miss Gibson?"

"Yes, sir," she replied, her voice shaking.

The hallway was stifling with the accumulation of days of summer heat. "May I come in and have a word with your father?"

"My father is not well," she faltered, even as behind her Gabe could see a man seated at a small table, his hand clasping a whiskey bottle.

"Please, Sarah, I've come to offer help."

Perhaps it was sheer shock that made Sarah step back and allow him to pass. Either way, he was inside the apartment that in total would have fit three times over into the foyer of his grand home. The man looked up at him and then went back to staring vacantly out the grime-covered window. "Who are you and what's your business here?" he asked.

Sarah hastily wiped the seat of the only other chair in the room and offered it to him. Gabe hesitated and then sat down.

"Mr. Gibson, my name is Gabriel Hunter."

That got the man's attention. His eyes blazed with fury. "Get out," he ordered hoarsely as he staggered to his feet. "Get out of my house."

Mr. Gibson took a swing at Gabe, but missed and started to fall. When Gabe caught him and eased him back onto his chair, the man started to sob. "Get out," he chanted over and over.

"Please, sir," Sarah pleaded as she ran to comfort her father.

Gabe sat down opposite the man and leaned forward. "Mr. Gibson, I have come to offer my help. I am well aware that I have come far too late to relieve you of the terrible grief your family has had to bear, but it is not too late for things to change. I need your help—yours and Sarah's."

The man's sobs abated slightly and Gabe could tell he was listening, so Gabe continued. "I need a list of every family who had someone working in the factory at that time—whether or not they were there on the day of the fire."

Gibson lifted his head and eyed Gabe suspiciously.

"Only then can I make sure that any of those people who need a job and are willing to work will have employment."

"My girl here worked for you," Gibson accused, "and you fired her."

"I did not hire her," Gabe said, "but I would like to hire

her now. I would like her to come and work for my parents, who live on Nantucket. She knows my mother and she also knows their…companion, Lucie McNeil."

"Lucie works for you?" Gibson asked.

"For my parents. My father is in the process of building an inn on Nantucket. He will need a large staff to run the place—maids and cooks and gardeners—and if there are people you know who have not found work since the fire, then perhaps—"

Gibson released a laugh of disgust. "Have not found work? How can we find work when there's nothing out there but that stinking hole in the ground?" he shouted.

In the silence that followed this outburst, Gabe was aware of the many sounds that filled the cramped building. The screams of crying babies, the squabbles of husbands and wives, the street noises of peddlers hawking their wares, rumbling carts and drays and the splash of dirty laundry water thrown off the fire escape all penetrated the paper-thin walls of the apartment. The need of these people was blatantly apparent to any passerby. The problem was that people like Gabe and Thurgood turned a blind eye to neighborhoods like this one. They had not cared where the workers came from or how they lived, only that they showed up every day on time and did the work.

"Mr. Gibson, I would like to help not only you and your family, but the families of those others who were… who lost loved ones or their own livelihoods because of the fire."

"You hear that?"

Gabe had been aware of a racking cough coming from behind a clean but torn curtain in the corner of the room. He nodded.

"That's my wife," Gibson said. "She's been down ever since the fire, and the streets are filled with apartments just like this one, where folks have no job, no money coming in regular and the landlord knocking at the door for the rent. So, how're you gonna help us, mister?"

Gabe faltered, searching for words. "I'm not sure yet. As a start I would like to offer Sarah the position with my parents."

"They'll pay her a decent wage? And give her room and board?" he asked quickly.

"And she'll have Saturdays off, on which day I shall personally arrange for her to come here to visit you and her mother. Further I would like to have a friend of mine—a doctor—examine your wife and prescribe some treatment. My mother has a condition that causes her to cough like that sometimes, and Dr. Booker has helped her."

"I can't pay," Gibson said.

"Dr. Booker runs a clinic for people like you—you pay what you can or when you can. No one is turned away."

Gibson studied Gabe for a long moment. "Why are you doing this?"

"It's a long story, Mr. Gibson. Will you accept my offer of help?"

"The job for my Sarah and the doctor for my wife?"

"As a start," Gabe said.

Gibson glanced at his daughter. "You say Lucie McNeil works there?"

"Yes."

"You want to do this, Sarah?"

Gabe saw Sarah nod, and the girl seemed to be holding her breath. Gibson then stuck out his hand to Gabe and Gabe shook it. "Thank you, sir. You won't be sorry. I'll have Dr. Booker stop by tomorrow, and please have Sarah ready to leave on Sunday morning at eight." He stood and moved to the door but stopped and picked up the bottle of whiskey. "One more thing, Mr. Gibson," he said, seeing that he had the man's full attention now. "You won't find answers to your problems in this bottle. If you're a man of faith, you already know that—and if not, take it from me, you can get a lot more help when you turn to prayer."

## Chapter Fifteen

As the summer passed, it seemed to Lucie as if there were a number of surprises. The first came when she returned from her Sunday off to find Sarah Gibson in the kitchen, finishing the washing and drying of the supper dishes. She had been bursting to tell Lucie in detail about Gabe's visit to her father, and of the way he had sent Dr. Booker, and now her mother was breathing easier.

"The same day he was there, a man came with a whole basket full of food," she marveled.

"But what are your duties here?" Lucie asked.

"I'm to take care of everything on Sundays, and then during the week do whatever you and Mrs. Hunter tell me to do. I get Saturdays off, and as part of my pay I get a ferry ticket every week to go visit my folks."

Her eyes glowed at the miracle of it all, and Lucie could not help but be happy for her friend's good fortune.

"And the best part is that he's got my pop working with the minister and some others in the neighborhood."

"On what?" Lucie asked, curious in spite of her determination not to be any more impressed with Gabriel than she already was.

Sarah frowned. "I'm not exactly sure, but it's something to do with a building he's planning for the place where the factory was."

"He's rebuilding the factory?" Lucie's heart sank.

"No. It's something else. You can ask him about it when he comes on Sunday."

The second surprise was one for Jonathan and Emma. A man arrived at the cottage one morning in late August and declared he had been instructed to install telephone lines for the cottage, as well as the inn. Once the phone lines were in, Jonathan and Gabe conducted nightly discussions about the progress of the inn, what materials might be needed and whether or not there were sufficient workers available to assure the place would be completely under roof and enclosed by September.

"No doubt," Lucie heard Jonathan yell into the phone. In spite of Emma's assurance that he did not need to shout, Jonathan remained unconvinced. Lucie smiled as she imagined Gabe at the other end holding the receiver several inches from his ear as his father reported the latest developments on the inn.

"How are the wedding plans coming?" Emma asked when Jonathan finally handed the receiver over to her. She waited for Gabe's answer, then gave a huff of exasperation. "Well, it takes time."

Emma smiled as she listened to Gabe's next message. "Why, that's a lovely idea, dear. I'll just put Lucie on and the two of you can discuss it."

She handed Lucie the receiver, but Lucie backed away.

"It doesn't bite, dear," Emma observed, and pressed the instrument into Lucie's hand.

"Hello," Lucie shouted, immediately understanding Jonathan's reaction to this strange box with its protrusions and wires. And the first sound she heard over a telephone wire was that of Gabe's laughter.

"I'm on the mainland, not in Europe, Lucie. There's no need to shout."

"Hello," she said in her normal voice.

"Hello," he said softly, then cleared his throat and continued. "Lucie, I would like for you to come to Boston on Thursday. I have arranged for you to be taken around to the showrooms of a number of merchants, where you can select the furnishings for the living quarters of the inn."

"I should think that—"

"My mother is in complete agreement with this plan," he continued as Lucie glanced at Emma, who was smiling broadly.

"If that's what Emma wants," Lucie said, setting Emma's head to bobbing in the affirmative.

"Excellent. Adam will call for you at seven and take you to the docks. My yacht will be waiting."

*And you? Will you be waiting?* Lucie shook off the unspoken thought. "All right," she said, and prepared to return the phone to Emma.

"Lucie? One thing more," Gabe said.

Lucie's heart skipped a beat, for there was something in his voice that alerted her to the fact that the "more" was more personal. "Yes?" she said warily.

"I have a project—a business project—that I should like you to see and give me your opinion on. Once you have finished your shopping the driver will bring you here to my offices so we can discuss the project before you return to Nantucket."

His offices were not his house, she thought, rationalizing that perhaps the impersonal business setting would temper the feelings that always seemed to lie like dormant ashes that could be sparked by a simple breath of air.

"I can't think how I might—"

"Just agree to come," Gabe said, and the weariness and pleading in his voice told her that whatever this was, he had done it at least in part for her. Her opinion was important to him.

"Very well," she said, and passed the receiver to Jonathan before Gabe could say another word.

Jonathan yelled goodbye and hung up the phone. "Well, everything seems to be falling into place," he said as he headed out the door and across the yard to where they could hear the hammers and saws of the workers putting the finishing touches on the inn.

"The Witherspoon girl is stalling," Emma muttered, more to herself than to Lucie. "She's stalling like a mule digging in its heels," Emma repeated as she took up the quilt, now finished except for the binding. "The question is why?"

"Well, it's given you the time you needed to finish the quilt," Lucie said, trying to lighten her sudden change of mood.

Emma blinked at her. "What has this quilt to do with that?"

"It's for their wedding—Gabe and Jeanne's."

"It's for a wedding all right, but not that one."

Lucie wondered for a moment if Emma's mind was slipping. She had been doing so well—thriving, actually, with all the activity around them and the improved connection to her beloved son. "Then which?" she asked quietly, fearing the answer.

"Yours," Emma replied. "Yours and Gabe's."

To Lucie's surprise and relief, Gabe had Fraiser meet her when the yacht docked in Boston, and the butler accompanied her on her rounds of the merchants. It did not take long for her to relent and permit herself to enjoy this journey through the shops and showrooms of beautiful furnishings and fabrics. Between stops she and Fraiser conferred over items they had just seen that might be appropriate. But Fraiser had to remind Lucie that it was not necessary for her to always choose the least expensive item, especially when it was evident that her heart had really been taken with a more luxurious choice.

By midafternoon she was exhausted but exhilarated, and had completely put out of her mind her meeting with Gabe at his offices. So when the carriage pulled up to an impressive granite structure with marble columns and massive arched windows, she assumed they had reached another stop on their shopping tour.

"Oh, Fraiser, I do believe we have what we need—more than is needed," she exclaimed. "Do you really think that—"

And then she saw the carved lettering on the cornerstone:

*Witherspoon and Hunter*
*Established 1875*

"I shall leave you here, Lucie," Fraiser said, stepping out of the carriage and offering her his hand to help her down. "It's been a pleasure."

"Oh, Fraiser, the pleasure was mine. Thank you so

much, and do give my regards to Mrs. King and everyone at the house."

Fraiser nodded and took his place in the carriage, leaving her standing at the entrance to Gabe's office.

Inside the lobby, where voices and footfalls echoed with importance, she approached the single desk. "I am Lucie McNeil. I have an appointment with Mr. Hunter," she said.

The young man smiled widely and came around the desk to face her. "He's been expecting you, Miss McNeil. Follow me, please."

He led her to an elevator and pressed the call button. He remained standing with her as the elevator made its way down the ten floors of the building to the lobby. The heavy doors slid open, and a uniformed elevator operator waited for her to enter.

"This is Miss McNeil," the receptionist said. "Mr. Hunter is expecting her."

"Am I late?" Lucie asked nervously as the elevator began to rise.

"Not at all," the operator replied. "Mr. Hunter has called down to the front desk several times, and whenever Darby gets a call directly from Mr. Hunter himself, the boy gets a bit flustered."

"I see."

"You must be mighty important, Miss."

"Not at all," Lucie replied, trying to study her distorted image in the black marble walls of the elevator's interior. She touched her hair, adjusted her hat and brushed off the front of her skirt.

"It's just that I've seen a lot of really big names come and go in this place and if he was anxious about them he never showed it. He might have his secretary call down to see if they'd come yet, but not himself." He glanced at her curiously.

"I work for his parents," she said, as if that should explain everything, and she was momentarily relieved when the elevator stopped smoothly and the doors opened as if separated by some unseen hand.

"Well, here you are, Miss," the operator said, and waited for her to step out of the cage and onto the thick carpet that covered the distance between her and yet another lone desk. A woman of indeterminate age was typing a letter.

"Ah, Miss McNeil," she said as soon as she heard the elevator doors close with a soft click. "I am Mrs. Groseclose, Mr. Hunter's secretary. Mr. Hunter is expecting you."

"So I have been told," Lucie murmured as she hastened to keep up with the long strides of the secretary as the woman led the way to the end of the hall. When they came to a wall of frosted glass etched with the design of waves and seagulls, Mrs. Groseclose tapped lightly and opened the door a crack. "Miss McNeil," she managed to say before the door was thrown open wide and Gabe stood there smiling the same confident, trusting boyish smile she'd seen in that photograph in Emma's parlor. "Thank you, Mrs. Groseclose. Lucie, come in. How was the shopping?"

Lucie stepped inside a room filled with light from the wall of windows that wrapped around on two sides and faced the harbor. In the center of the room was a large table, and on the table was the model of a building cut away to illustrate the interior, as well as the exterior.

"The shopping went well," Lucie reported, unable to contain her curiosity about the model. "Thank you for sending Fraiser along. He was so very helpful. In fact, you probably did not need me at all. His taste is impeccable."

"But did you find things you liked, Lucie?"

Lucie could not help but laugh at the ridiculous question. "Oh, Gabe, you have me shopping at the finest merchants in all of Boston and you have to ask if I liked anything?"

"Well, it's just that sometimes some of these merchants can be… It's difficult to find the exact right thing to suit the situation."

"We have found wonderful furnishings, and fabrics for curtains and upholstery that I think you will find quite suitable for Nantucket," she assured him. "What's this?" she asked, moving closer to study the scale model.

Gabe gave her a moment to digest the tiny street markers and the surroundings of the featured building. He watched as her eyes widened with surprise and disappointment.

"You're rebuilding the factory," she said, and it was not a question.

"I am rebuilding on the site," he said, "but look closer, Lucie."

She walked slowly around the large table, studying the cutaway to the interior, where she saw classrooms. "It's a school?"

"Among other things." He moved closer, following her as he gave her the tour. "See, there is also a small clinic. Charles is overseeing that. And over here—" He led the way around to the other side of the table. "That's where the library will be housed. And down here are more classrooms, for the adults to come to at night and learn skills they may need to improve their circumstances. Like reading or arithmetic, or in some cases, English."

"It's wonderful, Gabe. Is that a chapel?"

"A chapel and a food bank." He chuckled. "Believe it or not, Dolly Witherspoon has organized several ladies from her charitable groups to conduct food-and-clothing drives, so we should have an ongoing supply of items to offer people in the neighborhood who may be down on their luck." He pointed to a large part of the building nearest her. "That's a gymnasium, and out here—" he actually ran around to the other side and pointed to a part of the model where there were little trees, paths, blooming flowers and a pond "—that's the park." He looked up at her and grinned like a child eager for approval.

"I'm speechless. But Gabe, it must cost a fortune."

He shrugged. "I've been able to raise most of the money from business associates who were seeking a tax shelter, and there are friends who have come forward after hearing about Thurgood."

Lucie walked slowly around the perimeter of the table, studying the model from every angle as Gabe stepped aside and gave her the time she needed to take it all in.

"It will be finished in the spring," he said. "About the same time you'll open the inn for its first season."

Lucie shook her head in wonder. "Gabe, it's an amazing gift," she said.

"It's not a gift, Lucie. It's atonement. I realized that the only way I could ask forgiveness for the past was to create a better future for those who are still here." He paused and then added, "And I did it for you—for you and everyone who endured that day and suffered the loss of friends and family. It's a memorial, Lucie—a living memorial."

"It's beautiful, Gabe," Lucie whispered. "Thank you for letting me see it."

Gabe stepped closer and took her hands in his. He felt

her stiffen slightly as he pulled off her gloves and stroked the scars on her palms. "Whenever you look at these now, Lucie, I want you to think about the children and their parents who can come to a place like this and find help—real help. You did this, Lucie. You inspired this."

She had never loved him more than she did in that moment. If he had asked her to fly to the moon with him she might have agreed, but instead he said, "You have made me see that truly loving you means respecting your moral standards and values. I have made promises that I must keep, but I want you to know that you are the one true love of my life. Whatever happens, know this—it will always be you that I love."

Lucie could not stem her tears any longer. The day had been so filled with wonderful things, but nothing more wonderful—or more heartbreaking—than Gabe's declaration of the love they could not acknowledge or ever share.

She touched his cheek and then raised herself on tiptoes to kiss his mouth. "I love you, Gabriel Hunter," she said, and before he could take her in his arms she pulled back. "Please let me go now," she whispered when he reached for her.

Gabe hesitated and then nodded. He walked to his desk and pressed a button. "Mrs. Groseclose, please have the carriage brought round for Miss McNeil. She is going home now."

In a week filled with surprises, it was Gabe who received the most incredible shock of all.

That Saturday afternoon, as he was trying to complete some work before changing to escort Jeanne to the opera that evening, the doorbell chimed. He heard Fraiser open the door and then voices in the foyer—Fraiser's and Jeanne's. A light tap on his library door, and then the doors slid open.

"It's fine, Fraiser," Jeanne assured the butler as she firmly closed the door behind her, shutting the servant out.

"Well," Gabe said, trying hard not to sound irritated at the interruption. "To what do I owe this unexpected visit?" He put down his pen and glanced up.

Jeanne was still standing by the door, and there was something different about her, something that made Gabe get up and come around the desk. "Are you well, Jeanne?" he asked as he led her to a chair.

"Sit down please, Gabriel."

He was so surprised at her tone that he did as she instructed, taking the chair next to hers rather than his usual place behind his desk.

"Gabriel, do you love me?"

He opened his mouth to answer, but she ignored his effort.

"Because, dear Gabe, while I am enormously fond of you and have always thought of you in the most exalted terms, I do not love you. I never have."

"I see," Gabe said, his heart racing as he considered what this might mean.

"I doubt that you see at all," Jeanne declared, getting up and pacing the room while he remained seated. "Do you consider me a talented artist, Gabe?" she asked, after a moment in which she seemed to be gathering her thoughts.

The complete switch in the direction of the conversation confused Gabe. It had often occurred to him over these last weeks, when he had spent more time with Jeanne, that he was going to have to get used to her sudden changes of topic. He had attributed that to flightiness and an inability to stay on one subject, but perhaps he had been wrong. She certainly seemed focused at the moment.

"You know that you are a gifted portrait artist, Jeanne. Everyone says so."

She nodded but she did not smile. "I have talent but it needs the opportunity to flourish," she exclaimed, waving one hand in a dramatic gesture to emphasize her point.

"You could study with someone, perhaps," Gabe suggested. "Once we are married, you could—"

Jeanne stopped her pacing and came to stand directly in front of him. "Exactly," she said. "Gabe, I have friends in Paris, and they have friends who are successful artists and who are willing to teach me. Gabe, I wish to go to Paris to study."

Now it was Gabe's turn to stand and pace the room. "I'm not sure that's reasonable, Jeanne. I have a business that needs my attention here. We can travel, of course, once the business has recovered and we are more… solvent."

Jeanne burst out laughing.

"Oh, darling Gabe, I am trying to tell you that I do not wish to marry—you or anyone else. I want to go to Paris and study and find out if indeed I am as talented as our friends all believe me to be. I want to explore the possibilities, Gabe, before I settle down with anyone."

Gabe opened his mouth to speak, and then shut it. Was it possible that his prayer had been answered—and in the affirmative? For weeks, he had devoted himself to discovering Jeanne's finer points—her humor, her beauty, her gift of art—while denying himself the opportunity to see Lucie, to even think of Lucie. As it turned out it was unnecessary for him to say anything, for Jeanne was not finished.

"I have prayed about this for weeks, Gabe. Ever since your dear parents were here and I had the opportunity to get to know them. Your mother's wonderful stories about her courtship and marriage with the colonel—why, it took my breath away."

"Well, my mother can romanticize the facts, Jeanne," Gabe said.

"I asked myself why I was pursuing a match with you when there was no—forgive me—passion in it for either of us. You are devoted to your work and in a way, so am I, for my art is my work, Gabe."

"I see," Gabe inserted.

She laughed, and it was a sound of such pure delight that Gabe smiled at her. Jeanne stood on tiptoe and took his face in her palms. "I doubt that you see at all, Gabe. My father is perfectly horrified at the very notion."

"Jeanne, I'm sorry for—"

She released him and reclaimed the chair she had vacated, perching on the edge so she could reach his desk. "Now then, here is my proposal." She waited a beat, indicating with a look that he should take his place behind the desk. "You will stay true to your bargain to keep my father's name from being sullied."

Gabe was stunned that she had gleaned this information.

"Oh, don't look so surprised, Gabe. We women learn quickly that nothing is as it seems. Your sudden proposal, for example—" She quirked an eyebrow at him and Gabe had the good sense to look abashed. "Not your finest hour," she noted.

"What do you want?" he asked, amused now that this woman he'd always seen as a child was laying out the terms to a business arrangement as well as her father ever had.

"I want you to give me my freedom—and, darling Gabe, I want you to find happiness for yourself." She stood and offered him her hand. He took it and returned a firm handshake. Gabe laughed as he walked her to the door, feeling more carefree than he had in months. Surely this was the sign he'd been waiting for—God's message that he and Lucie McNeil were meant to be together.

Emma was on the porch, sitting in her usual rocker, with the hated wheelchair abandoned by the door. Jonathan sat opposite her, smoking his pipe and reading a newspaper.

"There's a hint of autumn in that breeze," he said. "I'll get your shawl." He got up and went inside the house.

"Where's Lucie?" Emma asked when he returned.

"She's at the inn, getting everything set for our move."

"The furniture has all come?" Emma asked.

"It has, and wait until you see what an excellent job Lucie and Fraiser did, my dear. I think you are going to be very pleased with your new home.

Emma snorted dismissively. "I am staying right here with you and our own things. Those things are for Lucie—and Gabe."

"Now, Emma," Jonathan said softly.

"Oh, stop treating me as if I've gone off, Johnny. Read this and then tell me I'm wrong."

Jonathan took the letter she handed him and scanned the contents. "Does this mean that Gabe has broken his engagement?"

"On the contrary, it's little Miss Witherspoon who has ended it. I knew that girl was stalling. I just couldn't understand why. She wants to be an artist. Well, God bless her. She finally found the courage she needed to stop trying to please the men in her life, and do what pleases her. I give her great credit for taking the time to write to us and give us the news herself."

"She says that Gabe is coming here today. Have you told Lucie this news?"

"It's not mine to tell," Emma said, and then pointed toward the harbor. "He's here," she said. "Sarah!"

Sarah ran to the side porch, wiping her hands on her apron. "Yes, ma'am."

"Our son is just arriving. Please be so kind as to meet him before he climbs all the way up here, and let him know that he'll find Lucie at the inn." She took Jeanne's letter from Jonathan and handed it to Sarah. "And be sure that you give him this."

Sarah beamed. "Yes, ma'am," she said, and took off at a run.

Together Emma and Jonathan watched as the yacht anchored and the crew lowered the dinghy. Emma reached back and placed her hand over Jonathan's. "Do you remember the day you returned to Charleston?"

"I do, love," Jonathan replied as together they watched their son beach the dinghy and start up the dunes toward the house. "It was the beginning of the very best years of my life."

Lucie laid the magnificent white quilt across the foot of the bed. Emma had insisted she take it down to the inn with several other treasures and put them all in the living quarters, where Emma and Jonathan would live now. Lucie and Sarah and the staff they would hire over the winter had rooms on the third floor, where they would settle in while they prepared for the opening of the inn in the spring.

Lucie assumed it was Emma's distress over the idea of Gabe marrying for anything less than love that was behind the older woman's stubborn insistence that she had made the quilt for Lucie and Gabe. Perhaps now that Gabe's wedding was only a few months away Emma would finally come to terms with reality. In the meantime the quilt was too fine to be hidden away in a chest or trunk.

She ran her fingers over the twin circles intertwining across the elegant silk and brocade fabrics in shades of white. "Double wedding ring," Emma had told Lucie. "That's the pattern name, although it might also represent a dual love story—mine with the colonel and yours with—"

"Now, Emma," Lucie had protested. "You only upset yourself by entertaining such fantasies."

Lucie moved to the door and opened it to step out onto the balcony that gave the best view of the bay. She saw Gabe's yacht anchored just offshore, and her heartbeat doubled. He had not come on a Sunday, but on a weekday. They had not seen each other since that day in his office. She closed her eyes and prayed for courage to face him.

"You'll catch a chill," Gabe said from the doorway behind her.

She shivered slightly, but knew it was not the sea breeze that affected her. "I was just airing the room—the painters…" she said, moving back into the room.

He opened the beautiful blue shawl he had purchased the day they had shopped for the anniversary gifts for his parents and held it out to her. "I've been saving this for you, Lucie," he said, and stepped forward to wrap it around her shoulders.

"Gabe, please—" But she could not resist pulling the shawl closer and surrendering to its warmth and softness.

"I have sold the mansion, Lucie, as well as the firm. The yacht, too, although the new owner agreed to allow me one last sail. I have come home to start again—with you, if you'll have me." He handed her Jeanne's letter. "Before you answer, Mama asked that I give this to you," he said.

Too emotional to face him, Lucie stepped back onto the balcony and opened the letter. The unfamiliar handwriting caught her off guard and she had to read through the contents twice to comprehend what the words truly meant.

When she finally realized Jeanne had relieved Gabe of his promise and he was truly free to love Lucie and to be loved in return, she had no words to express her joy. She turned and opened her arms to him, and he laughed and lifted her high in the air, kissing her face, her eyes, her mouth and swinging her around and around in the spacious room they would share once they were married.

"Put me down, Gabriel Hunter," Lucie protested, but her voice was filled with happiness and delight.

"Only if you promise to love me forever," he said.

"I do," she whispered, and kissed him.

# *Epilogue*

$A$s soon as Gabe and Lucie broke the news, Emma took charge. She was beside herself that the young couple had decided to be married as soon as possible.

"I'm ready to make our life here on Nantucket, where we belong," Gabe told her. "Lucie and I want to begin our life together, raising our family and—"

"That's all well and good, but you cannot stay in this house, young man. You must find a place in town. I will not have there be any gossip related to this union, do you understand me?"

"Yes, ma'am. I can get a place in town, but I'm coming here every day and I am spending every minute possible with Lucie. We've already lost too much time."

"Oh, Lucie, you know that I detest standing on ceremony in general, but there comes a time when the tenets of proper etiquette and procedure are necessary, and this is one of those times," she told Lucie later, after Gabe had ridden off to town. "Men," she fumed. "To them it's a simple matter to plan an event of this magnitude. They know nothing of what's involved."

"We don't want a fuss," Lucie said.

"Well, of course you want a fuss," Emma exclaimed, "and if y'all don't, then you will indulge an old woman who may never have another opportunity to plan such a joyous occasion."

"Emma is determined to turn this into the social event of the year," Lucie told Gabe later that evening as they walked along the bluff overlooking the beach. "She's determined to involve half the population of Nantucket in the planning. And I can't deny that I love it," she added shyly.

Gabe laughed. "That's good, because you certainly cannot fight it. We may as well just sit back and enjoy it, although—"

"You're worried about the expense," Lucie guessed.

Gabe nodded. "Oh, Lucie, I so wish that I could give you the most wonderful wedding you could ever imagine, but—"

"What you are giving me, Gabriel Hunter, is far more precious than a party. You are giving me your heart—your pledge to love me for the rest of our days. How could anything compare?"

He stroked her cheek. "Still—"

"Emma is quite aware of the financial circumstances. You'd be impressed with her ingenuity. For example, she has asked Mrs. King to provide our wedding cake as her gift, and Sarah to sew my gown as hers. Do you see the genius of that? She has provided them with things they can do to be a part of the wedding without straining themselves—or us—financially."

Gabe grinned. "I'll bet Mrs. King was delighted."

"What will happen to them—Mrs. King and Fraiser—now that you've sold the house in Boston?" she asked.

"I've given them sterling letters of recommendation. They won't have a problem finding other work."

"They could work here," Lucie said softly. "At the inn. We have Sarah, and us, of course, but it's a large inn, and the busy season will be here before we know it and—"

"Certainly they would not need to be trained," he replied thoughtfully. "Do you think they might accept?"

"To work for you? Of course," Lucie assured him. "Ask them."

"Speaking of asking, I have written to your father, Lucie. I have asked his permission to marry you."

"You didn't need to do that," Lucie replied.

"Yes, my love, I did. I agree with my mother on that point. I want everything to be done properly. I know your family won't be at the wedding itself, but I want them to feel a part of it. Perhaps one day we can travel there so I can meet them."

Lucie thought of the tiny, thatched-roofed house in the middle of fallow fields, where her parents lived with three of their seven children. "We'll see," she said, and smiled up at Gabe. "Thank you for writing them."

Gabe cleared his throat. "And while I am attending to matters I should have seen to before asking you to marry me, there is one more." He dropped to one knee and took her hand. "A proper proposal of marriage," he said softly, "usually includes some token that symbolizes that proposal." He slipped a ring onto her finger. "I hope this will serve that purpose, Lucie."

Lucie held her hand up until the moon caught the sparkle of a single stone set in a thin silver band. "Oh, Gabe, it is so beautiful."

"It was my grandmother's—Papa's mother. She was a lot like you, Lucie, beautiful and willful and so very devoted to others. Will you wear it?"

"Forever," Lucie promised.

Lucie had remained firm on the idea that she would wear a simple afternoon gown with wedding bonnet rather than the more traditional wedding gown and veil. So with sighs of exasperation, Sarah and Emma put their heads together and created a gown that left Lucie speechless.

"It's perfect," she whispered as she preened before the mirror in Emma's room. "I— It makes me look so—"

"Lovely," Emma said as she handed Sarah the matching wedding bonnet to position atop Lucie's upswept hair.

Lucie touched her fingers to the tiny pleats of the high chiffon neckline, then followed the lines of the gown out to the bodice of dotted swiss. The matching puffed sleeves narrowed just below her elbows into a delicate lace, fitted tight to her forearms and ending in points at her fingers. Her waist seemed tiny banded in the wide waistband of the skirt. And the skirt itself was a heavy poplin that ended in a narrow lace ruffle that matched her sleeves. The wedding bonnet was a simple arrangement of dotted swiss pleats capped by a wide tulle bow. But it was the color they had selected that set the entire ensemble off—a beautiful green that reminded Lucie of spring and the sea and Ireland.

"I told you it was the perfect color to show off those eyes and that hair," Emma told Sarah with a satisfied grin.

Sarah handed Lucie the final accessory, a matching parasol with a carved white handle. "Perfect," she murmured.

* * *

Over his career Gabe had managed business deals worth tens of thousands of dollars without so much as blinking an eye. In the face of economic ruin he had not only calmly found a way to sustain a portion of his fortune, but had also raised the necessary funds to make amends for the very actions that had led to his downfall in the first place. So why were his palms sweating beneath the white cotton gloves he wore? Why did the collar underneath his frock coat seem unusually tight? Why on this crisp, late-summer day, when a cool breeze from the bay floated through the tiny church, accenting the scent of orange-blossom bouquets in every open window, did he feel as if the temperature must have reached a hundred degrees?

Half the town, as well as several friends and associates from Boston, were waiting for the arrival of the bride. Gabe had been both surprised and touched by the presence of those he had expected to abandon him once they learned of his business reversals. It had been Lucie who had pointed out to him that in opening his heart to God, he had also opened himself to the kinds of unfettered friendships he'd known as a boy. To that end Gabe had gone one day in search of his old friend, Sean, and the two of them had shared many an evening recalling the adventures of their boyhood.

In the tradition of the day, guests mingled on the lawn of the church, and Sean came over to wait with Gabe. Finally, at the stroke of noon, Gabe looked up and saw his father's carriage, driven by Adam and gaily decorated with flowers and greenery. He could see his parents smiling and waving to friends. And then he saw Lucie, and his breathing settled back to normal. Ever since she had agreed to become his wife, Gabe had noticed that he went through each day with such joy, such calm, such assurance, as he had never known before, that life was good and that all things were possible for a union as blessed as this one.

He waited as his father assisted Lucie down from the carriage and led her into the church. Then Gabe lifted his mother into her wheelchair and followed. The music swelled as their guests completed the procession and took their places in the narrow pews, and as the wedding party walked the short distance to the altar.

Reverend Ashford led them in the repetition of the time-honored vows of matrimony, but Gabe was barely aware of the sound of his own voice as he looked down and into the violet eyes of his bride.

Lucie could not take her eyes off Gabe. He was her lifeline on this day that she had longed for, dreamed of and never dared hope would come. Her hand was shaking when Reverend Ashford called for the ring to be given. But she felt the sustaining strength of Gabe's fingers as he cradled her palm. She watched as he slid an intricate silver band onto her finger.

"Forever," he whispered, and Lucie's heart soared with the organist's triumphant recessional. Gabe reached for her and she remembered his promise of the evening before.

"Emma says you should not kiss me at the altar," Lucie had told him as they went over the details of the wedding ceremony.

"Ha!" Gabe had replied. "Let her try and stop me."

And so, to the stunned murmurs of some of the older

guests and to the delight of younger ones, Gabe kissed Lucie on the lips—and Lucie kissed him back.

The friend who had purchased Gabe's yacht insisted Gabe use it for a wedding trip. Now, after a week's sail along the coast, Gabe and Lucie had returned to Nantucket. They were laughing and walking hand in hand as they climbed up to the cottage from the beach the same way Gabe had the first day they met. Waiting to welcome them home, Emma and Jonathan could not help but recall their first years as a young married couple with everything ahead of them.

As Gabe scooped Lucie into his arms and she squealed with girlish delight, Lucie looked up and saw Jonathan and Emma. The older Hunters were silhouetted against the setting sun, and Lucie understood that, in some ways she was seeing her own future—hers and Gabe's. With God's blessing, they would grow old together in this place, telling their children and grandchildren their Nantucket love story.

Dear Reader,

I have always been fascinated by history—the history of nations, the history of entire societies, and most of all, the personal histories of individuals. In some ways, this is a love story within a love story, for as Gabe's parents come to the end of a long and happy life together, Lucie and Gabe are just finding their way. In my lifetime I have faced challenges that, when I look back on them from the vantage point of survival and even victory, would have seemed unimaginable to me when I was younger. What I know for sure is this: answers come when you stop the yammering inside your head and are quietly listening for the still, small voice of God within, showing the way.

I hope you will fall in love with Lucie and Gabe, dear reader, for their struggles are no different from those we all face today—the struggle for a secure home, the struggle to hold fast to our faith and the struggle to find our one true love. Do visit my Web site at www.booksbyanna.com and share your thoughts, or write to me at P.O. Box 161, Thiensville, WI 53092.

All best,

*Anna Schmidt*

P.S.: Be sure to watch for the sequel to *Seaside Cinderella* coming soon. Return to Nantucket in the throes of World War I as Gabe and Lucie's daughter faces the classic challenge of forgiving one's enemies.

# QUESTIONS FOR DISCUSSION

1. Imagine you are an immigrant alone in a strange land, and you've just lost your job and home. What would you do? How would you survive?

2. Think about the thousands of people in the world today who must face such challenges. How might their choices differ from (or be the same as) Lucie's?

3. If you have ever lost a job unexpectedly, how did you face that crisis? What helped you get through it?

4. Gabe was truly trying to consider what was best for his parents. How would you have advised him to change his approach to the situation? Have you ever thought you knew what was best for someone else? What did you do about it?

5. In today's aging society, many adult children are faced with caring for parents who stubbornly cling to their way of life in spite of ill health and frailty. How has this story helped you better understand why someone might make the choice to hold on to the past? Are there changes in your own life that you are reluctant to make? If so, what are they?

6. When Lucie realized her feelings for Gabe—a man who had turned his back on his faith—were becoming more complex, how did she deal with that? How did her faith inspire Gabe's return to God?

7. Have you ever had a relationship—romantic or not—where the other person's lack of faith was an obstacle? If so, how did you handle that?

8. How did Lucie's faith sustain her through everything she had to face? How has your faith helped you get through difficult times?

9. What qualities did Gabe's parents see in Lucie that made them think she—although not of his economic and social class—would make him a good wife?

10. Did you like this book? What about it did (or didn't) you like? How did the author's writing enhance the story?

# REQUEST YOUR FREE BOOKS!

## 2 FREE INSPIRATIONAL NOVELS
## PLUS 2
## FREE
## MYSTERY GIFTS

*Love Inspired*
# HISTORICAL
### INSPIRATIONAL HISTORICAL ROMANCE

**YES!** Please send me 2 FREE Love Inspired® Historical novels and my 2 FREE mystery gifts (gifts are worth about $10). After receiving them, if I don't wish to receive any more books, I can return the shipping statement marked "cancel". If I don't cancel, I will receive 4 brand-new novels every other month and be billed just $4.24 per book in the U.S. or $4.74 per book in Canada, plus 25¢ shipping and handling per book and applicable taxes, if any*. That's a savings of over 20% off the cover price! I understand that accepting the 2 free books and gifts places me under no obligation to buy anything. I can always return a shipment and cancel at any time. Even if I never buy another book, the two free books and gifts are mine to keep forever. 102 IDN ERYA 302 IDN ERYM

| | | |
|---|---|---|
| Name | (PLEASE PRINT) | |
| Address | | Apt. # |
| City | State/Prov. | Zip/Postal Code |

Signature (if under 18, a parent or guardian must sign)

### Mail to Steeple Hill Reader Service:
**IN U.S.A.:** P.O. Box 1867, Buffalo, NY 14240-1867
**IN CANADA:** P.O. Box 609, Fort Erie, Ontario L2A 5X3

Not valid to current subscribers of Love Inspired Historical books.

**Want to try two free books from another series?**
**Call 1-800-873-8635 or visit www.morefreebooks.com**

\* Terms and prices subject to change without notice. N.Y. residents add applicable sales tax. Canadian residents will be charged applicable provincial taxes and GST. Offer not valid in Quebec. This offer is limited to one order per household. All orders subject to approval. Credit or debit balances in a customer's account(s) may be offset by any other outstanding balance owed by or to the customer. Please allow 4 to 6 weeks for delivery. Offer available while quantities last.

**Your Privacy:** Steeple Hill Books is committed to protecting your privacy. Our Privacy Policy is available online at www.SteepleHill.com or upon request from the Reader Service. From time to time we make our lists of customers available to reputable third parties who may have a product or service of interest to you. If you would prefer we not share your name and address, please check here. ☐

LIH08R

# *Love Inspired.*
# HISTORICAL

## TITLES AVAILABLE NEXT MONTH

### Don't miss these two stories in August

**WILDERNESS COURTSHIP by Valerie Hansen**
Her unhappy marriage left widow Charity Beal leery of
men. But then Thorne Blackwell appears. His brother has
vanished, and his brother's wife and son are in danger. He
needs Charity's help to get the pair through the Oregon
wilderness to safety. Her kindness draws Thorne in. But
before he can win her heart, he has to save their party from
the sharpshooter stalking them.

**THE JOURNEY HOME by Linda Ford**
When Kody Douglas finds a vulnerable young woman in a
South Dakota farmhouse, abandoned in the darkest hours
of the Depression, he cannot simply ride away and leave
her. Charlotte Porter reluctantly follows this embittered
yet compelling man to his family's homestead. Could two
outcasts—brought together by hard times and shared faith—
truly find love in so cold and heartless a world?

LIHCNM0708